Betty,

THANK YOU VE[RY]

MUCH FOR ALL [OF]

SUPERB HELP — YOUR

ARE AN EDITOR

SUPREME!

# The Flames of Deliverance

John Schork

Jupiter Pixel Publishing

**ISBN 978-0-9843344-2-1**

First edition: July 2009
This book is a publication of the Jupiter Pixel Company


Jupiter Pixel
18380 SE Lakeside Drive
Jupiter, FL 33469
www.jupiterpixel.com
For enquiries:
info@jupiterpixel.com

For Cracker

My friend and true American

# Chapter One

Over Northern France
24 December, 1943

Ragged clouds whipped over the Mustang's shattered canopy, a thin trail of smoke marking the aircraft's descent into a solid grey mass of turbulent clouds. Captain Hank Mitchell figured he must be over the English Channel. He knew his engine wasn't going to run much longer and he fought the panic which threatened to overwhelm him as he continued to lose altitude.

"Blackbird Lead, I contacted Air Sea Rescue," crackled from the radio.

Chris Christiansen, flying on Hank's wing since they disengaged from a fight with two Messerschmitts over Bremen, knew they were in trouble. Still in tight formation, the two aircraft were instantly engulfed by the dark clouds.

Hank thought of the cold and stormy water he'd crossed many times on missions against occupied Europe. If the engine would only hold up for another twenty or thirty miles he could set down at one of the RAF dispersal fields that dotted southern England. At least if he had to bail out, he'd come down on solid land. He didn't want to think about ditching or parachuting into the Channel. Two pilots from his fighter group had gone down in that freezing wind swept hell and neither had survived.

He checked the oil pressure, 35 psi, well below the 50 psi the Merlin engine needed to run. Above the oil pressure gauge, he noted the altimeter passing through 6,000 feet. At this rate of descent he estimated eight minutes before he had to bail out or commit to ditching. But where was he? Ceilings that morning had been estimated at three to four thousand feet over England and northern France. They had to break out soon.

"I can see water," Chris transmitted.

Hank looked down through broken clouds and saw the forbidding grey green water whipped by a frigid wind from the northwest. Only ten minutes to England, he thought, just give me ten more minutes, baby. Images of ditching into heavy waves or being dragged by a parachute across open water kept forcing their way into his mind. Focus on what you can control he told himself, his hand pulling back slightly on the stick willing the Mustang to clear the watery nightmare below.

"I've got a good lock on the Hensley beacon, ten degrees port," came the radio transmission from his wingman.

Chris, doing everything to get me home, Hank thought as he carefully banked left to head for the beacon that marked the way to the RAF field at Gravesend, his first choice for an emergency landing.

As he leveled his wings, the compass needle locked on the beacon. The aircraft shuddered twice, the prop stopping almost instantly. Hank heard a loud bang and dark oily smoke began to billow from the engine compartment. He knew his decision had just been made for him.

"That's it, Chris. Gotta get out," he said over the radio, trying to keep the panic out of his voice.

"Hank, you're on fire!"

Suddenly the heat from a rapidly spreading fire just forward of the cockpit hit Hank like a hammer. Acrid smoke streamed back into the cockpit choking him, burning his eyes and forcing them closed. Fighting to remain calm he reached down for the emergency canopy release. Lowering his head momentarily, Hank pulled the handle and the canopy released into the wind stream. Flames shot over the instrument panel, the smoke and fire engulfing him. He coughed and fought to breathe, the oily smoke smothering him. Grabbing his harness release Hank desperately twisted it to free himself from the stricken Mustang.

Ripping at the microphone/oxygen cord Hank turned his head violently as flames whipped around his flying helmet. Panic began to overwhelm him, his fear turning into a desperate struggle to get out of the aircraft.

Trying to protect his face with an upheld hand he turned and dragged himself higher on the seat attempting to clear the cockpit. Hank jerked hard on his flight jacket realizing the radio cord was wrapped around his life preserver straps. Smoke and flames enveloped him as the aircraft nosed over toward the Channel. With one last violent push, Hank threw himself free of the cockpit.


Slowly tumbling, Hank sensed his fall toward the water as he searched frantically for the D-ring of his parachute. *It wasn't there!* Trying to stay calm he grabbed the left riser and ran his hand up until he felt the cold metal. *Got it!* A hard pull and he felt the sharp snap of the chute opening. He looked up toward the white canopy just as he hit the frigid water, his momentum plunging him down into the dark turbulence. Thrashing his arms, he clawed toward the surface, his lungs screaming for air. But before he reached the surface he was pulled forcefully up and into the light by the parachute, now inflated and on its side, the wind beginning to drag it across the waves. Like a puppet on a string, the parachute jerked Hank over the troughs and into the crests of the rolling waves. Coughing up water and grasping for breath, he fought to operate the release clasp on the harness. Pain crippled his left hand as he struggled to open the locking lever.

Slamming into the waves kept tension on the straps and Hank couldn't move the latch. Dragged into another wave, he swallowed more water as he coughed and gasped for air. One more twist and the lever released, allowing him to roll to the right and let the harness pull away from his body. The next wave hit him squarely in the face and he began to sink under the water.

The weight of his boots and clothes was dragging him down. His mind told him he was about to die if he couldn't find the lanyard to inflate his life preserver. Running his numb fingers down the rubberized material he located the small handle. One pull and the bright yellow vest inflated. Like a hand pulling him from the depths, he rose to the surface, coughing water out of his lungs and gasping for air.

Stabilized on the surface, still coughing, Hank began to shiver, the frigid water starting to numb his extremities. His face was pelted by freeing spray driven by a steady cold wind which blew foam off the crests of the heaving waves.

He knew survival time in the Channel wasn't long this time of year. The windblown spray forced him to close his eyes and he rose on the crest of a wave. The cold was like a knife plunging into his body. Never had he thought it could be like this, trapped in a freezing moving prison with no place to turn. A wave crest washed over his head and he coughed as water streamed into his nose and mouth. The panic he had fought off in the cockpit had returned and it threatened to overwhelm him.

Hank heard the roar of a Merlin engine as a lone P-51 flashed overhead at low altitude. *Chris.*

"Air Sea Rescue, Blackbird 02."

"This is Air Sea Rescue, go ahead."

"Pilot in the water approximately fifteen miles south of Gravesend."

"Roger, Blackbird, please standby."

For the first time since hitting the water he was able to get his breathing under control despite the violent uncontrollable shivering. He wrapped his arms tight against his body trying to conserve heat but knew it was a losing battle. *If someone doesn't show up quick, I'm done.*

The pain in his hand was joined by a burning sensation on the left side of his face. Again he heard Chris's engine overhead but couldn't see the aircraft. He's running out of fuel, Hank thought. Shit, we don't need two of us in the water. At least he knows I'm here, maybe he can do something. After living with the idea of violent death in the skies over Europe, Hank Mitchell realized he might soon die alone in this nightmare of wind and waves.

"Blackbird, we have two MTB's, call sign Specter Able about ten miles east of your position. Contact them on 126.7, over."

"Thanks, Air Sea, switching 126.7," Chris Christiansen transmitted, as he rotated the black radio tuner switches to the new frequency.

"Specter Able, Blackbird 02, come in please."

After what seemed like an eternity, Chris heard the receiver come to life, the British accent thick as he'd ever heard.

"Read you five by five, Blackbird. Understand one of your chaps decided to go swimming."

They must do this all the time, Chris thought. "He's been in the water about 10 minutes. I've got visual contact at this time."

"You'll need to direct us in, Blackbird. We are proceeding to your area."

"Roger." If I take my eyes off Hank, I'll never find him again, Chris thought. Below him the tiny yellow vest was barely visible in the green rolling waves.

Pushing the throttle ahead slightly, Chris began a climb to pick up the patrol boats as they closed on Hank's position. Leveling at 1000 feet, he looked east and saw the white wakes of two motor torpedo boats crashing through the waves at high speed. He estimated the boats were four miles away and heading almost at Hank.

"Specter, I've got you in sight, come port 15 degrees for the survivor."

"Port 15 it is...."

The two boat's wakes began to curve and they steadied heading directly at Hank.

"Estimating the pilot on your bow at three miles," Chris transmitted and for the first time thought Hank might have a chance.


Lieutenant Royce Archer called down to the pilot house from the exposed flying bridge, "Engines ahead slow."

A head appeared, coming up the starboard bridge ladder. Sub-Lieutenant John Mills called out, "Skipper, his mate said the pilot is on the bow at a half mile."

"Thanks, Number One. Let's get a net over the side and have Parmley ready to go into the water if the chap can't help himself."

Mill's "Aye, aye sir" faded away as he headed for the main deck.


Chris watched the lead boat slow, still heading directly for Hank. The second boat accelerated and began a wide turn to the right, apparently acting as watchdog for any hostile aircraft. As the first boat approached the yellow life vest, a white frothy wake erupted from the stern as its engines went into reverse. Figures were moving on the deck but Chris couldn't tell what they were doing. He saw Hank's vest moving closer to the boat. They must have thrown him a rope. At least he's strong enough to help them.

Two minutes later the MTB surged forward and began an immediate turn toward Portsmouth.

"Blackbird, we have your pilot on board. He needs to thaw out a bit but he should be fine. Air Sea Rescue will meet us on arrival and take care of him."

"Spector Able, thanks for everything. I'm diverting at this time."

The Mustang began a slow climb toward England, crossing over the two MTB's now at full speed heading north.


Royce Archer turned as John Mills climbed on to the bridge, the wind blowing the young man's hair askew.

"All buttoned up below, John?" Archer noted the other MTB closing to join on his boat.

"Secured for sea, Skipper." Mills hesitated as he looked over the bow which was now slamming into the waves, the speed picking up rapidly. "Looks like the pilot did a bit of a flamer."

Mills turned and looked at his second in command.

"One hand's pretty dodgy and the side of his face is badly burned.

"Better give him a little morphine, but let's not touch the burns, we'll be pier side in short order. Call Portsmouth Harbour Control and make sure they have an ambulance standing by at the fueling pier."

# Chapter Two

USAAF Station 373
Leiston
Suffolk, England
24 December, 1943

Major Robin Cunning, Commanding Officer of the 952nd Fighter Squadron, stood outside the door of Lieutenant Colonel Max Gogan's office. The tall, solidly built pilot held a telex from Eighth Air Force headquarters. He wondered how the 95th Fighter Group Commander would receive the news about Hank Mitchell. The report probably meant that Captain Mitchell would never return to the group, another casualty of the air war over Europe. Opening the door, Robin saw the short stocky Group Commander leaning over his desk looking at a group of charts. The room smelled of tobacco smoke and stale coffee. Standing next to him, the Group Intelligence Officer, Captain Farley Smith was pointing to one of the charts with a wooden ruler.

"Here's the final navigation check point on the mission route. You can expect heavy fighter opposition until the bombers hit the flak belt around Bremen. There are three German fighter fields within 75 miles of the ground track."

"I've got the report on Captain Mitchell whenever you're ready," Cunning said and walked over to the desk.

"Thank you, Farley. Make sure those fields are noted on the big chart for tomorrow's briefing."

Smith picked up several of the charts and headed for the door.

"So what'd you find out from the front office?" Gogan sat down and lit a cigarette, taking a deep drag and putting both feet on top of his desk.

"It's not good. Mitchell's in the Royal Naval Hospital in Portsmouth. Christiansen debriefed us that his ship was on fire when he jumped and he has pretty bad burns to his left hand and face." Cunning remembered the good looking Mitchell and then the disfigured faces of the men he'd known who had survived in-flight fires.

"With Anderson missing, that leaves your squadron two pilots short." Gogan had his finger on a printed piece of paper, running down vertical lines like a man checking baseball scores.

Cunning paused for a moment, keeping his anger under control.

"Yes sir, I guess that's about it."

Robin Cunning knew Gogan had never liked Mitchell, the only son of a banking dynasty. Robin didn't like the young pilot's cocky attitude either, but Mitchell was the leading scorer in the group with four confirmed kills

"Well, get on the horn to wing and make sure they know you're short. Tell those piss ants I expect replacement pilots down here right away."

"Yes, sir. What about Ambassador Winant?"

"What about him?"

"Don't you think we should make sure he's notified about Mitchell?"

Cogan pursed lips while he thought. "Yeah, I guess so." The U.S. ambassador to the Court of St. James was also a close friend of the Mitchell family. Connected by the money and politics of the northeastern patrician class, the Mitchells and Winants were more like family than friends. "Guess we have to tell him the young playboy's had his wings clipped."

Robin turned without replying and left the room. He suspected that the Group Commander also envied Mitchell's ability in the air. One of those natural pilots, he flew a Mustang like it was part of him. That was all history now, remembering the terrible disfiguring burns he'd seen from flying accidents. No one should go through that, no one, he told himself as he walked out into the frigid wind.

"You have to understand Captain Mitchell is still sedated. He suffered very serious injuries in addition to spending time in the Channel." Senior Nurse Supervisor Joyce Fleming smelled mildly of disinfectant, her manner just as antiseptic. Her shoes clicked on the tile floor as she walked down the hallway accompanied by Chris and Dan Wilskie.

"Yes, ma'am, I was there," Chris said. He'd known Hank Mitchell for over two years and flown as his wingman since they'd arrived in Europe. Wilskie was the Squadron Operations Officer and had been with Chris and Hank since the squadron stood up.

Nurse Fleming turned to survey the young man she had originally thought too young to even be an officer. Her eyes seemed to reappraise him. "My understanding was that one of our boats was able to pick him up in short order," she said, her voice losing some of its imperious tone.

"I don't know what would have happened if they hadn't been right there, the Channel was pretty bad," Chris said quietly.

They continued walking in silence, the click of Nurse Fleming's heels the only sound in the corridor. Chris's apprehension over what he might find grew the farther they walked into the hospital. He hated hospitals, hating being here and didn't want to think that someday he might be lying here.

Dan Wilskie wondered how Mitchell would react to getting shot down. That confidence you have to have as a fighter pilot was critical in air to air combat. Now Mitchell knew he wasn't invincible. Might be tough for him to take, Dan thought. He liked Mitchell, but sometimes Hank's cocky attitude was hard to take.

"You may spend five minutes with him," she quietly told them as they entered the two bed room in A Ward. "He needs his rest."

Christiansen saw only one bed was occupied, the other neatly made up with precise hospital corners. In the second bed, Hank lay on his back with a white tented affair covering his left arm and a patchwork of gauze bandages covering the side of his face. A light blue bedspread with a large white anchor covered Hank from the chest down. He must be sleeping; Chris thought and gently shook his left leg.

"Hank, it's Chris and Dan."

His eyes closed, Hank Mitchell lay on his back, the sound of people entering the room rousing him from a semi-sleep. Slowly he opened his eyes and turned his head slightly to the left. "Hey." His words were drawn out, showing the effects of a mild sedative.

"Hank, we've only got five minutes. Then the old battle ax said she'd throw us out."

"She can do it too," Wilskie added, feeling self-conscious.

Pain evident on his face, Hank slowly said to Chris, "Thanks for sticking around out there."

"You'd have done the same for me."

Hank turned his head to look up at the ceiling. "Yeah."

"What did the docs say?" Dan asked, concerned at the change in Hank Mitchell.

For a moment Hank continued to stare up without speaking, then said quietly, "They said I'm fucked up, what's it look like?"

"Sorry...." Chris's voice trailed off.

"Get me a drink, that's all I need," Hank said his voice now taking on an angry tone.

Chris looked down at his friend's face, the white bandages smelling faintly of petroleum jelly. "Yeah, I'll see what I can do." Only now did he realize this was the end of Hank's flying career.

The door opened and a tall man wearing a white hospital coat entered. His nametag said "Dr. Sinclair."

"Ah, I see you have visitors."

Chris stepped to one side to allow Sinclair access to Hank.

"We were just leaving," Chris said, edging toward the door. "Hank, get better."

"Take it easy, buddy," Dan added, following closely behind his friend.

"See ya 'round," Hank said, his head now tilted toward the door, watching the two men leave. "Shit," he said quietly to himself. Both of them were thinking the same thing, Hank thought, I'm done flying and they can't wait to get out of here. *I don't blame them; I'd feel the same way.*

As the door closed, Dr. Sinclair looked down at Hank and asked him, "How's the pain?"

"Get's bad sometimes, but the nurses have been taking care of it."

Sinclair read from the clipboard chart he had picked up from the table next to Hank's bed.

"One of your American doctors is coming over from the hospital at Whitchurch. Not sure what their plan is right now, but rest while you can.

Hank stared at the ceiling.

Christiansen and Wilskie walked down the corridor toward the entrance in silence. Both seemed to be trying to take in what had happened to their friend.

"Son of a bitch," Wilskie said as he reached the double doors.

"Yeah," Chris replied and angrily pushed the doors open to slam on their stops.


Hank's left hand ached, but it was tolerable with the morphine regimen the nurses had administered since his arrival at the hospital. He tried to forget the burning pain he'd felt in the water and during the trip ashore. Why didn't he wear gloves he asked himself? He knew the rules and like most fighter pilots felt those rules were only for the jerks. Flying without gloves allowed for a better feel in the cockpit when you were reaching for a switch, to say nothing about needing to have a good feel if you ever needed to find something critical like a parachute "D" ring. If I'd had gloves on I might never have been able to find that ripcord or get out of the chute, he thought.

The door opened and a tall, solidly built man in the uniform of a U.S. Army Major stepped into the room. He walked deliberately over to the bed.

"Captain Mitchell?" the man asked.

Hank nodded.

"My name is Roger Hanson. I'm with the 2nd General Hospital in Whitchurch." Hanson was in his 30's, muscular with a friendly face, his hair closely cropped.

"They said someone would be coming by. Are you gonna transfer me to Whitchurch?"

"That's standard procedure." Hanson stood with his hands in his pockets, his manner casual. "But there's something I want you to think about."

14

Hank looked up at Hanson and noticed he wore Army Air Forces Flight Surgeon Wings over his European Theater ribbon.

"You a flight surgeon?"

Hanson nodded. "I try to keep my eye out for any aviators on the casualty list."

"So what's there for me to think about?"

"Since I've been in England, I've done some liaison work with the RAF doctors at a hospital in East Grinstead."

"Never heard of it,"

"Not surprising," Hanson said. "It got busy during the Battle of Britain when the Brits had so many pilots burned in Spits and Hurricanes. The work they do is pretty impressive. It's allowed a number of their pilots to get back in the fight."

Hank remembered the RAF Flight Lieutenant who had briefed them on German tactics when the Group first arrived in England. The man's face had been reconstructed, but the results were only barely tolerable to look at. The man's skin was smooth, almost shiny. And it was clear his nose and lips had been the object of rebuilding by the doctors, but they didn't much resemble the original article. Hank never imagined his injuries could be that bad. The pain and now concern for his real condition made him queasy. Why was this guy talking about sending him to the place they only sent the worst cases?

"How bad are my burns underneath all of these bandages, Doc? What the hell are you telling me?" Hank had tensed his body tight, slightly rising off the pillow.

Hanson hesitated then said evenly, "I've talked with the attending physician and you have third degree burns to both your hand and face." The doctor let that sink in then continued, "There's concern about damage to the motor function of the hand and your left ear was severely damaged." Hanson's voice was steady, the rhythm very technical.

Hank lay back, his mind flooded with an avalanche of thoughts. His career, his life, how he would ever recover from this?

"How come you're the first one to tell me," he finally said, the anger coming through.

"I took Doctor Sinclair's initial report over the phone and asked him not to tell you the full extent of your injuries."

"Why the hell not?" Hank asked, feeling overwhelmed by what was unfolding.

"Because I wanted to see for myself," Hanson said very evenly.

"And you're some kind of damned expert?"

Hanson ignored the insult and went on, "I've been able to work with a brilliant doctor named Duncan Frazier at East Grinstead. He studied under one of the most famous doctors to come out of the war so far, Archibald McIndoe. Their work has been the driving force behind the newest techniques for repairing damaged tissue."

Hank stared at the ceiling, there was no escape, no where to run to make this nightmare end. He'd always valued his freedom, now he was at the mercy of strangers. Everything about his life was now out of his control. Maybe it was time to say the hell with it and go home to the family, he thought, they'd get the best doctors in the country. I've done my duty, four German planes knocked down. Now it's time to look out for number one.

"Suppose I just want out. Can you get me a discharge?" Hank asked, his voice very measured.

"Your injuries are certainly severe enough that a medical board would most likely recommend discharge," Hanson said after a moment.

"So I can go home and get taken care of at New York Memorial or the Mayo Clinic?"

"The Army will take care of you for as long as necessary."

"Doc, that's not what I'm asking. If my family can pay for it, I can go my own way."

Hanson nodded. "That's your decision."

"Then the hell with it. Send me home."

The doctor turned and walked to the door, turning as he grasped the knob and turned it. "Get a good night's sleep. I'll be back in the morning."

"I mean it. Send me home!" Hank yelled at the closing door.

# Chapter Three

Royal Naval Hospital Haslar
Portsmouth, England
25 December, 1943

"So what did you think about your chap?" Dr. Thomas Sinclair asked as Roger Hanson stepped into the Doctor's Lounge.

"Thomas, I honestly don't know. After the call from Major Cunning, I expected to find someone very different." Hanson poured a cup of coffee and sat down at the table.

"It's been my experience over the last few years that injuries like his affect everyone differently," Sinclair observed. "Why the special treatment for this one?"

Hanson took a sip of his coffee. "I've been visiting Duncan Frazier at East Grinstead since shortly after I arrived. They're doing much more advanced burn treatment than we currently offer our aviators. I know if I can get some results, our brass will be more inclined to let us set up the same type of facility."

"What do you do now?"

"We take care of the initial treatment here and then ship them back to the states. The problem is that once back home, they're at the mercy of whatever military hospital gets them. Some are all right, others aren't." Hanson rubbed his eyes.

Thomas Sinclair leaned across the table. "So this fellow is to be your guinea pig?"

"In a matter of speaking. Unfortunately it seems he doesn't want any part of it."

"I believe you Yanks have an expression....you can lead a horse to water..."

Hanson stood up and walked to the window. "Cunning told me Mitchell's a good pilot, almost an ace. Based on what you told me of his injuries and what I know they can do at East Grinstead, he might be able to get back in a cockpit. All he has to do is stay in England and undergo treatment. But it also seems he comes from a very wealthy family with influence both in the service and the government. It sounds like his father is on a first name basis with Roosevelt."

Sinclair laughed. "So, with a free pass home to the states, he can sign up with you, perhaps get back in the war and possibly get killed."

"Thomas, a lot of your pilots went back to flying duty after being treated by McIndoe."

"I rather think they didn't have the same situation to deal with."

Hanson nodded. "I suppose you're right." Perhaps his plan for changing the way the Army treated burned pilots would have to wait for another luckless aviator.


Nurse Fleming stood at the end of Hank Mitchell's bed with her arms crossed and a very stern look on her face.

"Mr. Mitchell, I understand you had words with Miss Edwards."

Hank stared straight ahead. "I simply told her I would appreciate some peace and quiet. She just kept chattering away and I didn't want to hear it."

Fleming, a tall woman, in her late 50's walked up to the edge of Hank's bed, her expression chilling.

"I will thank you to know that Miss Edwards is a volunteer at this hospital. She spends time here after a full day of work at Abercrombie's. I asked her to straighten up your room before the evening meal. I thought a gallant young pilot such as yourself would have appreciated her unselfish efforts."

Hank knew he'd over reacted when he raised his voice and told her to "Get out of here and leave me alone."

18

"I suppose it was the medication," he rationalized drily. "Would you please apologize to the young lady for me?" His response carried a tone of sarcasm.

Nurse Fleming looked back at Hank with a stern stare. "I would think that you would take that upon yourself tomorrow afternoon when she returns, if she returns. Now, how is your pain?"

"It's okay."

Nurse Fleming put her fingers on Hank's right wrist and checked her wrist watch. She said nothing as she let go of his arm and moved to the foot of the bed. Making a note on his chart, she walked over to the small table on the wall and removed a thermometer from an alcohol filled beaker.

"Let's check your temperature. Under the tongue and no talking."

After several other checks, Nurse Fleming left on her rounds with one final admonition to Hank to be nice to her young volunteers. "Or you'll have me to deal with, Mr. Mitchell."

Screw you, Hank thought as the door closed. He was tired of officious assholes and couldn't wait to get out of England and on his way home. He tried to tighten his left hand and immediately stopped as the pain shot up his arm. "Christ!" he yelled.


"Yes, sir, I've been assured that his injuries are not life threatening." Lieutenant Colonel Gogan stood by the window of his office holding the phone receiver close to his mouth.

"We suspect he'll be in the large Army hospital at Whitchurch until he's well enough to be shipped home." Gogan paused while listening.

"Yes sir, Mr. Ambassador, his family will be notified by Western Union..........No, sir, I don't know how long that will take."

Gogan looked over at Robin Cunning and rolled his eyes.

"Yes, sir.............Yes, sir.............. I'll notify you as soon as we have any further information.......Good evening, sir."

Gogan put the phone down.

"What a crock of shit. He wants to be kept updated on Mitchell's condition in anticipation of a call from Mitchell's father. How the hell would a civilian ever get an overseas phone priority just to check on his kid?"

"When that civilian talks to the Commander in Chief on a regular basis would be my guess," Robin said with a tinge of sarcasm. *Whether you like Mitchell or not, his family is connected and there's nothing we can do about it.*

Gogan lit a cigarette, throwing the match into the ashtray with a vengeance.

"Well I've got a fighter group to run. I don't have time for this bullshit."

John Gilbert Winant put down the phone, his face reflecting concern for Hank Mitchell. He remembered his young friend's visit in August. This would devastate his parents, Winant thought. And Margo Van Whiting, how will she take this? Hank and Margo were scheduled to be formally engaged on Hank's return to the states, with a society wedding to follow. He pictured the reaction by the Van Whitings to this turn of events.

He pushed the call button on his desk. The office door and his secretary, Alice Tinsley, entered carrying a steno pad.

"I need to visit Hank Mitchell. He's in the British naval hospital in Portsmouth. There's a chance he might be moved to the Army hospital at Whitchurch shortly."

"Yes, sir. Will that be all?"

"My gracious, I lost track of the time. Please be on your way. Have a merry Christmas, Alice."

The sound of Christmas carols drifted in from the hallway, but Hank wasn't in a holiday mood. Despite the morphine, his hand hurt more than yesterday. He still hadn't seen the damage to his face. Between bouts of self-pity and fear he thought about taking the dressings off himself, but there was no mirror in the room. And, he was afraid of what he would find.

Hank Mitchell didn't think he was a coward. He had volunteered for the Air Corps in 1941. He always knew there was a chance he could die, but that came with flying. In combat he'd learned to live with the threat of death each time he took off. But he never thought something like this could happen. If he survived the war, he would move on to the world of business and banking. That's the way his life had been laid out by the family.

His education at Harvard was one more step in the expected path for the heir to the Mitchell dynasty. The war turned out to be one wrinkle no one had anticipated, but his desire to fly and natural ability in the air became a plus. Being a war hero would open up the world of politics in addition to banking. His family was comfortable with the plan, as was Margo. It was a situation from which everyone might profit. Now, disfigured and handicapped, neither the boardroom nor political landscape would welcome him.

The word cripple kept returning to Hank. This morning when the nurse helped him use the bedpan he felt ashamed and helpless. Struggling to move his body without pain so that she could help him relieve himself, he wanted to scream in frustration. Yesterday he'd been an active duty fighter pilot. Today he was a helpless invalid. He picked up a glass of water on the stand and threw it against the wall, shattering and throwing glass shards across the floor.

The door opened and Roger Hanson entered, his eyes shifting to the broken glass and water on the floor.

"Good morning, Hank," Hanson said, ignoring the mess. "How'd you sleep last night?"

"Not worth a shit." Hank felt in a nasty mood, why not take it out on Hanson.

"Be more specific, Hank. I can't try to fix 'not worth a shit.' I need a little more to go on." Roger stood at the side of the bed his hands clasped in front of him.

All right, Hank thought, I'll give him a chance. "I can't roll over with this contraption over my hand. Sleeping on my back is killing me."

"We can do something about that. I'm going to check the burned areas this morning. After we finish I will rig up a soft bandage to protect your hand."

"Okay." Hank tried to add a tone of civility to his response. He couldn't read this guy, the straightforward, no nonsense manner seemed to mask a different person.

"How about the pain? We have you on a fairly low dosage and I'd like to keep it that way if it's tolerable.

Hank thought about his hand, the damn thing did hurt, but it wasn't unbearable. "I can get by for now."

"Good. Now I'm ready to get on with this if you are. I know it's Christmas morning, but I figured you didn't have anything else to do."

"Can I see my face?"

Roger paused for a moment and then said, "If you'd like."

Hank wondered what he meant by that, why wouldn't he want to see the damage? "I'll see it sooner or later, right?"

"Of course you will. Just be prepared, burns like yours aren't pretty," Roger said.

Feeling nauseous, Hank felt a cold sweat break out despite the cool temperature of the room. "Just give me a minute."

"No rush." Roger uncovered a metal tray on the side cabinet. He seemed engrossed in examining the instruments, his back to Hank.

"How long have you been over here?" Hank asked.

Roger looked back over his shoulder. "Got here in the summer of '42. I was part of the Eighth Air Force's advance party. We had to figure out how to provide medical service for all of the different bases and fields that were popping up all over the island. It turned out we had to rely on the Brits initially until we ramped up the number of trained medical personnel we could get over here."

"So that's how you met the Brit doctor?"

"Pretty much. We didn't have many patients and it was a good chance to upgrade my clinical skills."

The doctor turned around, a set of stainless steel scissors in his hand. "I'm ready to take a look at that hand, if you are."

"Let's get it on with it."

Gently Roger cut and removed the gauze bandages. A nurse stood to one side with a tray to collect the discarded material. In less than a minute Hank's hand was exposed, it's red and black blistered flesh coated by a layer of petroleum jelly.

Hank couldn't take his eyes off what used to be his hand. It would never be the same. If he lived another fifty years, he would have to carry this claw every day. He wondered how he would button his pants.

Roger carefully examined Hank's fingers. He asked him to move each one individually and then collectively.

"Try to extend all your fingers fully."

Hank tried, but his hand was frozen.

"That's it."

"Fine, relax."

The Doctor picked up Hank's chart and made several notes in it.

"We'll reapply some ointment, and then put on the first layer of dressings. It appears your motor functions are not compromised too badly. The large burned area on the top of the hand is going to be the biggest problem. If you're ready we can take a look at your head."

Hank only nodded, the shock of his hand still gripping him as the nightmare continued.

It took longer to remove the dressings from the side of Hank's face. Adhesive tape had to be carefully removed along sensitive areas of the face and some of the tape had adhered to Hank's hair. The used bandages began to fill the metal pan. As Hanson worked, he carefully examined the damaged skin. Although he hadn't commented on it to Mitchell, Roger Hanson's optimism increased after seeing Hank's hand. Perhaps the damage to his face wasn't as bad as described. Now he stood back, holding the other side of Hank's face so he could get a full view of the burned area.

"How's it look?" Hank tried to sound relaxed, but his pulse was racing.

"Not as bad as I was led to believe. The damage to the area above your jaw should heal on its own with proper treatment."

Hank waited, sensing there was more to follow.

"I'm afraid your ear is pretty bad. How much of it we can save is hard to say."

"I want to see it," Hank said.

Hanson turned to the nurse and nodded. She walked over to the side table and picked up a large hand mirror. Handing it to Hanson, she picked up the discarded gauze and left the room.

Hank took the offered mirror and without hesitating held it out to view his face. He was stunned at the apparition that stared back at him. It was if someone had taken red and black wax and smeared it across the side of his face to the edge of his mouth. A shiny layer of protective jelly covered the burned area adding to the macabre vision. Then he saw his ear. The lower lobe was gone, the remaining flesh shone red in the stark light. Blackened pieces of flesh highlighted the charred edge. Hank handed the mirror back to Roger.

"You doing all right?"

Hank simply nodded, his worst fears now confirmed. He was a freak and no matter what anyone did, he would never be the same.

"With the exception of your ear, the actual tissue damage is not what we had originally feared. It's that way sometimes, the first evaluation doesn't really tell the story."

"You're saying it's okay?" Hank asked sarcastically.

"Not at all. You've had a severe injury. But with what we know now, we can do a great deal to get you back on your feet. My real concern is your hand."

Hank continued to take part in the conversation, but it was if someone else was talking. His mind kept returning to the horrible sight of his burned face.

"Why's that?"

"The face, as long as functionality isn't compromised, is cosmetic. But a severely burned hand that compromises the tendons and muscles will render the hand useless. Your hand is severely burned. Luckily the damage is confined to the upper layers of the skin. That tells me we can rehabilitate it to full functionality with proper treatment." Roger looked at the expression on Hank's face and knew what he would say next was critical. "In fact, I see no reason that you couldn't return to flying, in time."

Hank turned his head to look at Hanson, his frustration erupting. "What makes you think I'd ever want to?"

Roger looked up, surprised by the vehemence of Hank's reply. Slowly he said, "Because I talked to Major Cunning and he told me you were probably the best pilot in the Group and they needed you back."

Turning his head to look out the window, Hank said nothing for a minute. Then he looked back at Hanson and said, "I'm done flying and I'm done with this stinking war. Let someone else do it." He turned back to look out the window.

"I'll check back on you later." Hanson put the mirror on the table and reached for the door knob.

"And, Doc......."

Hanson turned.

"Merry fucking Christmas."

# Chapter Four

Royal Naval Hospital Haslar
Portsmouth, England
27 December, 1943

Doctor Roger Hanson opened the outer door to the Naval Hospital Commander's office. Inside a young WREN sat at a desk, reading a military phonebook.

"I'm Major Hanson. They told me at the ward that the Admiral wanted to see me.

"Oh yes, sir. We couldn't find you earlier."

"I just drove in from Whitchurch."

"Let me tell the Admiral you're here." She got up and knocked lightly on the closed wooden door that read, "Senior Surgeon." Without pausing she turned back out of the door, opening it wide. "Major, you may go in."

Rear Admiral Hugh Prescott sat at a small coffee table. Next to him sat a man in a superbly tailored suit, a crisp white shirt accented by a British regimental tie.

"Doctor Hanson, do come in and have a seat."

Roger sat down, folding his hands in his lap.

"This is Ambassador Winant," the Admiral said.

"Roger Hanson. Pleased to meet you, sir."

Roger recognized the name from the news magazines where the activities of the U.S. ambassador were constantly chronicled.

"The Ambassador has been down visiting Captain Mitchell."

"Yes, sir," Roger said, not sure where this was going.

Winant hesitated. "Doctor Hanson, I've known Hank and his family for many years. In fact his father and I attended college together and the families have stayed in very close contact."

Roger nodded, saying nothing.

"I've been assured that Tyler, Hank's father, will have been notified of his injuries by the Air Corps by now."

"Yes, sir, I would expect the telegram would have been sent by now."

"Quite so. But I wanted to get a clearer picture for myself so I might send Tyler an update."

"Yes, sir."

"Doctor, I'm stunned at his condition and I'm concerned."

"How so, Mr. Ambassador?" Roger asked.

"He's angry, morose and sullen. That's not Hank Mitchell I know. He was always a fire cracker, if you know what I mean." Winant leaned forward, his expression very serious.

"People react differently to serious injuries, sir. I've seen the same reaction many times before. An injury that can affect your capability to function, to say nothing of your appearance, evokes a panorama of emotions such as anger, self-pity or hopelessness. That depends on how that person is put together. How a patient eventually deals with the injury has a lot to do with their attitude. One of my jobs is to try and figure out the best course of action for that person. What works for one may not work for the other."

"Well, I hope when he gets back to the states that he can perk up. My God, he's down in the dumps. But I know his family will spare no expense to care for his injuries."

"Sir, he has a long period of rehab in front of him to regain full use of his hand. His face will heal, although there will be significant scarring. And I think he'll lose most of his left ear."

"My God," Winant said, sitting back in his chair, his gaze fixed on Roger. "That will be very difficult on the family."

"Yes, sir," Roger said trying to keep the sarcasm out of his voice. Continuing with his thought, he said, "I think returning him to the states right now is not in his best interest."

Winant's expression changed to puzzlement. "Why not? Surely he's better off with his family, to say nothing of the best medical care money can buy."

Roger leaned forward. "There're other things to consider, sir."

"Such as?" The Ambassador now sounded like a senior government official whose judgment was being questioned.

"Sir, the British have rewritten the book on burn treatment. I'm convinced there's no better place for a positive burn protocol than right here, right now."

The Admiral spoke up, "The work they've done at Grinstead is remarkable. Many of our lads owe their lives and futures to their efforts. The Doctor has a valid point."

Roger continued, his enthusiasm showing. "Sir, if Hank Mitchell goes back to the states, he loses the support of men who are going through the same battle. No offense intended, but the medical world back in the states doesn't understand combat injuries like the Brits do. They've had this war in their front yard for four years. They not only know how to treat the injury, they know how to treat the man."

The two older men sat without saying a word.

"If I can keep him here, take him to Grinstead and let them work their magic, I think you might get the old Hank Mitchell back. If he goes back to the states, I'm not sure."

"When I talked with him, he left no doubt in my mind he intended to return home," the Ambassador said.

"It's been three days since he saw his face for the first time. He's been withdrawn and angry ever since. I'm concerned that if I don't start the treatment soon, it'll be too late. But I'm at an impasse; he insists he wants to go home. I think in his mind the sanctuary of his former life can overcome this turn of events, but he's kidding himself."

"What do we do?" Winant asked.

"We can't do anything, sir. But I have an idea."

Squadron Leader Thomas Baden-Smythe knocked twice and entered room 623 of the Royal Naval Hospital Portsmouth.

"Hello there, may I come in?"

Hank looked up and was shocked to see a burn scarred face come from behind the door. He realized his expression showed his reaction.

"Don't worry, I'm used to it. I don't take offense anymore. I'm Thomas Baden-Smythe. My friends call me "Q". Roger Hanson thought you might like to hear a little bit about East Grinstead from a graduate."

Hank watched the man walk across the room, his stiff left leg making his gait slightly awkward. He extended his hand, which also bore the scars of fire. Gingerly accepting his hand, Hank felt very uncomfortable.

"Don't worry, it looks a bit bum, but works just fine. Mind if I sit down?"

"There's a chair over there."

The man smiled widely as he slid the chair up to the bed and sat down. He moved his head closer to Hank's looking at both sides.

"Only one side, that's a good thing. And only one hand. All things considered, you could have been much worse off."

His comments made Hank angry, but how do you react to someone who has clearly been burned worse than you have?

"So tell me what happened?" Baden-Smythe smiled and waited for Hank's response.

"P-51 escort on a mission over the continent. Didn't see the son of a bitch who got me over Bremen. Made it as far as the Channel before my Mustang decided to turn into a torch."

"You never see the one who gets you. Same for me. We jumped a flight of Heinkels over Dover and before I knew it, the entire cockpit was on fire. Lucky to even get out."

"When was it?" Hank asked, warming to Baden-Smythe's personality.

"October 23, 1940, one day I shan't soon forget."

Hank looked at the shiny scars and tight skin of Baden-Smythe's face. The man's eyes were bright and sparkled when he talked.

"So they treated you at Grinstead?"

"For almost a year. But without them, I probably wouldn't have made it."

"Why's that?" Hank found himself captivated by the outgoing flyer.

"Everyone there's in the same boat. It takes good medicine, but it also takes the right situation to get over a brew up like this...or yours. And I know of what I speak."

"So did you ever fly again?"

"On active service with 666 squadron at Tangmere right now, flying Spit Mark Nines. A tremendous aircraft. Holds its own with your Mustang D's. The only thing that Jerry has to compare is the FW-190."

Hank noted several ribbons beneath his embroidered wings, including the Distinguished Flying Cross. "Was it hard to get back in a cockpit?"

Baden-Smythe stared at Hank for a moment. "Was I scared? Without question. Terrified is a more apt description. But I figured that I'm still ahead of the game by just being alive. So bugger it, I'm flying until the war ends or I buy it. Simple as that."

Hank had never heard anyone being so honest about the fear he knew everyone felt in combat. Nor had he ever encountered a pilot who was so black and white on his future. No wonder these guys whipped the Luftwaffe in the Battle of Britain, he thought.

"Q" spent the next hour describing the treatment at East Grinstead, from the physical layout to the normal sequence of treatment. The more he talked, the more questions he received from Hank.

"Well, I best get on my way. I'm on alert later today."

"Thanks for taking the time to talk to me. I honestly don't know what I'm going to do, but at least I've heard it from the horse's mouth."

Baden-Smythe looked askance at Hank. "Horse's mouth?"

"One of those Yank expressions."

"Quite so." He laughed. "Hard to believe we had the same ancestors! Good luck."

"And to you."


Later, as he lay in bed, Hank thought about what Baden-Smythe had said. What should he do? It sounded like they had a good program. But wouldn't the top flight clinics at home be the same? He had to admit he missed the family and he'd be able to see them again. If the doctors were successful at East Grinstead, he might regain flight status. Every night since the accident, vivid memories would flash back to him. The flames roaring back over the cockpit wall, struggling to find the parachute rip cord and the freezing water in the Channel.

There was a sharp knock on his door, which swung open.

"Hank, you look much better than the last time I saw you." John Winant carried a small box of toffees which he put on the bed stand next to Hank. "These are marvelous. Hope you like toffee."

"Thanks," Hank said, although he couldn't have cared less about the candy.

"I wanted you to know I got through to your father. He'd been notified by the War Department, but there weren't any details. I filled him in and he'll let the family know." Winant smiled.

"What did he say?" Hank asked.

"He wanted specifics on how bad you were hurt"

"What did you tell him?"

Winant hesitated. "Hank, I told him it was serious. I also said I thought you'd be coming home for treatment."

Hank's voice became very soft. "Did you tell him I was burned?"

The ambassador nodded.

"And he was going to tell Margo?"

"That was my understanding."

"That'll be an interesting conversation," Hank said, his tone mildly sarcastic.

"What have you heard about going back home?" Winant asked, trying to change the subject.

"Doctor Hanson told me it would be a minimum of two weeks before I should travel. I guess I'd go home then if the damn Army can figure out how to get me on a ship."

"Well they're all looking forward to seeing you." The ambassador smiled, clearly uncomfortable.

"You think that applies to Margo?

Winant's expression changed to frustration. "Hank, I honestly don't know. I've known Margo and her family for a long time. They're good people. But this is something that many people have trouble dealing with."

"I appreciate your honesty. But who wants to be seen with a circus freak?"

The two men said nothing.

"Hank, cross that bridge when you come to it. Right now, just work on getting better."

Hank nodded, fighting hard to keep his anger and frustration in check.

The wail of air raid sirens punctured Hank's thoughts. He'd been thinking about Margo.

"All right, Mr. Mitchell. Ambulatory patients must proceed to the shelter at the end of corridor six. You haven't been on your feet much lately. Do you think you can manage?" Nurse Castle asked from the doorway.

Hank glared at her. "Why in the hell would I want to go to a shelter?"

"We are quite close to the naval piers and they are a frequent target of the Germans." She sounded very business like.

"Well I'll tell you, I don't particularly care if they do drop a bomb on my room. Might solve a lot of problems."

"Mr. Mitchell, you are in the care of the Royal Navy. We're responsible for you and you will go to the shelter. If you can't manage on your own, I'll be happy to get the orderlies to carry you down there."

The tone in her voice reminded Hank of a drill instructor. She wasn't going to take no for an answer.

"Yes, ma'am," he said.

He walked slowly down the corridor watching the staff going about their duties. He saw several of the nurses wearing helmets and realized they were staying with the patients that couldn't be moved. Signs directed him down a well lit stairway, past a wall of sandbags and into a large room full of people sitting on benches or standing. Most were wearing hospital garb, ranging from robes to pajamas. Several of the nurses were checking on patients, making sure they were comfortable.

"Captain Mitchell, sit down over here. We could be here for some time." He turned to see Nurse Fleming motioning him to a padded bench.

"How long do these things last?" he said as he sat down carefully.

"Longest was almost two hours. If this is just a nuisance raid, it should be over shortly. But we never know."

Hank watched the staff going around the room. Most patients were sitting calmly. In the distance, he could faintly hear a steady crack which he knew were long range anti-aircraft batteries taking the attacking aircraft under fire. He felt the ground shudder once, then three more times in quick succession, each more pronounced. The anti-aircraft fire picked up in intensity and the room started to shake. He saw Nurse Fleming look with alarm at one of her fellow nurses who nodded. Four more explosions shook the room, sending debris down from the rafters. Hank looked around trying to understand what was going on as a violent crash split one of the overhead beams. One end of the lower section fell straight down, knocking Nurse Fleming to the ground. Another crash, then silence. A light cloud of dust filled the air, the room now totally quiet.

"Everyone all right?" Someone asked.

"No," Hank said, taking two steps over to Nurse Fleming. She lay on her back under the beam which now was in danger of detaching at the other end which would crush Fleming. "Help me move her."

"Here, mate," he heard a man say and another patient helped him pull her to safety.

Hank knelt down at her side.

"Are you all right?"

She lay still, staring up at the ceiling.

"I can't seem to move. Please call a doctor," she said softly.

Hank stared down at her. She lay on the concrete floor motionless, her arms at her side. Blood ran down the side of her face from a cut on her head.

"I need a doctor over here, right now!"

He leaned over so she could see him. "You're gonna be fine, just be still."

"Thank you, Mr. Mitchell," she said.

The next morning Hank walked to the end of wing five to see the bomb damage. One stick of bombs had hit within the confines of the medical compound. Miraculously only one person was killed, an ambulance driver who had chosen to stay out of the shelter.

He saw Nurse Castle walking toward him.

"Ma'am? Any word on Nurse Fleming?"

She stopped and looked up at him.

Hank could see her eyes were red.

"It's too early to tell," she said, her voice tenuous.

"I'm sorry."

Nurse Castle looked at Hank with curiosity. "You were with her when the beam fell, weren't you?"

He nodded.

"Would you like to see her?"

"Is it okay? I don't want to intrude on her family."

"Her husband was killed at Dunkirk and her only son is a prisoner in Singapore. Come along."


Joyce Fleming was alone in the single room when Hank and Nurse Castle arrived. The open window allowed bright sunlight to illuminate the white sheets which covered her to the neck. There were no pillows under her head, but a padded block sat on each side of her head and a small towel supported her neck.

"You have a visitor, Joyce."

"It's Hank Mitchell, Nurse Fleming. I wanted to see how you were doing."

"Quite well, Mr. Mitchell," she replied, her voice strained.

"Joyce, I have to make rounds. I'll check back on you later. Mr. Mitchell, you are welcome to stay."

Hank would have normally jumped at an excuse to leave a hospital room, but something made him want to stay with the injured nurse. "Can you use some company?" he asked.

"Yes.....thank you."

He pulled a chair up to her bedside and sat down. "How are you really?"

For a moment he thought she hadn't heard him.

"A bit scared, quite honestly," she finally said.

"I think I understand."

It was quiet in the hospital. The only sound came from a buffing machine being used on the tile in the corridor.

"You've been a nurse here for a long time?"

"Since 1922. My husband was in the Navy. His ship was here and I was just out of nursing school."

"This is a Navy town?"

"My goodness, yes. For four hundred years or so."

He saw a slight smile on her lips. "I'd never been in an air raid before."

"I guess we've become used to them. Jerry has been dropping bombs on us for five years."

"It seems like England has been in the thick of it from the beginning."

"Second time in twenty years. I remember the first war, I was a teenager. The terrible casualties, men coming home with no legs or arms, their lungs destroyed by mustard gas. The Germans have caused a great deal of pain over the years."

Hank got up and walked over to her side.

"Is there anything I can get you?"

She smiled. "Why Mr. Mitchell, you have the makings of a nurse."

"Please call me Hank. And I don't have what it takes to be a nurse. Now can I get you anything?"

"Truly, I'm fine. It's been nice talking with you. Takes my mind off...."

"Then I'll stay if you don't mind. Takes my mind off it too."


Roger Hanson stepped into Hank's room later that morning. Hearing about the bombing the night before, the doctor had been on the road from Whitchurch as soon as he could round up a driver.

"You had quite a night," he said as Hank looked up from a road atlas he had spread across his lap.

"Doc, glad you're here. I was just checking to see where East Grinstead was on the map. Not too far from here."

"No it's only about an hour and a half by car. But why are you looking at that?" Roger walked over to the side of the bed. "You aren't going to tell me you changed your mind, are you?"

"I want to get back in this war."

Roger shook his head. "I just received your orders sending you back to the states."

Hank snapped back, "I changed my mind."

"It's not that easy. Once you've been approved for out processing from theater, lots of things happen to arrange that move. It's a paperwork nightmare, but it's a fact. Trying to get the order rescinded before it's time for you to leave is almost impossible."

"You're kidding," Hank asked looking for a positive response.

"Wish I was. Your orders were fast tracked, I suspect because of the ambassador. Medically you're fit to travel and that's all they needed."

"Christ."

"You're scheduled to depart Southampton in one week."

"How can I get that changed?" asked Hank.

"Honestly?"

Hank nodded.

"I'll deny ever saying this, but you need to back door the system using the ambassador."

"Will you go see him for me?"

Roger laughed. "If they find out a lowly major went around the entire chain of command, directly to the U.S. ambassador, they'll lock me up in Leavenworth and throw away the key."

"Will you do it?"

"Yeah, what the hell," Roger said as he shook his head. This must be the Hank Mitchell that the Ambassador and Major Cunning had been talking about and he liked this version.


Later that day, Major Roger Hanson U.S. Army called at the Embassy of the United States in London. He carried a personal letter for the Ambassador Winant and requested to deliver it in person. John Winant, while surprised and disappointed for Tyler Mitchell, was supportive of his request after a brief explanation by Roger Hanson. A phone call that afternoon from the Ambassador to General Ira Eaker,

Commanding the Eighth Air Force in England, resulted in a series of phone calls and telexes back and forth between organizations in England. Two trans-Atlantic telegrams closed the loop on the proposed transfer of Captain Henry Tyler Mitchell, III to the United States for treatment of combat injuries. One day later a military ambulance delivered Hank Mitchell to the Queen Victoria hospital in East Grinstead.

# Chapter Five

Queen Elizabeth Hospital
East Grinstead
West Sussex, England
31 December, 1943

Doctor Duncan Frazier pulled off a set of rubber gloves and threw them on the table. Hank Mitchell lay in a dental chair with his head supported by two cushioned pads. The bandages covering his head had been removed exposing the damaged area.

Frazier pulled up a chair. Roger Hanson stood to one side, his arms crossed on his chest.

"You were lucky. Doctor Hanson has spent time here and his treatment was exactly in line with our protocols. The salve he used on you at Portsmouth is something we developed early in the war. It's mostly petroleum jelly, but we also add several unique compounds that we have found to be beneficial to the healing process and preventing infections. A word to the wise, many of the things we do here might seem more than is needed, but we are very sensitive to preventing infections during the treatment."

Hank nodded.

"I think that Doctor Hanson's prognosis is accurate. We should be able to restore full use of your hand. There isn't much we can do about your ear. It's mostly cartilage and we just don't have anything that can replace it. My biggest concern is the large area of third degree burns on the top of the hand. I don't

38

see any option but to graft skin over the damaged area when it's ready. It does take time, so you'll have to be patient."

"How long are we talking, doctor?" Hank asked.

"I should think three months to get your hand up to full functionality. During that we'll time continue with the healing and cosmetic restoration of the face.

"Suppose I don't care about being pretty right now? How long will it take to get me to where I can fly an aircraft again?"

Frazier looked first at Hank then at Roger.

Hanson nodded.

"Very well. I should think with hard work on your part you should be quite capable of passing an RAF flight check in six months."

"Then that's what I want to do."

"Is there something pressing?" Frazier asked.

"A score to settle."

Frazier stood up. "Motivation takes many forms, Captain Mitchell. I've seen patient recoveries driven by every emotion from hate to love. We try to take that into account, but it's really the results that count.


One hour later, Hank returned to his room. Although it was a two man room, the nurse told Hank his roommate, Flight Lieutenant Trevor Mahan had been granted an overnight pass to London. Hank preferred to be alone, but he could handle a room mate. He didn't plan on being at East Grinstead that long.

As he sat back on his bed, Hank thought about Duncan Frazier's words. Six months to get back in action. Not me, pal, he thought. I'll do it sooner than you think. These people seem to know what they're doing and Hanson says he wants to get me back in a cockpit. He remembered Joyce Fleming lying on the floor of that shelter.

"They told me to expect a bunk mate."

A tall RAF pilot walked into the room carrying a small valise. His uniform looked hand tailored and his shoes gleamed from a recent polish. He put his case down on the bed and turned to face Hank. No one warned Hank that Trevor Mahan had been severely burned in a crash landing of his crippled Mosquito fighter. The skin on his cheeks showed the shiny evidence of Doctor Frazier's repairs. His nose looked as if it were made from pinkish clay, the nostrils unduly visible. One ear looked partially damaged, while the other looked normal.

"Name's Mahan, Trevor Mahan." He held out his hand to Hank, who quickly noticed his hand appeared undamaged.

"Hank Mitchell. They told me you'd be back today."

Mahan turned to put his hat on the top shelf of a clothes cabinet.

"It's all that keeps me sane quite frankly, my little trips to the city."

He came back and sat down on his bed, loosening his tie. "Freshly arrived and still sporting that new guy look. Let's have a look at you." He leaned forward and looked at both sides of Hank's face. "Right, you most definitely belong in the Guinea Pig Club."

"Did you say Guinea Pig?"

"Quite right, those of us who have been through the often trial and error course of treatment here, like to feel we belong to an exclusive club."

"Not something that sounds too inviting to me." This guy almost sounds happy, Hank thought.

"You'll quickly find that no one here is going to feel sorry for you or let you feel sorry for yourself. Once you get past that, it's tolerable."

"How long you been here?"

Mahan stood up and removed his coat, hanging it in the locker under the cap.

"Almost fourteen months. I was flying Mosquito night fighters out of Church Fenton and crash landed after tangling with a Heinkel. Too much petrol in the tanks and the fire crew had a time getting me out. Since then it's been a steady treatment of grafts, saline baths and therapy."

A wave of discouragement swept over Hank. Suddenly the task in front of him seemed overwhelming and his anger returned.

The door opened and a young woman wearing the light blue smock of the hospital volunteers entered. She was the same age as the two patients, a wisp of a girl with dark brunette hair and beautiful smile.

"Miss Murray, I haven't seen you around lately, I thought you might have run off to London to seek your fortune."

She crossed the room to hand him a mimeographed piece of paper.

"You know I normally work in Ward Three, Mr. Mahan. I'm only helping Sister Angela today." She turned to Hank and handed him an identical sheet. "This is the menu for the week. Sister Angela asked me to remind you that it is subject to change." She smiled quickly at Hank, her deep green eyes friendly but wary.

"Thanks," he said finding himself at a loss for words. Hank realized he was self conscious of his bandages and the smell.

"Hank, this is Miss Katherine Murray one of our lovely volunteers who are here to minister to our every need. I've longed for her since my arrival, but alas she has spurned all my advances. I remain distraught and discouraged, but then love is a fickle thing."

Kate Murray turned toward the door.

"Are all pilots incorrigible, Mr. Mahan?"

"Only in the Royal Air Force, my dear," he said with a hint of pride. "Now the Yanks are entirely different and you'll find Captain Mitchell here irresistible."

"Without a doubt," she said and swung the door closed.

"She's quite the dish, wouldn't you say?" Mahan asked.

Hank didn't respond. No woman will ever look at me like they used to, he thought. Seeing that lovely young woman reminded him how his life had changed.


"The saline bath does several things. It allows us to remove dressings with minimal disruption to the skin surface. The water also promotes granulation of the skin and helps combat infections." Roger sat on a small chair watching Hank, whose hand was immersed in a large washtub equipped with a circulating motor which kept the water moving.

"What next?"

"I want you in the bath for one hour. Then we'll sprinkle on a light layer of sulpha powder and reapply the gauze dressing."

"And I keep working the fingers?"

"Right. One of the biggest problems the Brits saw at the beginning of the war with burns to the hand was a loss of motor functions as the skin healed and contracted. They were using a tannic acid treatment back then, so the danger now isn't as great. But I don't want to take any chances. If you want to be holding a throttle with that hand in three months, keep flexing those fingers."

"Okay, Doc."

The quiet hum from the motor and light gurgle of water kept them company as the minutes ticked off.

"So you're from New York?" Roger asked as he closed the medical book he'd been reading.

Hank opened his eyes and looked over. "Yeah, grew up on Long Island. My Dad works in the city. How about you?"

"Other side of the country, Seattle."

"We're both a long way from home."

"So what really changed your mind about staying here? According to Cunning, you had it made back in the states."

"Maybe I have a score to settle."

Roger looked at the young pilot, wondering what he meant.

Hank added, "What difference does it make anyway?"

Getting up from his chair, the doctor walked over to the bookcase with the book.

"There's more to doctoring than just treating the wounds, Hank." Roger moved over by the saline bath. "A lot of what will determine whether or not you recover fully from this comes from right here." He put his finger on the side of his head. "The more serious the injury, the more important the patient's attitude. Simple as that."

"And you think I'm doing this for the wrong reason?"

"I don't know. I suspect you don't know for sure either. Maybe you're afraid for your family to see you. Maybe you have a death wish and figure if you stay here it'll come true. People do things for different reasons. I think both of us need to remember that as we deal with these burns."

Hank looked up at Roger, "Just fix my hand, Doc. Nothing else matters."

Roger turned and walked out the open door. Hank's angry he thought, but that could be a good thing.

Looking down at the swirling water, Hank's anger returned. Every time he seemed to have turned a corner the depression returned to put a black cloud over him. He couldn't help his reactions and that made his outburst at Roger that much more distasteful after the fact. He'd never felt so out of control and it was destroying his outlook on life.

"Shit," he muttered and pulled his hand out of the bath. He held the awful claw in front of his face and tried to move his fingers. There was movement, the pain shooting up his arm. Water dripped on the floor as he stood up and went to find Roger.

Later that afternoon, Hank walked down to one of the communal rooms that had become a combination lounge, ready room and public house for the servicemen undergoing treatment at Queen Victoria Hospital.

As he entered, two men who were playing cards looked up. Except for their obvious facial injuries, they almost looked like they were in a club. Both wore RAF uniforms, their shirts open at the collar. Trevor mentioned the standard practice of wearing uniforms as much as possible instead of pajamas and robes. He had to admit that it felt better to wear trousers. Somehow he felt more like an aviator than an invalid.

"I heard we had a Yank here." Hank's khaki uniform included his captain's bars and silver wings.

The other man, whose back was turned, twisted and looked. Hank saw the horrible scars on the man's face and tried to hide his reaction.

They returned to their cribbage game and Hank walked over to a small bookshelf and looked at the titles. Glancing out the window at the covered walkway that ran between the wards, he saw Katherine Murray carrying several blankets in her arms. He watched her as she crossed the walk and met two patients going in the opposite direction. She smiled at them and stopped for a few words. Funny, Hank thought, in the middle of all this crap she can smile. He pulled a book from the shelf with his good hand. Without looking at the title he turned to walk back to his room.

A week later, Hank had settled into a comfortable routine of saline baths, dressing changes and physical therapy. The novelty of being the only American in the hospital faded and he was happy to be left alone. Trevor Mahan was at the very end of his treatment, with his release expected within the next two weeks. Despite the British pilot's happy go lucky demeanor, Hank could detect edginess as the time approached to leave the hospital and return to active service. Was he wrestling with the same fears that Hank had already considered?

"So what happens when you actually get out of here?" Hank asked.

"Two weeks of leave, then report to 11 Group headquarters at Uxbridge." Mahan seemed to drift off into thought as if he was considering the assignment.

"Any idea what you'll be doing?"

"Some kind of admin work I should suppose."

They lapsed into silence and both continued their reading.

"Have you thought about flying again?" Hank asked.

Mahan looked up from a magazine.

"If they ask me, I'll give it a go. But quite honestly I was never the greatest pilot, probably better to leave it at that."

Hank wondered how he would feel when his time came.


"Your range of motion is not increasing as I would have expected," Doctor Hanson said as he wrote in Hank's chart. "Have you been running through all of the exercises four times a day?"

"Yeah, pretty much," Hank said as he tried to extend his fingers upward and outward from his palm, the pain shooting up his arm.

"Well 'pretty much' isn't going to get the job done," Hanson snapped.

"Get off my back," Hank's voice rose, aided by the pain he felt.

"I'll leave you alone when you decide to take full part in the program. You can't pick and choose what you will or will not do, it doesn't work that way. This is about more than Hank Mitchell, even though that's as far as you can see. If this treatment is successful, I might be able to persuade the Air Corps to adopt McIndoe's methods. That'll make a lot of difference for the men who are going to get burned in this theatre. You ought to do it for yourself; God knows you're self centered enough. But at least do it for the guys who will need this treatment in the future." Roger turned and slammed the door as he left.

Hank sat stunned for a moment then stood up, upsetting the entire tray of instruments which crashed onto the floor along with a water glass that shattered. "Shit!"

The door swung open and Katherine Murray looked in, her face showing concern. "Is everything all right?"

Hank pushed past her, "Absolutely, couldn't be better."

The young woman turned to watch Hank walk down the hall. He didn't look back.

Hank found Roger Hanson at the nurse's station. The Doctor stood with his back against the wall, arms folded over his chest. He looked at Hank.

"I didn't understand what this was all about," Hank said.

Roger didn't say anything, but stood up straight from the wall. He turned to face Hank. "Don't ever forget that I will do everything I can to help you get better. But I've also got a responsibility to every man out there who's going in harm's way." He turned and walked away down the corridor.

Hank walked slowly back down to the treatment room. *Sometimes you're an asshole, Mitchell. This is one of those times.*

He opened the door to find Miss Murray picking up the instruments from among the glass, carefully placing each one in a sterilizer pan.

"Here, let me help you," he said, bending down to pick up a large piece of broken glass.

She looked up, but didn't say anything, her expression hard to read.

Hank was embarrassed and said quietly, "I'm afraid I lost my temper."

"You're not the first. In fact it's rather common around here. We try to pay it no mind."

They continued in silence and shortly had the floor cleaned up and instruments ready for cleaning.

"Miss Murray, thank you."

Turning, he saw surprise on her face. "You remembered my name."

"I did, Katherine Murray." He smiled at her. "Am I forgiven for my terrible behavior?

She returned the smile. "You are. But only if you'll call me Kate."

# Chapter Six

Queen Elizabeth Hospital
East Grinstead
West Sussex, England
14 January, 1944

Doctor Duncan Frazier examined Hank's hand very slowly.

"This has been a good two weeks. Doctor Hanson and I feel it's time to graft healthy skin to cover the large area extending from your knuckles back to the wrist. Over the last three years we've done many of these. We don't expect any problems."

Roger stood to one side, watching his colleague.

Frazier continued, "We'll select an area on your right side about five inches above the waist," Duncan Frazier said as he drew on a plain paper tablet with a pencil. "Then a flap will be lifted and your hand taped in place such that the flap will align and cover the top of your hand. Your body will continue to support and nourish the flap while the underside will be attaching itself to the damaged area of your hand. At the eight to nine day point we'll be able to cut the remaining skin linking the flap to your side and now you have healthy skin on the hand. Your side will of course heal in due course with our monitoring for any problems."

"Any questions?" Roger asked.

Hank shook his head no, knowing that he would do whatever they told him to and accept whatever happened.

"We're both very encouraged by the increasing flexibility and range of motion you've gained. I know it's a painful process, but as you can see it does work. This is particularly important because we'll have to curtail your exercises completely for the first four days after surgery. Can't afford to disturb the healing process. During that time you'll lose some of the flexibility you've gained, but it will come back when we allow you to work your hand on day five. Any questions?"

"Just tell me what to do. Now when are we gonna get to it?"

"In about an hour. I'll have the orderlies stop by to get you when it's time."

"Right," Hank said without emotion.


"Strange chap, Roger," Frazier said as they walked down to the operating theater to scrub.

"I haven't figured him out yet. Major Cunning tells me about this upbeat, cocky fighter pilot, but I sure haven't seen it. All I see is anger and very little of anything else. Maybe because his life was so promising, it hit him harder than most."

"So the rich are going to be more depressed by being burned than the milkman's son."

"You know that's not what I meant. But just consider. His future was on a gold plated road. New York society, the opera, debutante balls, and he was going to be right in the middle of all of it. Now he sees himself as a circus freak who will never be accepted by his world.

"That's absurd," Frazier sharply.

"We know that, but it's his perception and that's all that matters right now. His room mate, Trevor Mahan, actually came to see me because he was worried about him."

Frazier turned to Roger. "But you still think surgery is a good idea?"

"I think it's his only chance. Getting back into a cockpit may be the only thing that will allow Hank Mitchell to reclaim his life. Even that might not do it, but I say we give him a shot at it."

"Then let's get on with it. I haven't worked any miracles today and I'm in the mood."

The two doctors pushed open the swinging door to Operating Theatre Three.

Hank lay on his back. Adhesive tape secured his left arm to his side. In spite of the restraint, he'd had a quiet night, the sedative allowing him to sleep almost straight through. Staring at the ceiling, the sounds of morning came from the hall, a hospital waking up. A neatly made up set of covers on the other bed told him Mahan was out on another jaunt into the world. "Must be nice." Hank thought. Wrinkling his nose, he moved his facial muscles in response to the slight itch under the bandages on his face. Winking his eye seemed to help and he alternately winked and wrinkled as he stared up at the ceiling. Then a face stared down at him.

"Are you quite all right?" Kate Murray asked, a look of alarm on her face.

Closing both eyes he felt the humiliation rise. How could he have missed her entering the room?

"I'm fine, Miss Murray.....Kate," he said quickly, trying to act as dignified as possible under the circumstances.

"If you say so," she said skeptically. "I have a breakfast tray for you."

His stomach rumbled and she smiled at him.

"That sounds like a 'yes' to me," she said and turned to go get the tray.

Hank wondered why he felt so awkward around this woman. He'd only seen her three times since their first meeting, but each time she'd been able to pull him out of his foul mood. What was it about her that touched him?

She was back, placing the tray on his bed stand. Moving to the bed, Kate said, "Here, let me help you sit up."

Hank began to twist.

"No, wait. Let me help you so you don't pull your bandages."

He stopped and looked her in the eye, their faces now close and a look of concern on hers.

"This is kind of awkward trying to move with one good arm."

48

"That's what I'm here for.  Now slowly roll to your right and I'll help pull you up and back."

She put her hand under his right hip and the two of them slid him to a more upright position.

"There we go.  Now let me get another pillow for behind you."

He watched her go to the closet and open the door.  She turned back and saw him staring at her and smiled. "Everything all right?"

"Yes, fine.  Thanks."

As she fluffed up the pillow behind his back she commented that he was the first American on the ward.

"That's a distinction I would just as soon have avoided," he said quietly.

"Well, just plan on being the first American patient to be released from here, good as new."

"I don't think 'good as new' is every going to apply to me again."

Her expression turned serious.

"They do wonderful work here, they really do."  There was an intensity to her voice that reinforced her words.

Hank smiled ruefully.  "Some things can't be made right again.  I just want to get back in an airplane."

She walked over beside the bed and picked up his good hand in hers.  "I've been at this hospital for three years.  While the men from here don't leave looking like they were never burned, they all leave stronger and better inside and I think that's what counts."  With a quick smile, she let go of his hand, turned and started for the door.

"Miss Murray, thank you," he said much more formally than he intended

She turned and said, "Captain Mitchell, you're welcome, and my name is Kate."


An hour later, Trevor Mahan returned to the room.  He wore his service uniform and carried a manila envelope in his hand.

"Well I'm off, all checked out and ready for the road."  Walking over to Hank's bed he offered his hand and the two men shook hands silently.

"You watch your ass out there," Hank said as Trevor reached down to pick up his valise. "But it's hard to get hurt in a cushy staff job, right?"

"Actually, this is a change of orders." He held up the envelope.

"And..."

"Seems that Fighter Command is short of experienced Mosquito pilots and they are expanding the number of squadrons. So two months in the RTU and back on operations."

His voice was matter of fact, but Hank could tell he was upset.

"Where will you be," Hank said trying to engage his friend.

"Right back to Church Fenton, site of my last little smash up."

The two men looked at each other, each understanding the implications of what was happening.

"You could turn in your wings. Flying is still voluntary, right?"

Trevor put on his overcoat. "Simply not something that's done, old man."

Hank understood. "Yeah, I know."

"Well, I'll make the best of it. Find myself a crusty old navigator and make sure we both survive this war." He flashed an exaggerated smile, but Hank could see the anxiousness in Trevor's eyes.

"You take care of yourself. We'll meet in London sometime for a drink."

Trevor picked up his bag and moved to the door. "Your treat?"

Hank laughed. "My treat."


"So how long before they cut your hand loose?" Chris Christiansen asked Hank.

"Doc said tomorrow and none too soon. I'm getting real tired of hugging myself."

Chris laughed. "Wait 'til I tell the guys about this."

"This is something those jokers don't need to know about."

"You think they'll let you fly again?"

"Hell, I haven't forgotten how. As the invasion gets closer they're gonna need every pilot they can get."

"In the last two weeks the krauts have been getting desperate. They've been pressing their attacks even after the bombers have flown into the flak belts."

Hank could see the strain in Chris's face and let him talk.

"Pat Madison had to jump out over Soligen, but we saw a good chute. One of the new guys, you never met him, got bagged on his second mission, never knew what hit him. Larry Campbell got hit on an escort mission two days ago, a cannon shell went off right below the wing root, but he got back and landed at Biggin Hill. He's in the hospital down there for now. We're damned lucky that Wilskie's been there the whole time. He really helps keep everyone settled down."

"How're you holding up?"

"I'm doing okay. They made me a division lead, so I guess I'm doing something right."

Hank had always been impressed with Chris's flying skill and knew he'd be a good flight lead. But Hank could sense his friend was tired. Chris had been in constant combat for almost four months.

"You just keep watching your six, buddy."

"Well if you'd get your butt back in a cockpit, you could watch it for me."

The two men laughed, comrades still, only separated for a time.

"So when they gonna let you get out of here and get some fresh air?"

Hank knew the answer, "Once I get this hand back, Doc Hanson said I could go into town, maybe even London. I'll tell you though, anywhere is fine. I'm going stir crazy in here."


Dr. Duncan Frazier snipped one final piece of adhesive tape and stepped back.

"All right, why don't you work your arm and shoulder a bit. Then we'll take a look at your hand."

Hank brought his arm forward and carefully stretched it horizontally in front of his chest. Slowly he began to work it back until he held his hand out directly sideways from his body.

"It feels good to move it, but the shoulder is a bit stiff."

"Good," Frazier said, "Now show me your range of flexibility with your fingers."

Over the next fifteen minutes, Duncan Frazier and Roger conducted a thorough check of Hank's motor functions.

While he felt some pain at the edge of extension, Hank was surprised his hand was working better. The fresh skin moved like the original, only the whitish red scar that ran along the entire graft indicating the extent of the former damage.

"Splendid, Captain. I believe we have crossed a major hurdle and in a relatively short time."

"You were lucky there was no damage to your palm. With your graft protecting the major part of the damage, the remaining peripheral burns will continue to heal naturally. It's more important than ever to keep at your exercises to increase the flexibility and range of motion during the healing process." Roger took Hank's wrist and rotated his hand back and forth examining the other burned areas.

"Also, don't begin to think that the danger from infection is passed. You must continue with all of the procedures you've been shown to prevent problems. It would be a bloody shame to suffer a setback at this point."

"I won't take any chances," Hank said. "Does this mean I can get out of here on a little liberty now?"

Frazier nodded. "I shouldn't see why not. Trips into town at first, I want you back here each night. You're not ready for much more than that. And you will follow all hospital orders while you're out. We've had too many chaps start mucking around with our work and create problems."

"Don't worry, Doc. I'll do whatever you say. I just want to get out of here and see real people." Hank hadn't realized how much he really did want to escape the ward, even if only for an hour.

"One advantage of going into town is that no one here stares at wounded men any more. They've seen everything and have gotten quite used to it," Frazier added. "And it's time to stop wearing your face bandage."

"Hank, if you want to go out tomorrow, I'll get a pass ready for you. Besides, it's supposed to be a nice day," Roger said.

Without the bandage, Hank thought, that's gonna be tough. But I've got to get used to it at some point.


Armed with a set of directions from the senior nurse, Hank turned down the offered ride. She told him to follow Hollye Road for about a mile to East Grinstead.

He enjoyed the walk although he wasn't used to so much exercise. The last five weeks, much of it spent in bed, had taken its toll. Enjoying his freedom, Hank walked past neatly kept houses on both sides of the road. Just like small towns everywhere, he thought.

Thirty minutes later he saw a series of buildings and decided he had found the town. The brisk winter morning began to chill Hank, despite his gloves, scarf and raincoat. Ahead a single story brick building carried a large green and white sign noting "Geo. Hunicutt – Bookseller." Books or no books, Hank thought, a little warmth was in order. He opened the door to the sound of a small bell which hung over the sill.

Inside he found a small shop lined with rows of bookshelves. He was the only customer and no one attended the small counter at the rear. What the hell, he thought; maybe I'll find a book.

Slowly the warmth returned as he examined the shelves for a potential purchase. He'd always enjoyed book shops back home, the shelves always promising the potential of new adventures or knowledge to the reader. He found himself looking at a shelf of British novelists. He'd studied economics when he attended Harvard, and novels were never high on the list of required reading, particularly British novels. A nicely bound black volume with gold lettering caught his eye, "A Tale of Two Cities" by Dickens. He pulled it off the shelf with his right hand and cradled the book in his left elbow. Checking the cover page, it read: "Printed in 1937 by H. Christie and Sons, London/Newcastle." Hank looked around at the shop, must be tough to make a living like this, he thought.

"May I help you," a familiar voice asked from behind him?

He turned to see Kate Murray behind the wooden counter.

"Oh, it's you," she said, a slight flush rising on her cheeks.

"Hello," Hank said, feeling very self conscious, she had never seen him without his bandages. "I was just looking for a book." He held up the volume of Dickens as he walked back to the counter. "Actually I was cold and this looked like a good place to warm up."

"So you don't really want a book?" She asked, not seeming to notice the scars on his face.

"No, I think some books would help the time pass at the hospital," he said quickly.

"Perhaps I can help you find one?"

"Thanks," Hank said. She seemed totally oblivious of the damage to his face. Had she seen so much that it didn't bother her anymore?

Kate picked up the book. "Do you enjoy Dickens?"

"Haven't read a lot of him, but I think so."

"I was just fixing some tea in the back. Why don't we have a cup of tea and decide which books you might like?"

Hank returned her smile. "I'd like that."


Like many English shops, there were living quarters in the rear for the owner and his family. Kate showed Hank to the kitchen which overlooked a small garden.

He sat leafing through the volume of Dickens as she finished making two cups of tea.

"I know you Americans love coffee, but it's hard to get in our markets."

"I've developed a taste for your English tea. It's a lot better than the tea back home."

She carried a small pot over to the table and set it on a trivet. Two white china cups sat to each side of the pot, and she poured the steaming liquid into them.

"Would you like milk or sugar?" she asked, setting the pot down.

Hank shook his head. "No, thanks."

"So this is where you work when you're not at the hospital?"

"Actually it's my family's shop, but I tend the shop for my father."

"I thought the sign said George Hunicutt. Your name is Murray."

She put her cup down after taking a sip.

"Murray's my married name, George Hunicutt is my father."

"You're married?" Hank hadn't noticed a wedding ring on her hand.

"My husband was killed in North Africa. He was a tank commander in the 7th Armored Division. One day a letter arrived from the War Office and told me he'd been killed in action. No details, nothing. But I guess that's the way it's done." Her eyes misted over and she looked away.

Hank put his cup down.

"I'm sorry."

"This is a terrible war, Captain Mitchell. I just want it to end so people can get on with their lives."

They sat in silence for a moment.

"So you volunteer at the hospital when you're not working here?"

She nodded. "My father and I share the duties here when I'm not at the hospital. Working at the hospital is the least I can do."

He looked across the table and realized how different this woman was from Margo.

"And you, Captain Hank Mitchell, tell me about yourself. I've never really gotten to know an American."

"Not much to tell. I'm from New York, come from a normal American family and signed up for the Air Corps right after the attack on Pearl Harbor."

"And is there a Mrs. Mitchell?" she asked.

"Only my mother," he said not wanting to think about Margo right now.

She laughed. "Then, Captain Mitchell, I think another cup of tea is in order."

They both laughed.

"Would it be okay if you called me Hank?"

"You're Hank?"

"Actually it's Henry, but everyone calls me Hank."

"All right, Hank. Let's find a book for you."

"It's got to be more than response to treatment. Captain Mitchell is a different fellow from the one we first treated." Duncan Frazier stood in front of the deep sink scrubbing up prior to treating his next patient.

Roger laughed. "Contrary to what we'd like to believe, the ministrations of the opposite sex can provide a tremendous boost to the morale of your average fighter pilot."

Frazier turned and looked at Roger quizzically.

Roger took Frazier's place at the sink and began to scrub.

"I am intrigued, pray go on."

Continuing to scrub his finger nails with a small brush, Roger went on, "It's quite simple really, our sullen and withdrawn patient has responded to the friendship of one of the volunteers."

"Indeed. Whatever it takes, of course. Any details?"

"Her name is Kate Murray. She's a local. Her father's the town bookseller, George Hunicutt." Roger finished washing and picked up a freshly laundered hand towel.

"I know her quite well. Their shop is just down the road. Lost her husband in Africa in '42. She's been one of our steadiest volunteers for several years now."

"Well it appears the two have struck up a friendship and perhaps it's progressing beyond that. What I do know is that Hank Mitchell seems to be happy for the first time since I've known him. And you're right," Roger continued, "I'll take an attitude improvement any way I can get it. Of course he was healing nicely anyway, but I think this can only speed the process and get him looking past the immediate."

"Remarkable business we're in, Doctor Hanson."

"I would agree completely, Doctor Frazier."

The two laughed and walked into the treatment room.

# Chapter Seven

Queen Victoria Hospital
East Grinstead
West Sussex, England
21 February, 1944

The sunlight streaming through window of his room matched Hank's mood. The last two weeks had proved to be engaging in a manner he would never have expected prior to the accident. He found himself totally taken with Kate Murray. They'd been able to spend time with each other every day and last weekend he'd walked to the shop and met her father. It seemed right and normal that he should see her, while at the same time he knew his relationship with Margo had not ended. Never one to play the field like his Harvard fraternity brothers, he found himself unsettled that he could so easily start a relationship with a different woman.

He turned as the door opened and saw it was Kate. She dropped by his room during her shift if the workload permitted and he found himself looking forward to her visits.

"Hello," she said, "Am I disturbing you?" She carried a book and walked over to the window, holding it out. "I thought you'd like this." The black leather binding carried the gold lettering "A Christmas Carol."

Hank laughed. "I hate to admit I've never read it. But I did see the movie before the war."

Kate exaggerated a frown. "While the cinema can be quite entertaining, true joy will always come from the written word."

"Why Katherine Murray, I do believe you have touched me."

She laughed and he joined her as they stood in the late afternoon sunlight.

He found himself looking into her eyes as they both stopped laughing at almost the same instant. They said nothing, but they both stood very still as if caught in a spell.

Kate raised her hand very slowly and gently pulled Hank's face down while never taking her eyes from his. In the afternoon quiet, the two kissed once and she put her hand on the side of his face very carefully and quietly said, "My dear man."


Several days later, Chris Christiansen and Dan Wilskie arrived from Leiston, bringing the reality of the war home very quickly. They reported two more of the 'old gang' had gone down over Germany, only one chute was seen. The squadron's primary mission was escorting the B-17's and B-24's that were now making regular bomb runs on German industry. Chris told him about the increase in Luftwaffe aggressiveness as the Eighth Air Force shifted their targets into the heart of the Third Reich. The three of them had lunch together before they had to get back on the road to Leiston.

After they had left, Hank Mitchell sat with a book open on his lap in the day room of Ward 3. He slowly squeezed a tennis ball while he read, oblivious to activity around him. His face was uncovered. A patch work of pink skin ran from behind his left eye to what remained of his ear. The external ear tissue was a small stub that protruded from the top of the ear canal and extended approximately ½ inch outward. Both of Hank's attending physicians had been pleased to discover he still had a full range of hearing, certainly enough to pass an Air Corps flight physical.

As Hank worked on his hand, he thought about what his two friends had said. The squadron was fighting the Germans and losing men every day. While he couldn't fly in his condition, he felt guilty not being with them. He'd always heard you fight for your comrades more than any thing else. Now he realized it was true.

"How's the hand," he heard someone ask from behind him.

Hank turned and smiled. "Feeling stronger every day."

Kate knelt down next to his chair and picked up one side of his book.

"You started it," she said. "I loved the story as a girl. It made Christmas much more special."

Hank closed the book and rubbed the back of his neck.

"I think Mr. Dickens is on to something, being able to see the future. I like that idea. You could make a bundle in the stock market."

Kate stood and came around his chair, her hands running lightly over the back of Hank's neck. She leaned back against the window sill.

"I don't know if I'd like to be able to see into the future. Just enjoy each day and don't worry about what you can't change," she said.

"That's just the point," Hank said. "Scrooge was able to change things. That's what I like."

"And suppose you see something you can't change, like your own death. Do you keep going down the path that leads to your own destruction?"

The serious look in her eye unnerved Hank.

"I guess it would depend on what you died for? There are things worth dying for, right?"

"My husband thought so, but he never asked me. I wasn't ready to have him die in a desert thousands of miles from England, in a war that may or may not have even been necessary."

Hank looked at her with surprise.

"You don't think this war was necessary?" he asked.

"Hank, it's all about politics and power. Do you think Hitler would have declared war on England if we hadn't stepped in to defend the Poles?"

He was surprised by the emotion in her voice.

"I guess I never thought about it. But I know the Japs bombed Pearl Harbor and we didn't have any choice."

"Hank, there's always a choice." Kate stood up, smoothed her smock and said, "I really need to be on my way. I'll stop by and see you before I head home."

He took her hand and she looked down at him.

"Did we just have an argument?"

"We've never talked about the war. There are some things I feel strongly about and we don't share those opinions."

He released her hand.

"I guess not."

She turned and walked away toward Ward 4.


Upon completing a thirty minute exam of Hank's hand and face, Colonel Hugh Ridgeley, the senior physician on the Eighth Air Force staff stood washing his hands in the sink. Roger Hanson and Duncan Frazier waited for him to finish.

Ridgeley dried his hands and walked over to the coat rack where his uniform coat hung. Slipping the coat on, he began buttoning it and turned to the two doctors.

"Remarkable job, gentlemen. I saw the initial reports from Portsmouth and the pictures taken two days after the accident. Before the war, we would have written off an aviator with injuries like that. I want to get our people completely familiar with your protocols and we will implement them immediately. Doctor Hanson, I'm going to pull you back to headquarters temporarily as my project officer on this. I know you don't like leaving your patients, but it shouldn't take too long to get the word out to all the station clinics and level one treatment facilities. I'm pretty sure I can get our new boss, General Doolittle, to sign the orders which will get everyone jumping to, if you know what I mean."

"Yes, sir, I can be wrapped up here by tomorrow afternoon."

"Splendid. And Doctor Frazier, my thanks for what you have done to show us the way. I would like to meet Dr. McIndoe at some point to thank him personally."

The two men shook hands.

"Now, I need to get on my way. Have to make it to London by 1830." Ridgeley turned to leave.

"Excuse me, Colonel. About Captain Mitchell and his request to return to flight duties?"

"Approved, Doctor, of course. Prepare the release and bring it with you when you report."

He turned to Hank.

"Good luck, Captain." He started to leave then stopped. "And the next time you go flying, wear your gloves."

"Yes, sir."


Telex orders arrived the next morning from Eighth Air Force Headquarters directing Captain Henry Tyler Mitchell, III to report back to the 95th Fighter Group at Leiston on flight status.


"Oh, excuse me. I didn't know you were here, Doctor." Kate Murray said as she stopped at the door to Hank's room.

"I was just leaving, Kate. I had to drop off Hank's orders," Roger replied. A manila folder lay on Hank's neatly made bed.

She looked confused. "Orders, where are they sending you?" she asked, looking at him with concern.

"They just came in. I'm going back to the Group at Leiston."

The look on her face showed surprise then confusion.

"I don't understand. You're going back to flying?"

Hank nodded. "The doctors gave me my flight clearance yesterday. I'm leaving in about an hour. Chris is coming down to get me."

"Hank, you don't have to do this. You've been wounded, you're just healed and your air force has plenty of pilots. Doctor, surely they don't need him that badly."

Roger looked confused. "I better leave you two to talk about this."

"But you think he's well enough to go back to flying?"

"Not just me. The senior flight surgeon from headquarters thinks so too." Roger picked up his cap and moved toward the door.

"Hank, you can fight this can't you?" Her eyes now looked desperate.

He looked down for a moment then into her eyes. "Kate, I'm going back because I requested it. No, I don't have to go back, I want to."

She looked shocked, her face showing disbelief. Turning, she ran from the room.


He found her at the end of Ward 4, sitting in one of the small alcoves, her arms wrapped around her body as she stared out the window.

"This is a bigger hospital than I thought. I was afraid I wouldn't find you before I had to leave." He sat down next to her.

Kate continued to stare out the window.

"All of this happened very quickly. But I thought you knew I intended to fly again."

"I know you said that", she said softly, "But I never thought they would actually let you."

He didn't know what to say. Now he realized how she truly felt and where she thought their relationship was going. How could I have been so stupid, he thought. Now he didn't know what to say.

Several tears ran down her face as she turned to face him.

"I know I'm being silly. I just thought that there was something between us."

He looked at her, wishing he could be anywhere in the world but where he was, telling her he was leaving.

"Kate, you're very special to me. Maybe there's a future for us, but right now I can't think about that. It's time for me to get on with the war."

"So once again it happens," she said, turning back to the window. "I've loved two men in my life. One died in the desert and now you're returning to that awful, bloody war."

Hank felt helpless. There was nothing he could do or say.

"And you could have taken yourself out of it. I guess that makes it even harder for me." She turned to face him, "You don't have to do this." Her face showed the pain she felt, tears running down her cheeks.

"Yes, I do, Kate. There're a lot of reasons and I'm not sure I understand them all. But I do know I have to go back. I'll write you when I sort this out, but I've got to do this."

He gently kissed her cheek, stood up and walked away.

# Chapter Eight

USAAF Station 373
Leiston
Suffolk, England
23 February, 1944

The Army sedan made its way down the dirt perimeter road which circled the Army Air Corps base at Leiston. Through the barbed wire fence Hank saw two P-51's in the warm up area waiting to take the runway.

"Stop here a minute, Chris."

Christiansen slowed to a stop, not bothering to pull off to the side of the road.

Hank heard the engines run up on the two aircraft as they pulled on the active runway. Hank's mind remembered each step, how automatic each of the pre-takeoff checks had been.

Delaying only five seconds, the lead aircraft began to roll, the roar of its engine echoing off the hangars. As the first Mustang passed a thousand feet of roll, his wingman released brakes and also went to full throttle, his aircraft rapidly accelerating down the tarmac.

"Looks like a training hop. Must be one of the new guys," Christiansen said.

"Easy on the new guy comments. I'm one of them, remember?"

"Right," Chris said and put the car in gear, heading for the main gate.

Two Army sentries manned the wooden guard shack which sat next to the road. Across the road, a wooden sign said, "Welcome to Leiston - Home of the 95th Fighter Group."

"May I see your ID card, sir?" A Corporal, wearing the white webbed belt of the MP's over his long brown overcoat, stood next to Chris's opened window, the look on his face showing bored indifference to his job.

Chris said nothing as he pulled out his wallet. He showed his card to the guard who had leaned down to look across at Hank.

"I'll need to see yo...." The guard's words froze in his throat as he saw Hank's face. Trying not to look repelled, the man recovered to say, "I have to see your card, sir."

Hank had seen the look on the man's face. He fumbled for his wallet, pulling out his identity card and holding it up for inspection.

The guard, now very animated, snapped a sharp salute. "Proceed, sir."

Chris pulled away. "Asshole."

Hank stared ahead, wondering how he'd be received. During his visits to East Grinstead, he'd felt very comfortable with people's reactions. Maybe the local Brits were so used to seeing disfigured aviators for the last three years that it didn't matter to them. Perhaps the rank and file of the 95th Fighter Group might not feel the same way.

"Let's stop at the squadron and let the Major know you're back," Chris said. He pulled up next to a single story, dark green wooden building. Next to the door, a replica of the 952nd Fighter Squadron's patch hung on a metal suspension frame. Hank had always liked the patch, a gold lightening flash with blue wings striking a red and white bull's eye.

They found Robin Cunning sitting in his small office reading from an opened folder on his desk.

"Skipper, look who the cat drug in..."

Cunning looked up, saw Hank and smiled.

"Hank, come on in. Good to see you." He stood up and offered his hand over the desk.

"Glad to be back, Skipper," Hank said.

"Here, sit down," Cunning said removing his leather flight jacket from a chair and hanging it on a wall hook.

"I'm gonna check tomorrow's flight schedule," Chris said. He stepped into the hallway.

"So, how're you feeling?" Cunning asked, sitting back in his chair.

Hank nodded. "I'm okay. Actually I feel good. Guess the rest helped more than I realized."

"The docs put any flight limitations on you?"

He shook his head. "No, sir. Clean bill of health, by the Eighth Air Force Flight Surgeon no less. He told me I was fully qualified to return to operational flying."

Cunning looked at his young pilot, the terrible scars still livid on the side of his face. What the hell does that guy know, he asked himself? How do you have part of your face burned off then get back in the cockpit like nothing ever happened?

"You ready to do that?"

Hank hesitated before answering Cunning. He respected the older man and wanted to be square with him.

"I think so."

"Okay, Hank. Take as many hops as you need to get yourself refreshed. When you feel ready, let me know and we'll put you back on ops.

"Yes, sir."

"And don't push it."


After Mitchell left his office, Cunning sat back in his chair. Something was different about Hank. More than just the burns, he didn't sense that cocky attitude anymore. But the young pilot didn't seem too concerned about getting back in the air and into combat. Either he's putting up a hell of a front or we might have the makings of a first class aviator and leader on our hands. Wonders never cease, he thought, turning back to the pile of papers on his desk.


Two days later, Hank flew his first flight since bailing out over the Channel. A slight case of nerves disappeared as soon as the wheels indicated up and locked following takeoff. A scattered layer of clouds and a reserved flying area allowed Hank to take the P-51 through her paces. The procedures came back very quickly, but he knew he needed to log some time to get comfortable again. An hour into the flight he felt good with his flying skills. His concern about his hand tiring was unnecessary. Other than a little stiffness, it worked fine. The rough cloth of the flying cap irritated his face, particularly his ear, or at least what was left of it. Need to get some kind of liner, he thought, as he pointed the Mustang back toward the field for landing practice.


Hank stopped by the parachute loft on his way back from the flight line. He couldn't find Technical Sergeant Tuchman, the squadron's senior parachute rigger.

He stepped behind the tall set of lockers that separated the room into front and back. Opening a large cabinet, Hank looked for any kind of soft material the Sergeant might be able to use for a cap liner. On one shelf, he saw a roll of green cloth that looked almost like flannel. That might do it, he thought.

Hank heard someone enter the shop, assuming it was either Tuchman returning or another pilot dropping off gear for repair. He kept checking the shelves, but the soft green cloth seemed to be the best candidate.

"Did you see that guy Mitchell?" a voice came from the other side of the lockers.

"Christ, what a mess. Why don't they just send the guy home?" a second voice said.

"Damned if I want to see that every day. Makes me fucking sick."

"Hell, he probably doesn't have anyone at home who wants him now."

The two men laughed.

"Tuchman must be at lunch, let's come back later."

Hank heard them leave and realized his body was shaking. His hand gripped the locker shelf so hard it was painful. The pain and frustration of the last seven weeks was a cruel joke. He was a circus freak, and that would never change. Hank turned and came face to face with a square mirror mounted on the far wall. Staring back at him was the creature he had become.

"Hi, Captain, can I help you?"

Hank turned to see Sergeant Tuchman standing at the edge of the lockers. Tuchman was older. He'd been in the Air Corps before the war and the two men had always enjoyed a good relationship. The Sergeant appeared not to be bothered by Hank's burns.

"Sergeant, do you have your camera?"

"Yes, sir," Tuchman said.

"I think I need a new picture," Hank said. The parachute riggers kept a squadron pilot picture board outside the ready room.

"Ah, yes sir, whatever you want." The Sergeant opened a drawer pulling out a camera bag which contained a small bellows camera, and flash unit. "You sure about this," he asked when he'd loaded a flash bulb into the reflector housing.

"Absolutely," Hank said, smiling at Tuchman. He assumed a pose in front of the small squadron plaque, where all pilot pictures were taken.

"Okay, here goes."

The bright pop accompanied by the shutter click captured the new Hank Mitchell for the pilot's picture board and posterity.

The cap liner forgotten, Hank walked toward the door, stopped and turned.

"Sergeant, how about getting me an extra print of that picture.... I want to send one to my girl." He spun on his heel and left, leaving Technical Sergeant Tuchman staring after him.

"Yes, sir," he said under his breath, knowing Mitchell couldn't hear him, "Sure thing."

"That about covers it, any questions?" Chris asked as their pre-flight brief concluded.

"Nope, I'll get the weather," Hank said and stood up abruptly.

"Hey, you okay?"

"I'm fine."

"Bullshit, pal. You haven't said two words this morning." Chris threw the briefing book on the table. "What's eating you?"

"Nothing, let's get going," Hank said and walked into the hall.

Chris picked up his flying cap and followed Hank.

Hank Mitchell's anger had simmered all night long. He felt like his life was slowing slipping out of his control. All the plans for the future, everything all blown to hell. Well at least these sons of bitches were gonna know he could still fly circles around them. Taking it out on Chris didn't make him feel any better, but he couldn't help himself.


The radio chatter had been minimal as the two Mustangs flew formation, conducted rendezvous practice and then shifted to tactical maneuvering. Perhaps it was the anger that focused Hank's flying, but he flew the big fighter as well as he ever had. Several compliments from Chris told him that his friend felt the same way.

"I'm ready if you are," Chris transmitted.

"Roger, as briefed." Hank broke right and pulled hard to separate from Chris who was flying lead. Pushing the throttle forward, ensuring the mixture rich, he pushed the stick forward slightly to unload the wings and accelerate faster. One minute later he reversed back hard toward Chris, and called, "Two's turning in...."

"Lead, roger."

The two Mustangs closed each other head on, each aircraft at full power, making almost 400 knots. Hank picked up Chris just left of the nose, banking slightly left to pass as close as possible to the other aircraft. In a blur, they passed, and Chris transmitted, "Fight's on."

Chris Christiansen's solid aviation ability coupled with his currency gave Hank a test for three minutes as each aircraft tried hard to convert their airspeed or location to an advantage over the other. But Christiansen made a mistake when he momentarily lost sight of Hank, who promptly pitched up into the sun, bleeding off airspeed allowing him to pull his nose around at Chris's tail.

Christiansen saw his plight and tried a hard turn to force an overshoot, but a quick pitch up allowed Hank to keep Chris in front of him and within 15 seconds the pipper of his gunsight was on the other aircraft.

Hank keyed his transmitter and said, "You're dead, lead."

The debriefing between the two aviators took only ten minutes. While Chris wanted to take longer, he soon realized Hank felt they were wasting time.

"Seems hard to believe, but you're better than most every pilot in the squadron. I'm not sure what else you can accomplish by drilling holes in the sky over England." Chris was trying to be conciliatory, sensing his friend needed support.

"My thoughts exactly," Hank said curtly. "You wanna tell the Skipper or me?"

"I'll stop by and see him," Chris said, his tone now all business.

The two men looked at each other momentarily, each knowing things weren't right, but also knowing there was nothing they could do about it.

"Thanks."


"So he goes back on ops, Chris. I don't care if you do think he hasn't adjusted to his injuries. The flight surgeon said he's ready to go and you said he could fly circles around you, right?" Robin Cunning had listened to Chris Christiansen's concerns about Hank for ten minutes before letting go with both barrels.

"Yes sir, but...."

"Chris, we need pilots and we need experienced pilots more than anything else. With four kills, Hank's the second highest scoring pilot in the group. We both know he's probably the best stick. So if he wants to go out and kill Germans, that's fine with me, no questions asked." He remembered the encounter the day before with Hank. Yes, something had changed. It unsettled Cunning, but at the same time as a squadron commander it was his job to make sure his pilots were effective in combat and he had no doubt Hank would do that. But this was certainly a different Hank Mitchell than he'd ever seen before.

Chris realized he was wasting his time. The pressure to protect the bombers that were now expanding their attacks deeper into Germany was intense. Daylight bombing by the Eighth Air Force began with very little fighter support and the losses reflected it. Now with the P-47's and P-51's in theater and capable of staying with the bombers most of the way to the deepest targets, the brass wanted and needed to minimize future losses. Each fighter group commander knew he was expected to launch full divisions for each raid, find their charges, and defend them against everything the Luftwaffe could throw at them.

The survival rate for fighter pilots in combat over Europe went up very quickly as they accumulated missions under their belts. An experienced flight leader like Hank was expected to protect the bombers and train his wingmen at the same time. While the training squadrons stateside were turning out solid flyers, they weren't combat effective until they had ten missions behind them.

Hank's name appeared on the squadron flight schedule the next afternoon listing him as the leader of one of the four P-51's divisions launching to escort the 91st Bomb Group on a mission against the metal fabrication works at Hanau, just north of Frankfurt. The mission measured 410 miles one way and the Mustangs would provide close escort for the entire route of flight.

# Chapter Nine

USAAF Station 373
Leiston
Suffolk, England
1 March, 1944

"Sir, it's 0445, time to get up. The chow hall opens at 0500 and all crews are to be in the briefing hut at 0600."

Hank opened his eyes to see Corporal Wanamaker kneeling by his cot.

He yawned and asked, "How's the weather, Corporal?"

Wanamaker laughed as he moved to the door.

"Colder than a witch's tit at the North Pole, sir, and dark to boot."

*You asked for this, Mitchell.*

He swung his legs to the floor, his woolen socks providing some protection against the cold tiles. In a smoothly developed ritual, Hank pulled on his wool trousers and long sleeve shirt, rolling up the arms and heading for the wash basin. Quickly shaving and brushing his teeth, he toweled the cold water from his face and rolled down the arms of his shirt. Feels okay so far, he thought and grabbed his flight jacket and cap.

In the officer's end of the mess hall, he saw Chris sitting at a table with two young First Lieutenants. Setting his tray down, he saw one man's nametag said "1st Lt. Sam Tesore."

"Morning, Chris."

"Hank, meet Sammy T. and Phil Wakefield. They're in our flight this morning."

They shook hands over the mess trays, and returned to eating. Both men obviously self conscious and they avoided looking at Hank's face.

"How long you guys been with the group?" Hank asked.

"We both got here mid-January," Tesore said, his eyes not leaving his plate.

Hank knew he recognized Sammy T's voice from the paraloft yesterday.

"We both have eleven missions," Phil Wakefield volunteered, looking briefly toward Hank.

"The Skipper had to rearrange flights after we lost Jensen and Hartfield. This will be our normal flight for now. I thought I'd take Phil as my wingman, put Sammy on your wing," Chris said.

Hank nodded, but said nothing.

In a minute he finished his plate and slid it to the middle of the table.

"We've got a few minutes before heading over for briefing and this'll save us time after the big brief. As you can see, I had a very unsuccessful episode with our friends in the Luftwaffe. I don't intend for that to happen again. I expect two things from you: keep your eyes open for Jerry and stick with your leader no matter what. Too many pilots have their head up their ass thinking the lead has look out responsibility for the flight and everyone else is just flying formation. I hope you've learned by now that whoever sees your opponent first generally wins. A wingman's job is to make sure his lead survives to shoot the other bastards down. You do that by sticking to your lead like glue and keeping your eyes open. I don't expect verbal diarrhea during a fight, either. If it's critical, talk, if not, keep your trap shut. Clear?"

The two young pilots both looked anxious, neither saying anything.

"Well?" Hank asked again, his voice hard.

They nodded, Lieutenant Wakefield saying quietly, "Yeah."

Hank continued, "By now you've probably figured the Krauts are pretty good airplane drivers. But we know attrition is taking a toll from their combat experienced pilots. Well, gentlemen, we're gonna do our best to help that attrition. This flight will single out the lead aircraft and go after them. If we can shoot down their squadron commanders and flight leaders, the combat effectiveness of their fighter squadron will go down the toilet. That's why it's even more important for you two to stick to Chris and me like glue. When we single out their leaders, their wingman will do their best to protect them and converge on us. That means they're not shooting at the bombers and that will win the war for us. If either one of you don't think you can handle the heat, let me know now. I don't need some pansy son of a bitch pulling out of a fight and leaving my ass uncovered. Understand?"

Now the two men looked very uncomfortable. They looked at each other then back to Hank.

"How 'bout you, 'Sammy T?" Hank's voice was tinged with a hint of sarcasm. "Think you can handle it?"

Tesore raised his chin a little and said, "Yeah, I can handle it."

Hank turned to Wakefield.

"And you?"

"I think so."

Hank abruptly got up.

"Now there's confidence if I've ever seen it. Come on, we'll miss the brief."

Chris watched Hank walk out the closest door, wondering what had happened to the Hank Mitchell he used to know.

"Come on you two, this should be a real experience….and he is a hell of a stick, so pay attention."

Following a forty minute brief by Colonel Max Gogan, pilots from the three fighter squadrons which made up the 95th Fighter Group changed into flying gear and manned their aircraft. A low ceiling mandated a staggered departure from Leiston, the P-51's of the 951st Fighter Squadron taking off first, climbing to the highest rendezvous circle overhead the field at 16,000 feet. Major Cunning led the 952nd off in order, the twelve Mustangs climbing to 15,000 feet in groups of two. Arriving at altitude, the four plane divisions slid into position on Cunning's wing as he maneuvered the squadron to the right side of the group formation. In less than twenty minutes, thirty four fighters were joined together and on course to rendezvous with the B-17's of the 91st Bombardment Group.

Once clear of the low layer of clouds and fog, the fighters found a clear morning over England, frost forming on their cockpits as they climbed to 26,000 feet. Inside the aircraft, the cold began to soak into the pilots, the small cockpit heater ineffective at the extreme temperatures found in the winter skies over Europe.

Hank ran a finger of his gloved hand under the bottom seal of his oxygen mask, which was already beginning to chafe his face. Looking ahead, he saw a line of white contrails against the dark blue sky. Those must be ours, he thought, the bombers were on the pre-briefed course. He checked his watch, right on time. The fighters rapidly closed on the tight formation of B-17's cruising at 24,000 feet.

Robin Cunning, in the lead Mustang of the 952nd, banked to the right and put the squadron in its pre-briefed position on the bomber's right side. Once in position, the squadron flight leaders loosened up their formation, the squadron spreading out over a half mile of sky.

Checking his engine instruments, Hank realized that despite the cold and chafing oxygen mask, he felt good. For the first time in almost two months, it was as if he was almost normal again. For the next five hours he could forget about his face and try to kill Germans. Looking left at the closest bombers, he could see the crews through their windows and in the upper turret. It was a strange kinship, two groups of men on a common purpose both facing potential death, but continuing on to the target. This was the time he hated the most, waiting for something to happen. He tuned in the strike frequency and waited for a transmission to tell him the radio was working. Not surprising, it was quiet on the air. Intelligence had warned everyone that the Germans were very good at monitoring transmissions to gather information. The less everyone said the better. He knew that would change as soon as the action started. It was human nature to talk when you were scared. He wondered how his new wingmen would react when the shit hit the fan. The one kid seemed pretty cocky. Sammy T. my ass, Hank thought. We'll see if they can fly worth a damn, that's what counts. The other guy, Wakefield, seemed pretty straight, let's hope he's not some kind of Boy Scout.

"Lead, Tango Able One Two is losing oil pressure on number four, returning to base."

To his left, a B-17 slowly descended from the formation and began a slow turn to the left toward England. He noted the remaining bombers in that defensive box changed their formation slightly, closing the distance between aircraft. With ten .50 caliber machine guns on each Flying Fortress, it was important to maintain a formation that allowed each gun to defend the box. Soon he could see the gunners testing their guns, the bright tracers arcing into the blue sky.

Weaving slowly left and right to maintain position on the bombers, the P-51's could now look down and see the fields of France through breaks in the clouds. Hank knew this would give the lead navigator a chance to verify their flight track. He'd been on several missions that never got visual contact with the ground and couldn't verify their targets when the time came. The clouds continued to break up and he could see a large river down to his left, winding through rolling hills. Okay, we're in Messerschmitt territory now, get your head out of your ass and start watching for Germans. Quickly he checked his guns switches and ran his fingers over the drop tank jettison switch.

"Blackbird, bandits, two o'clock level," Chris Christiansen transmitted.

Hank looked right and saw five black specks moving fast in the direction of the bombers.

"Blackbirds, jettison tanks, now."

Ramming the throttle full forward, Hank turned his flight right to meet the threat. Allowing for the bandit's speed, he put the nose of his Mustang in a point of space where the two flights should cross.

"Chris, take the two on the right, I'll take left," Hank said.

"Roger," was the clipped response.

The two flights were closing on each other at over 400 knots and Hank now could see the dark green shapes were 109's. They had bright white spinners on their propellers and red cowlings. The Germans kept their course, apparently unaware of Hank's flight. Suddenly the five aircraft began to turn toward them, now realizing the danger.

Okay, you son of a bitch, Hank thought, let's see how big your balls are. The aircraft were now on opposing courses and

Hank banked slightly left to put his nose directly on the leader's aircraft.   Squeezing the trigger, he felt the airframe vibrate as the machine guns fired, tracers flying forward directly through the German formation.   For one brief moment he thought he'd misjudged and a collision seemed imminent.   Hank's aircraft flashed between the leader and his wingman, no more than fifty feet separating the two.   Immediately he pulled hard left, throwing his head back to keep an eye on the Germans.  The two 109's on the left kept going toward the bombers, but the leader and two on the right began a right turn back toward Hank. Bleeding off fifty knots in a quick climb, he pulled the nose of the Mustang around toward the bandits.  Full throttle and unloading to zero "g" allowed him to accelerate back to 350 knots and gain a pursuit angle on the last German.   As the three Germans passed, he reversed and again pitched up, now able to get his nose back down on tail end Charlie.  Squeezing the trigger, he saw pieces begin to fly off the Messerschmitt, smoke erupting from underneath the cockpit, followed by flames.

Seeing the flames engulfing the other fighter, Hank felt nothing but pleasure.  Pulling hard, he looked for number two who was nowhere to be seen.  The German leader was turning right and Hank pulled as hard as he could without bleeding off airspeed to get behind his opponent.   My wingman better be covering my ass, he thought.

"Blackbird Two, you got lead?" he asked, doubt now in his mind.

"I've lost sight, lead," came the crackling response from Lieutenant Tesore who was apparently not engaged in the fight.

Shit, Hank thought, just as tracers arced over his right wing.  Viciously he pulled up, the Mustang shuddering violently as its airspeed rapidly bled off.  Hank felt the fighter losing yaw control, the rudder becoming more ineffective.   His assailant went by him, down and to his left.  Hank's rapid loss of airspeed had caught the German off guard, and the attacker now found himself on the defensive.  Taking a quick look for the leader and seeing no threat, Hank nursed the nose down, now completing the roll with right rudder as the German slid into his gunsight reticle.  Once more the .50's opened up, hitting the German in the left wing root.  The wing suddenly failed, snapping off into the wind stream, the stricken German now twisting toward the ground with bits of aircraft continuing to shed from the doomed fighter.

Where's the lead, he asked, frantically searching above, then rolling the aircraft to look below him. Hank's air sense told him it was only a matter of time before the leader attacked, so he pitched over to build up as much airspeed as possible. As the airspeed passed 320 knots, he began a left turn searching high and low to no avail. He can't be out of ammunition, maybe fuel, he thought. Pulling the nose up, he began to gain altitude, now passing 17,000 feet, the sky still empty of planes, friendly or enemy. Checking the fuel gauge, he realized it was time to start the trip home. If the weather didn't break up, getting back into Leiston might take some time. Reaching for his small map, he estimated a course home and turned to 245 magnetic, leaning the mix on the engine and pulling the throttle back to 46 inches of manifold pressure.

Two Spitfires intercepted Hank as he finished crossing the channel. He realized that he'd forgotten to turn on his IFF as he left France. British radar stations must have thought he was a lone German recon aircraft. He wasn't on one of the approved return to base routings after his fight took him so far from the main navigation route. Reaching down, he switched the MK III to "on" and stared back at the two pilots on his right. He saw the leader show a thumbs up and the two aircraft rolled away from him. Guess I can still make rookie mistakes after all, he thought, embarrassed more than angry, better not do that with the Krauts.

As the propeller slowed to a stop, Hank slid the canopy open. After four hours of being assaulted by the smell of fuel, cordite and sweat, the fresh air was like a tonic.

"Any ammo left in the guns?" Billy Thackery asked from behind the wing. The tall skinny Sergeant hailed from Texas and had been Hank's crew chief since arrival in Europe.

"Not much," Hank said, standing up in the cockpit and stepping out on the wing.

"Gun camera film?"

"Yeah, they better take a look." Hank slowly pulled his flying helmet off, the cool air feeling good against his irritated skin.

"You okay, Captain?"

"I'm fine, the others back yet?"

"You're the first. Ops said the first ones should be back on deck in about twenty minutes." Thackery had climbed up on the wing and glanced in the cockpit.

"Any gripes?"

Hank shook his head.

"I talked to Sweeney last night. For a case of beer, he'll do the artwork." Corporal Ted Sweeney was the group's unofficial artist for customizing aircraft.

The big fighter currently was devoid of nose art or any indications of victories over the Germans. Hank now rated six downed Germans painted under his cockpit.

"Good idea, Billy."

"You want 'Margo' Two on this one?" The aircraft Hank bailed out over the Channel had been painted 'Margo' in honor of his girlfriend.

He laughed. "No, Sergeant, I have a special request. I want this ship named 'Flaming Death.' And instead of swastikas, I want a skull and cross bones for each kill. Think he can do that?"

Sergeant Thackery looked down at him without saying anything. He climbed down off the wing. "You sure about that, Captain?"

"Dead sure, Sergeant and make sure he uses plenty of flames. And another thing, I want the bastards to know who I am, so how about painting the outer three feet of each wing bright yellow."

"The skipper gonna be okay with that?"

Hank slapped his crew chief on the back as he started to walk toward the debrief hut. "As long as I keep shooting down Germans, I don't think he'll give a shit one way or the other. By the way, tell Sweeney to put six skulls under my name."

Only one intelligence officer was sitting behind the debrief table when Hank entered. On a side table, a large pot of coffee vented steam, its metal lid rattling slightly. Beside the coffee several trays of sheet cake waited for the incoming aircrews. The Lieutenant looked up and motioned to Hank.

"Captain, grab a cup of coffee and I'll take your report. You can beat the crowd."

The coffee smelled good and he filled a white china mug on his way to the debrief table.

"Just a few questions," he said as Hank sat down. The man's pencil was poised over a mimeographed form.

The questions rolled over all the standard areas, observed weather, navigation route, enemy reaction, radio discipline and any pertinent intelligence noted.

"We'll pull the gun camera film to check for confirms on the two Jerries."

Hank stood up and as he did the man's eyes betrayed his reaction to Hank's face.

"By the way, Lieutenant, did I mention the first Kraut was fully engulfed in fire as he was going down? Burning like a roman candle." He stared hard at the man.

Looking down at his paper he said, "Uh no, sir. I'll make a note."

"You can say that the German probably looked worse than I do by the time he got out, if he got out."

Hank turned and walked out of the hut, the Lieutenant watching him go.


"Give the guy a chance, Hank."

Robin Cunning still wore his flight suit as he sat on the couch in his office relaxing after debriefing.

"The little piss ant cut and ran as soon as we merged with the 109's. How the hell can I kill the bastards if I'm always watching my own back cause my wingman can't hack it?"

Cunning's calm demeanor began to change.

"Damn it, Hank, how come no one else has bitched about Tesore. He's flown a dozen missions on a couple of different leads. You're the first one who's not happy."

"Maybe those leads aren't pressing the Krauts like they should." Hank knew he was pushing Cunning, but he had to have a reliable wingman.

"What the hell does that mean?"

"How many kills has the squadron tallied up lately?

The skipper didn't reply, but stood up and walked over to a green metal cabinet on the wall. He opened a door and took out a bottle of bourbon and two glasses. Filling both glasses, he turned to Hank and handed him one.

Cunning looked angry, his mouth set in a grim line.

"Hank, if you and I didn't go back to the beginning of this group. And if you weren't the top scorer, I'd have your ass for what you just said. Instead we're going to toast your two kills today. The intel types confirmed both of them."

He raised his glass and touched Hank's tumbler. The two men both drank in silence.

"Now as a friend, tell me. Are you trying to set a record as the biggest asshole in the European Theater? Relax, would you?"

"Robin, I've got something to do, and that's kill Germans. I want a new wingman and also your permission to pursue the Krauts when they break away after their attacks." Normal procedures tied the fighters to close escort of the bomber formations which most fighter pilots found frustrating as the Germans could attack and then run back to their bases.

"I can get you a new wingman, but quit chewing up my Lieutenants because you're pissed off. And you know close escort is standard operating procedure. Even Gogan can't do anything about that."

"Every pilot worth a shit knows that policy is crap. Maybe if we start going after them full tilt, the results will convince the arm chair aviators that it makes sense to never give the Krauts a free ticket. Kill them when they attack, on their way home, and in the landing pattern. Then drop bombs on their fucking mess hall. It's as simple as that, quit playing bullshit games and do what it takes to beat these bastards."

Cunning looked at him, then turned away to grab the bottle.

"Then let's drink to our personal attempt to fix the Eighth Air Force," he said as he filled their glasses.

The two men drank deeply.

"Hell, I never wanted to be a colonel anyway," Cunning said.


Hank turned his head toward the door of his room as he heard two quick knocks. He laid on top of the blanket, still in his flight suit, his boots on the floor next to his bed. The door opened six inches and he heard Chris.

"Anybody in there?"

"Yeah, come in," Hank said, swinging his feet to the floor.

"What in the hell were you doing out there today?" Chris asked, his voice angry. "How about telling me you're going to start trying to ram the Krauts before I find out the hard way. Son of a bitch, I don't think I missed hitting a 109 by more than 20 feet."

Hank stood up and walked to the wash basin, splashing water in his face.

"I'm getting rid of Tesore, he can't handle it as far as I'm concerned."

"He can't handle it? Who the hell do you think can handle a lunatic with a death wish?"

"Chris, we're letting the Krauts dictate how we defend our bombers. Unless we change the rules, there're gonna be a lot of dead bomber crews before this thing is over. I told you we were going to go after the leader, that's what we did. And I think it worked pretty damned good. I got two and I heard you got one."

"Yeah, I did," Chris said and sat on the bed.

"Then let's go over to the club and have a drink to celebrate that three of Adolph's best won't ever bother our bombers again."


"Sir, my name is Clement Dunmire. Major Cunning told me I have been assigned as your wingman."

Hank and Chris looked up at what Hank later said was an officer, just scaled down a bit. While Second Lieutenant Dunmire showed no reaction to Hank's burned face, both of the experienced aviators were stunned at the short stature and slight build of the man standing in front of them. Chris doubted if he tipped the scales at over 135 pounds and would bet money shaving was not a requirement. The set of silver wings on his left breast were real enough, it was just hard to believe this youngster was a fighter pilot.

"Is that so?" Hank asked, taking a deep drink of his fourth bourbon and water. "And what makes you think you can handle being my wingman?" the sarcastic tone of his voice slightly slurred by the alcohol.

"Lay off, Hank," Chris said, extending his hand to Dunmire. "I'm Chris Christiansen."

Dunmire shook hand with Chris. "Nice to meet you, sir."

"My question stands, Lieutenant, what makes you think you can be my wingman?" Hank sat back in his chair, his eyes boring into the young officer.

"Sir, I've been told that a good wingman has to fly wing and shut up. I can do both."

Chris laughed.

Hank paused; maybe this kid had some balls after all. "Where're you from Dinmeyer?"

"It's 'Dunmire,' sir and I'm from Charleston, South Carolina."

"I'll be damned, Chris, a gentleman from the old south. Tell me Mr. Dunmire, you willing to fly with a couple of damned Yankees?"

"Sir, you may be damned Yankees, but you drink bourbon, that's all I need to know."

Now Hank laughed.

"Sit down, Mr. Dunmire; I'll buy you a drink."

"Thank you, sir."

# Chapter Ten

USAAF Station 373
Leiston
Suffolk, England
4 March, 1944

Walking across the grass toward his Mustang, Hank tried to focus on the mission brief. Today the Group would escort a heavy bombardment group of B-24's. In an effort to more quickly tip the balance of the air war over Europe, a concerted effort was being made at destroying the aircraft production factories of the Reich. Located in the heart of Kassel, a Daimler Benz engine facility produced power plants for Germany's principal fighter, the Me-109. Over one hundred Liberators, using a mix of high explosive and fragmentation bombs would try to destroy the ability of the plant to produce engines. The 95th's job was to make sure they made it to the target and back. Southwest of Kassel, one of the Luftwaffe's premier fighter groups was based at Rothenburg. The intelligence estimate expected "heavy" fighter opposition.

"Hank, hold up," Robin Cunning called from across the parking area.

Hank stopped as the Skipper walked up. Cunning's yellow Mae West stood out against the dark green grass. In his hand he carried his charts and flying helmet.

"I talked to Gogan. He's not crazy about your idea, but he knows that we gotta try something. Your flight is cleared to operate at your discretion. You okay trying this with a new kid on your wing?"

"Hell, let's teach him the right way from day one. I'm still trying to get over taking a seventeen year old munchkin into combat."

"You still doing okay?" Cunning eye's showed the concern he felt.

Hank nodded. "Don't worry about me, there's a bunch of Nazis that are getting ready to die for the fatherland."

Cunning turned and began to walk toward his aircraft then turned back to Hank.

"You watch your ass, bucko."

Hank's normal pre-mission jitters didn't bother him. It was the letter in his shirt pocket that scared the hell out of him.


Today's forecast of good weather could be an advantage to both sides in different ways. Clear weather meant the lead bombardiers would be able to refine their aim approaching the target and with the new bombsights clobber them. At the same time, clear weather always meant the Luftwaffe would be out in strength and there were no cloud layers to provide cover for the bombers.

While he never wanted to fly multi-engine bombers, Hank had the greatest respect for the bomber crews. With no ability to maneuver, the big bombers flew on through the anti aircraft fire and fighter attacks with nothing to protect them but the thin metallic skins of their Fortresses and Liberators. Flying daytime raids for more accurate bombing, the firepower of the bomber formations had to provide the last line of defense against the Messerschmitts and Focke Wulf's thrown against them by the Luftwaffe. If Hank and his fellow fighter pilots did their job well, the German fighters would never get near the bombers at all. Unfortunately the Germans were good and the missions were long. The longer the mission, the greater the exposure to fighters standing alerts at the many fields across Germany. At the target, they had to run the gauntlet of German 88mm flak guns, which could hit them with lethal shell fragments up to 26,000 feet.

A bomber damaged over Germany then had to survive the fighter onslaught for sometimes hours in an effort to make it back to England. If a crewman was severely injured, his chances of survival were slim with loss of blood, shock and freezing temperatures all working against him.

When the Air Force started offensive operations against the continent, the loss rate on some missions was over 10%. No fighter existed that could stick with the bombers on long raids into the continent and the losses almost reached a breaking point. With the arrival of the P-47 and P-51, the playing field began to level. Bomber crews could now hope to survive a tour and rotate back to the states. It took a different breed of aviators to face the certainty of death or capture constantly and still continue to go out day after day.

Hank rechecked his instruments, everything still looking normal. To his right "Clem" watched from behind goggles and oxygen mask. Adjusting his mirror, Hank could see Chris and Wakefield in trail about a mile and stepped up a thousand feet. The four Mustangs were in an unusual position four miles from the main formation and about 4,000 feet above. In Hank's mind they were outriders, the first line of defense who would be in a position to attack hostile fighters before they got to the bombers.

So far the kid had done well. He kept his mouth shut on the radio and flew a good tight formation. Estimating an hour to Kassel, he thought they would have been attacked by now. For the hundredth time he swept his eyes from 9 o'clock over to 3 and back. Each time he would elevate his scan, systematically covered every piece of sky in front of them. Every fifteen seconds Hank twisted to look behind and below his aircraft.

For one moment he hesitated in his scan, seeing aircraft at 3 o'clock low, paralleling the bombers. Two flights of five 109's were maneuvering for an attack run. Quickly he charged the guns and jettisoned his drop tanks.

"Blackbirds, bandits 3 o'clock low. Lead's attacking."

Rolling hard right, Hank looked back and saw the kid sliding behind and matching his roll.

"Chris, I'll take the lead formation, you take trail."

The aircraft began to accelerate as Hank unloaded and pushed the throttle full. A mile ahead the ten German fighters maintained their formation, five in a line abreast with the second five perhaps half a mile in trail. Hank could see their markings, yellow cowls and a yellow tip on the vertical stabilizer, combat veterans.

Hank knew this was a desperate gamble. Their speed advantage should allow one burst before the trail 109's came after them. His heart pounded as the rage of battle griped him.

The outline of the lead Messerschmitt filled his gunsight. At 200 yards, Hank squeezed the trigger, feeling the aircraft shudder from the recoil of six Browning machine guns. His shots hit the leader's cockpit. Pieces of canopy shredded as the bullets tore through it, killing the pilot instantly. The 109 snapped violently to the right, smoke coming from the engine as the German entered a death spiral.

Hank watched the remaining four aircraft break right and left, the loss of their leader destroying the formation. Pulling up hard, he slowed his potential overshoot, then reversed violently back to the right. He knew a shot might open up if the second German didn't pull hard enough. The other 109's would be on him shortly. Hank pulled the Mustang right, fighting the "g" forces, his target sliding into the cross hairs of the gunsight. A three second burst scored hits, but Hank knew he couldn't press his attack until he located the other Germans.

Looking right he saw two Messerschmitts at his three o'clock, bright flashes telling him they were firing at their extreme range.

"Black lead, break right, break right, one behind you." Clem's voice was urgent but not panicked.

Hank strained to look behind him, seeing a 109 at almost dead six. He took a deep breath and pulled as hard as he could, forcing the German into an overshoot. As he reversed back he was now canopy to canopy in a rolling fight with the 109. Suddenly tracers laced past his adversary, pieces of the German's left wing detaching into the wind stream. The kid!

Small flames appeared on the 109's wing and he spun off to the left. Hank looked right to see two more Germans attacking, with at least five more aircraft in his field of view.

Hank turned with the two Germans for five minutes with no shots by either side. A third 109 slashed through the fight, trailing smoke from his engine and clearly in trouble. Finally Hank pulled his Mustang almost vertical and the lead German made his fatal mistake by reversing the wrong way. The German must have realized his error, but it was too late. Twisting desperately, he couldn't shake Hank. Hank hit the German with a full 3 second burst from less than 100 yards. The enemy fighter snapped to the right, pieces leaving the aircraft as it dove toward the earth. The second German saw his opportunity to escape the fight and dove toward a deep valley that ran to the north.

Hank quickly scanned the sky, but there were no aircraft to be seen. In his mirror, Clem flew a loose trail formation and appeared to be undamaged. Hank realized he was soaked with sweat, his left hand sore from constantly jockeying the throttle.

"Black Two, how's your fuel," he asked, simultaneously checking his own. Twisting to see the fuselage gauge, Hank noted it was about ½ full. He should have guessed, the aircraft was flying great and that always happened after about half of the fuselage tank burned down. The wing tanks were 2/3's full, giving him about 160 gallons, plenty to make Leiston if they didn't tangle with any more Germans.

"I'm okay, lead."

"Roger."

Turning the Mustang to the left, Hank estimated where the return route would be for the bombers. If they could pick up another group or any stragglers, they could add their firepower to help the bombers home.


"The kid got one, first time out." Hank climbed out on the wing, and Billy Thackery reached up to take his oxygen mask and helmet.

"We need to add any skulls to this beast?" Thackery asked.

Hank looked down at the row of six black skulls with crossed bones beneath them.

"Let's wait til they confirm 'em, but there should be two more." He jumped down from the wing and walked over toward Clem Dunmire's Mustang, now parked next to his. The young pilot knelt down by one wheel, making Hank wonder if he had a religious zealot on his hands.

"Thanking God for getting back in one piece?"

Clem stood up.

"No sir, I wanted to see if the cut in that main mount was any worse. Don't want them to change the tire for no reason."

Called that one wrong, Hank told himself. This kid's got the makings of a damned good aviator if he can stay alive for a few more missions.

"Let's get in there and debrief the mission."

"Yes, sir," Clem said, following Hank across the tarmac.

The two walked in silence for a minute.

Funny, Hank thought, most rookies would be jabbering like a monkey, especially after their first kill.

"Good job out there," he finally said as they approached the door of the Nissan hut.

"Thanks."

Hank stopped as did Clem.

"You okay?" he asked, wondering if the kid had some kind of combat shock.

"Yes, sir, just fine."

Hank looked at the clear eyes, the face lined only with marks from his oxygen mask. It was obvious that Second Lieutenant Clem Dunmire was indeed doing fine, his first successful combat mission under his belt with no ill effects.

"Don't forget to tell them to pull your gun camera film."

"Yes, sir."

Back in his room, Hank sat down at his desk with a tumbler of bourbon and the letter. Why did he dread what might be inside? In the last week he'd tried not to think about Kate. When they parted he wasn't sure where things would end up. Her anger and bitterness about the war and his decision to rejoin it seemed to have thrown a wrench into any possible relationship for them. He told himself that finding someone now didn't make sense. His future was flying missions against the Luftwaffe, probably with a good chance of dying or getting captured. If he survived the war, there was still his disfigured face. Why would any woman want to look at that for the rest of her life? But there was something about Kate Murray that made him want to look past all of that. Was she the one? Did this terrible turn in his life open a door for him and he was being too stupid to recognize it? And don't forget about dear Margo. Life would certainly be simpler without women, he decided.

Hank took a drink and picked up the envelope which showed the effect of being in his pocket, now wrinkled and moist from his sweat. Her name was in the upper left corner, but there was no return address. He pushed his finger under the flap and carefully opened the letter. Withdrawing the single sheet, he quickly unfolded it and let his eyes race over the text. He stopped and stared out the window, then read it again slowly ".....I know how you feel about the war and doing your duty. Understand why I feel the way I do. Having lost one man, I never wanted that kind of pain again. What I didn't know was that I would find you and fall in love. Now that sword would be over my head again. Hank, I just can't do it. I hope you understand........please take care of yourself, I will not try to see you or write. No matter what happens, I will always remember you, my wonderful Yank...."

He felt empty. I guess that's it, he thought, but just as well. It wouldn't be fair to her, right? Let her find some nice guy and live happily ever after. Hank downed the rest of the bourbon and flung his glass into the wall where it shattered. The anger proved he was only kidding himself. This wasn't what he wanted.


"Okay Hank, your tactics seem to be working. Eight kills in one week and we've only lost one B-17 from fighter attack. Gogan thinks we should give it two more weeks and then take it up the chain." Robin Cunning sat across from Hank at the deserted end of the chow hall. Lunch concluded over an hour prior, only the mess cooks remained in the building.

"I want to get more aggressive," Hank said. "The more I think about it, the more I know we can take this farther. If we can follow them back to their airfields, it will start to affect how they deploy their aircraft. Think about it, anytime you attack the Americans; someone's going to track you down where you live. That's never been done in this war. I heard it happened in the first war, makes it more personal."

Cunning held his empty coffee cup, staring down at the table in thought.

Hank continued, "And we plan it so if there are no attacks on the bombers, we have pre-planned fields to strafe on the way home."

"You really don't like those people do you?"

"The Krauts?"

"Yeah, what did you think I meant?"

Hank shook his head. "I thought you might have meant my flight. Beating up airfields has always been dicey if the triple A's ready for you."

"Well it's still easier to kill the sons of bitches while they're parked on the ramp than rolling in on you."

"My thoughts exactly. And the more planes we destroy and pilots we kill, the fewer bombers we lose."

Cunning stood up. He looked tired, the pressure of combat leadership catching up with him.

"All right, let me talk to Gogan. This may be more than he's willing to do right now, but I'll try. By the way, I keep meaning to tell you. A friend of yours is transferring into the Group."

Hank looked up at the Skipper and said, "I don't have many friends anymore, you know that, don't you?"

"I think this guy qualifies. Doc Robertson got transferred to Kenley. The 354th lost their flight surgeon and he knows their Group Commander pretty well. We're getting Major Roger Hanson as our new Group Flight Surgeon.

# Chapter Eleven

20 Miles East of Münster
Germany
23 March, 1944

Hank checked his mirrors and then the sky to his front, all clear for now. Blackbird flight cruised north in a battle box after breaking off from bomber protection at Münster. Colonel Gogan's comment on the plan to strafe airfields had been, "In for a penny, in for a pound."

Luftwaffe attacks that day had been light and so far no one in Hank's flight had fired their guns. Perfect day to try the new tactic, he thought, plenty of fuel and ammo. Looking over to Clem, he saw the bright yellow wingtips all four of the flight members now wore. When he asked Thackery during the man up, his crew chief simply said, "They all wanted to look like you, so I said what the hell."

Knowing they would now be showing on the German radar net, he pushed the nose over to take advantage of a valley up ahead. Checking the chart, Hank felt confident this was the Cheine Valley. Following the valley would funnel them into a pronounced gap in the hills and just beyond was the Luftwaffe airfield at Salzwedel. They planned to attack in groups of two, using different attack heading to complicate tracking for the German anti-aircraft guns. Hank decided to limit this first attack to one run by each aircraft. He hoped the gunners would

91

be caught with their guard down long enough to do real damage to the parked aircraft.

Looking ahead, he relaxed slightly as the large bend in the valley came into view, confirming he was in the right place. Hank estimated fifteen miles to the field. Looking at his airspeed indicator he did a quick math problem and estimated they would be at the target in about two and a half minutes. Flashing over the rolling trees at 350 knots, he watched the sweep hand on the instrument panel clock.

"Lead's breaking," he transmitted and simultaneously pulled up hard right, knowing Clem was right behind him. The Mustang's nose climbed to 20 degrees above the horizon and now Hank could see the large open area used for takeoffs and landings. Pulling the nose back left and lining up on a line of parked fighters, he squeezed the trigger and watched his tracers flash into the first parked Me-109. Walking the fire up the line of parked aircraft, he watched one fighter explode into a mass of flames. Hank banked left, lining up on a row of buildings facing the aircraft. Squeezing the trigger he saw men run left and right seeking cover as the .50 caliber slugs tore into the wooden buildings. One last course correction allowed him to target a sand bagged emplacement near the perimeter road. Concentrating his fire into a gun pit made him feel good. Bastards, he thought, as his Mustang flashed over the smoking gun emplacement and clear of the airfield.

Turning hard left, Hank saw Clem pulling up as he crossed the perimeter road, the young pilot's Mustang barely twenty feet above the ground.

"Two, check left 10 o'clock."

Dunmire's Mustang pitched left.

"In sight," Clem called on the radio.

Banking hard to the right, Hank looked for Chris and Wakefield, expecting to see them completing their runs. He spotted one Mustang at the end of the field. Looking right he found the second crossing the runway. Tracers from automatic weapons floated skyward, but the four Mustangs were now well out of range.

Hank felt his pulse slowing, as he set a course north for Rheine. They might be able to catch up with the bombers for the rest of their flight over the continent. The results of their attack on Salzwedel would be clearer after reviewing the gun camera films, but he knew his guns had scored multiple hits on parked fighters in addition to the support buildings. We're going to make life a little less enjoyable for the Luftwaffe, he thought, and I want them to know we are coming.

"Aircraft at our left 9:30 low, Blackbirds," Chris called over the radio.

Searching forward of his left wing, Hank quickly picked up a four engine transport aircraft tracking southeast toward Frankfurt.

"Chris, we'll fly cover, you saw it first, it's yours," Hank said.

"Roger, let's go Four."

The two Mustangs smartly rolled left and established an attack heading on the unsuspecting transport.

Hank watched them make a rear quarter attack, both fighters flashing by the lumbering transport. Smoke began to trail from the German's number four engine as Chris pulled around for another attack.

"Lead, the Kraut just dropped his landing gear." Chris called.

Over Europe, an aircraft dropping its landing gear signified submission to the attacker. The aircraft would then fly to the nearest enemy base, land and surrender.

This makes no sense, Hank thought. The nearest "enemy base" lay across the English Channel, 300 miles north of where they were now. He watched the German turn slowly north, his airspeed not more than 100 knots.

"We don't have time to play games, Three. Finish him," Hank said.

The two Mustangs were now flying an easy circle around the German, an Arado 232.

"There's a red cross painted on the fuselage, Lead. Maybe this is a medical flight."

"I don't care. Finish him."

Chris and Wakefield continued to circle, the transport continuing its northward course.

"Watch out for bandits, Two," Hank said as he rolled his Mustang over almost inverted and pulled the nose down toward the German. His airspeed built up quickly and he watched the lumbering transport move under the reticles of his gunsight. He squeezed the trigger, immediately seeing hits on the fuselage. A slight back pressure walked the tracers into the cockpit and pieces began to fly off the fuselage of the doomed Arado. Rolling left, he dove past the transport, his speed allowing him to roll back to the right and gain altitude while watching the German roll inverted and begin a spiraling dive toward the green valley floor.

"Join up, Blackbirds."

The flight back to Leiston was quiet and uneventful. Blackbird flight arrived at the field as the rest of the group was landing from the mission.

Hank knelt under the wing, making a quick survey during his post flight inspection. No evidence of combat damage, despite the heavy anti-aircraft fire from the gun emplacements around Salzwedel.

"What you did out there was bullshit."

Turning, he saw Chris standing next to the Mustang, hand on his hips.

"And why's that?"

"That plane commander had surrendered; he'd dropped his gear and wasn't taking any evasive action."

"Your opinion, my friend." Hank stood up and saw the anger in Chris's expression.

"What the hell's wrong with you? You think that by becoming a butcher you'll get even for what they did to you?"

"Maybe it will, Chris. But that's not what changed how I look at this war. When we first got over here, I thought we were the knights of the modern age, chivalry and all that crap. Well I figured out that's a bunch of shit. This is a fight to the death, no holds barred. Until we figure that out, those bastards are going to keep doing what they've been doing since 1939."

Chris looked at him.

"Now get into debrief." Hank brushed past Chris and began to walk toward the debriefing hut.

"So you're no different than the krauts."

Hank stopped and turned to face Chris as Clem Dunmire walked around the tail of the Mustang.

"We didn't start this war, Chris. There's a difference. If you can't understand that you belong in a monastery not a cockpit."

Hank turned and walked away toward debrief. "Come on, Clem."

The two men walked away from Chris who stood watching them, anger on his face.

"Clem, our job is to shoot down German aircraft and protect the bombers. Don't let anything get in the way of that, understood?"

"Yes, sir."


"You want to do what?" Colonel Max Gogan asked, his face reflecting his surprise.

Hank Mitchell and Robin Cunning stood in front of the group commander's desk, both looking ready for an argument.

"It makes sense, Colonel," said Cunning. "After reviewing the gun camera films from Blackbird flight, I'm convinced that beating up the German fighter fields is something we've got to do."

"Okay, I'll look at the films. When the Krauts attacked the Brit airfields in 1940 it almost broke the back of the RAF. If we can destroy them on the ground, so be it. Give me specifics."

Robin placed a chart of Europe on Gogan's desk.

"As part of the main bomber mission, we detail several flights to head out on their own to hit the Krauts while they're getting ready to launch."

"Catch em with their pants down?" Gogan pulled a large cigar out of his desk and began to unwrap it.

"Exactly. If we can disrupt the normal flight launch, it will throw off every part of their defensive network. The controllers will have to route fighters from farther sectors, pilots will be unfamiliar with their normal operating areas. It'll throw a wrench into the whole works."

"Worst case, Colonel, they'll start putting more aircraft in the air at all times, which will kill their maintenance to say nothing of the fuel they'll burn." Hank knew they were getting Gogan's attention.

Puffing hard as he lit the cigar, Colonel Gogan seemed lost in thought.

"We think tomorrow's mission to Magdeburg would be a good time to start," Cunning said.

"Okay, I'll talk to the front office. Robin, if we get the go ahead I want your squadron to lead this effort. Get your pilots together and bring them up to speed on everything they'll need to know before tomorrow."

"Yes, sir."

The two pilots saluted and left Gogan's office.


Hank opened the front door of the headquarters building.

"Get the word out for an all pilots meeting at 1900 in the briefing room."

"Right," Hank acknowledged.

"We'll show the gun camera films from your flight. That'll give the new guys an idea what they'll be seeing during low altitude strafing runs. Plan on briefing anything you learned from that mission. No sense reinventing the wheel."

They continued to walk toward the squadron area, both lost in thought.

# Chapter Twelve

USAAF Station 373
Leiston
Suffolk, England
23 March, 1944

    The informal briefing lasted over an hour. The pilots of the 952nd appeared intrigued with their new mission. A long question and answer period allowed Hank to cover every aspect of low altitude attacks on an airfield.

    "Let me say it one more time. Don't make multiple runs against an airfield that has active anti-aircraft. We may not like the bastards, but they've got good triple A and they're not stupid. Try multiple runs, particularly from the same direction and you'll be pushing up daisies or eating sauerkraut in a Luftwaffe POW camp."

    Robin stood up and walked out in front of the group.

    "Okay, that's it. Remember, this is still on the drawing boards and we haven't been given the go ahead yet. If we get the green light tonight, I'll have intel prepare charts and any pictures for the briefing in the morning. This could be a real chance to hurt the enemy where it counts. Try and get some sleep tonight. Dismissed."

"Hey," Hank called to Chris as they filed out of the briefing room.

Christiansen turned, his face grim.

"Yeah?"

"Let's talk," Hank said, falling in next to Chris.

"What's there to talk about?"

Hank grabbed Chris's arm, turning him around so they were face to face.

"Don't give me that bullshit, you're still pissed about the Kraut today. We better agree on what rules we're gonna use in the future so someone doesn't get killed out there for no good reason."

Chris pulled Hank's hand away.

"Rules! Who are you kidding? You don't have any rules. As far as you're concerned you do whatever you can justify to yourself – that's not what the rest of us call rules."

"So you think we should have let that aircraft go?"

"I think we should have thought about it more than you did."

Hank shook his head, his friend's words exasperating him.

Slowly he said, "What in the hell was there to think about?"

"That was an unarmed transport that appeared to be on a medical mission."

"And what the hell difference does that make?"

Chris stepped closer to Hank. "Perhaps you forgot about the Geneva Convention, buddy. It's just like a hospital ship. You can't fire on the red cross."

The two men looked at each other.

"I'm tired. If you don't have anything else to say, I'm gonna hit the rack," Chris said as he turned to walk away.

"You want out of the flight?' Hank called after him.

"I'll think about it," Chris said, not looking back and continuing to walk.


"They say drinking alone is bad for your health."

Hank sat alone in his room which was lit only by a small desk lamp. He poured a measure of bourbon in a glass and pushed the cork back in the bottle. Picking up the glass he held it up in a mock toast.

"Well I say bullshit to them."

He took a drink, grimacing as he swallowed a full measure of the strong liquor.

"Besides, who wants to drink with the Butcher of Leiston?"

For a moment he recalled what Chris said about the Geneva Convention. Shit, he thought, maybe I did break the rules. But you can bet those sons of bitches have broken a lot more.

Hank heard a knock at his door. For one moment he thought about ignoring it. He didn't feel like seeing anyone, but it could be about the mission tomorrow. Getting up, he reached for the door knob and opened it to find Roger Hanson standing in the hall.

"Hi, Hank," the doctor said.

"Hello Doc, welcome to beautiful Leiston," his words slightly slurred. "Come on in, I'm just having a drink to relax. Sit down, let me fix you one."

"Not me, I have to go see Colonel Gogan."

"Well, sit down and relax for a minute. Gogan can act like an asshole, but he's a pretty straight shooter. Just wish he could fly better."

Roger looked surprised as he pulled up a chair.

"Why do I guess there's a story behind that?"

Hank shook his head. "No story," he said. "I just think that he's working so hard to fly his aircraft and lead the group when we're on missions that he misses things."

Roger didn't reply for a moment, and then said, "How have you been?"

Hank tossed down the rest of his drink and reached for the bottle.

"No ill effects at all, Doctor. What now passes for skin does get chaffed as hell under my oxygen mask and my hand aches sometimes. But all things considered, I'm doing fine."

"Robin Cunning told me you named your plane, "Flaming Death."

"Kind of catchy, don't you think?" Hank filled his glass with whiskey.

"I know several psychiatrists who might disagree with you."

"Yeah? And I bet they don't look like me either," the humorous tone leaving his voice.

"I think you and I need to do some talking."

"What in the hell's there to talk about?"

"Hey, I can ground you for medical reasons if I have to."

Hank turned to see that Roger's expression had turned hard.

"I'm fine, just having a little fun with folks."

Roger stood up. "I gotta go see Gogan. Come by and see me after tomorrow's mission. I want to take a closer look at our repair job."

"Sure thing, Doc, whatever you say."

Stopping in the door, Roger turned and said, "And lay off the booze tonight if you want to make it to the debrief." Doctor Hanson pulled the door shut.

Hank started to take a drink then thought better of it.


Forty seven Mustangs launched from Leiston, the first aircraft rolling down the runway at 0645. Once the Group rendezvoused, Colonel Gogan turned south to find the 90th Bomb Group which was already almost an hour along the track toward the railroad marshalling yards outside of Bremen. Robin Cunning had taken the flight lead for the squadron and detached from the larger group at 0755, taking up a pre-flighted heading of 077. The navigation plan called for the squadron to split into three divisions of four aircraft who would each strike a Luftwaffe field in the Bremen area. Hank's flight would hit the most heavily defended of the three fields, Bruchaven. The Group Intelligence Officer briefed Hank that the Germans had reinforced the field defenses with a number of quadruple 20mm guns mounted on half tracks. These guns had been first seen in North Africa and proved lethal to the RAF.

Hank adjusted his oxygen flow to full, trying to erase the hangover from the night before. Flying at 10,000 feet, he didn't need the oxygen to survive, but he hoped it would speed his recovery from too much bourbon. At least the queasy stomach no longer bothered him after a large dose of Bromo Seltzer.

Unfortunately he knew passing on breakfast would come back to haunt him later, but he'd have to face that when the time came.

Looking to the right he could see Clem flying a loose wing position about one hundred feet slightly aft of the wing line. Clem's goggles were down and his oxygen mask attached. Scattered low clouds covered part of the terrain, but at altitude the brilliant blue sky almost let Hank forget they were on a combat mission. Chris and Wakefield trailed on the port side, 300 feet behind Hank's Mustang.

The discussion this morning between Hank and Chris had been short, both men ready to forget the anger of the day before and focus on the mission. Despite the proximity of enemy airfields, Hank found himself wondering how he and Chris had hit it off so well. They came from very different backgrounds and their personalities were completely opposite, but both could fly a Mustang better than most. Perhaps that's it, he thought, we respected each other as flyers and so the friendship grew. Checking his mirror he could see "Glorious Ginny," Chris's Mustang, in position to prevent any attacks on Hank from behind. Watching the sleek fighter make the small corrections to stay in position, Hank knew they were as good as anyone in the skies over Europe.

Robin began an exaggerated wing rock which told flight leaders to detach and proceed on their individual missions. Hank immediately pulled power, trimming the P-51's nose down slightly to commence the descent to low altitude. Many of the other pilots felt that coming in low cost you precise navigation and wasn't worth the trade off. After several attacks, Hank knew that the surprise afforded by a low altitude attack more than made up for increasing the nav problem. "Just make sure you know where the hell you are," he told the other pilots. His attitude didn't increase his popularity with the squadron, but he couldn't have cared less.

Descending through 2000 feet, Hank checked his chart one more time. He'd selected the navigation route because it allowed him to follow the river to a very distinctive bend, which was only eight miles from the airfield at Bruchaven. From that point, a turn to attack heading and one minute of flying would put them over the field.

Turbulence buffeted the aircraft as the four fighters descended. The short stubby wings made for a hard ride. At times the instruments were difficult to read. Ahead Hank saw the river, the water a greenish brown, its banks lined by trees. Descending to 200 feet he began to follow the terrain of the river valley. A small barge flashed past on the left side, its journey downriver aided by a small boat tied to one side. Hank strained his eyes, always on the lookout for cables or wires strung across the river. At this altitude enemy fighters would have trouble seeing them and even more trouble mounting an effective attack.

Checking his gun switches one last time, Hank passed over the river bend and turned for Bruchaven. In succession, Clem, Chris and Wakefield followed him, all aircraft now making over 350 knots. The clock doesn't lie, he told himself as the second hand passed 12. Pulling up hard he simultaneously took a sharp cut to the right, immediately reversing hard.

Just right of the nose three FW-190's were holding at the end of the runway. They're launching, he thought. He made a quick correction to the right and depressed the gun trigger. At this short distance against stationary targets the effect was dramatic. His bullets tore into all three, smoke and dust rising from the impacts. The closest aircraft blew up, flipping the second into the third, flames breaking out of the dust. Hank flashed over the burning aircraft and hurtled down the runway 30 feet above the concrete.

Remembering the control tower was to the right. Hank carefully dipped the right wing, bringing his gunsight over the three story brick building. His tracers flew into the upper level, throwing glass, bricks and wood high into the air. Pulling up he cleared the shattered tower by fifty feet and only then did he see the tracers coming from his right. He felt the aircraft yaw hard to the right and he fought for control, the stick fighting his effort to correct left. *Shit!*

Struggling to get the wings level, Hank watched as more tracers arced past his canopy as German gunners found their mark. He fought the nose down and put the Mustang on the tree tops, trying to evade their fire. Suddenly he was clear of the tracers and over an open valley. This thing is still flying, he told himself, but there's a problem with the controls. Can I keep it flying? Gingerly he raised the nose and started a gentle turn using only rudder. If I get jumped on the way back home, I'm dead, he thought. Then he realized he didn't care if he lived or died. It just didn't matter.

Twisting in the cockpit, he looked back to see the other three aircraft had joined him in the climb. I really don't care, he repeated to himself, the words giving him a feeling of freedom.

"I don't give a shit if you don't think you don't need a rest. I think you do and so does Hanson. Hell, go sit in your room for two days, I don't care. But you're not going to fly for 48 hours. Chris took a demotion to get back in your flight. Let him lead a couple of missions, he's earned it." Robin signed a pass and handed it to Hank. His tone softened. "You're no good to me or the squadron in a smoking hole somewhere in Germany. If a couple of days rest gets you back in fighting trim then it's worth it. I'm still on your side, remember?"

Hank picked up the slip.

"I probably could use a break. Maybe a trip to London."

"There you go, good meal, smell some perfume, get lucky...."

"Yeah, London, home of Dr. Jekyll and Jack the Ripper, I'll fit in fine." Hank turned and walked out, closing the door behind him.

Robin broke his pencil and threw it against the wall. The son of a bitch makes me crazy, he thought, then he remembered the visit from Roger Hanson.

"Skipper, he's on the ragged edge," the doctor had said. "I don't know whether it's something that he can get past or not. It may come down to pulling his wings. But something's got to change."

Robin hoped Hanson was right. Neither he nor the group could afford to lose Hank Mitchell.

Ten seconds after walking out of Robin's office, Hank knew what he needed to do.

# Chapter Thirteen

East Grinstead Township
West Sussex, England
25 March, 1944

Hank stood up as the small bus pulled to a stop outside the Post Office, one of four stops in East Grinstead on the London to Eastbourne bus line. The elderly bus driver had told him this stop was the closest to the Excelsior Hotel on Hyde Road.

"A nice little establishment, I've heard," the man had said in a heavy cockney accent.

Carrying a small bag, Hank walked toward the hotel, surprised at enjoying his absence from Leiston. Maybe Cunning and Hanson had been right, a short break couldn't be bad. He found himself anxious to check in and be on his way to find Kate.

The Excelsior reminded him of the small inns of New England, run by a family, more like a large home than a hotel. Other than a quick reaction to his face, the middle aged woman behind the counter proved to be very friendly and was most insistent that Hank just let her know what he needed. He asked for directions to the book store, which she wrote down on a small piece of paper.

"Wouldn't want you lost on your first day, now would we."


Slightly disoriented when he first departed the Excelsior, when he turned on London Road, Hank recognized where he was. Everything looked the same as that day he first walked in to find Kate behind the counter. What would he find today?

Opening the door, the bell jangled to announce his arrival. Glancing behind the counter he saw it was deserted. Hank turned to carefully close the door, his emotions confused.

"May I help you?"

He turned to see a tall man with short cropped hair standing behind the counter. The man smiled pleasantly, waiting for Hank's reply.

"Hello. Yes, I was looking for Kate Murray."

"She's at the hospital today. Is there anything I can do?"

"Are you Mr. Hunnicutt?"

The man's expression changed slightly. "That's right, George Hunnicutt."

"Sir, my name's Mitchell, Hank Mitchell. I met your daughter at the hospital."

Hunnicutt didn't reply.

Hank walked back to the counter and removed his gloves.

"I was in town and wanted to say hello."

George Hunnicutt extended his hand over the counter.

"I know who you are, Captain. Kate should be back shortly. Might I offer you a cup of tea while you wait?"

Hank followed him into the kitchen.

"Kate said that you had returned to your unit. Back in the thick of it, I s'pose?"

"Yes, sir. I'm based at Leiston."

"Nasty business, war."

"Yes, sir, I agree with you."

"Spent my time in the Royal Artillery in the last war. The war to end all wars.....cripes."

Hunnicutt placed a cup in front of Hank and returned to the stove.

"Damned Huns. You'd have thought they did enough damage last time and here we are again."

"Well, maybe we'll break them for good this time."

"Bloody well hope so," he said, pouring tea into Hank's cup.

Sitting down heavily, he poured a small amount of milk into his tea, stirring it with his finger.

"My daughter seemed quite taken with you." Hunnicutt stared over the top of his cup, his comment almost an afterthought.

"She's quite a lady," Hank replied, embarrassed by her father's comment.

The two sat quietly taking small sips of their tea.

George Hunnicutt put his cup down and looked directly at Hank. "Dan's death in Africa almost killed her. I was worried she might never recover. I knew what she was going through, lost her mother in '34."

"I'm sorry; she never talked much about her mother."

"Not surprising, that's the way she is, keeps everything inside."

The sound of the door bell tingling came from the front.

"Better go see who that is," he said getting to his feet. "Just relax."

Looking out the window, he could see small buds starting to grow on one of the trees by the flower bed. Spring had always been his favorite season.

"Hello, Hank."

He turned, Kate, her cheeks rosy from the cold, her smile soft and reserved.

"Hi," he said awkwardly, starting to get up.

"Sit down. Can I get you some more tea?" she asked.

"Sure," he said.

She removed her scarf and coat, hanging them on a peg behind the door.

"I saw Doctor Frazier today," she said, pouring tea for the two of them. Returning and sitting down, she stirred her tea, her eyes on the cup.

"Roger Hanson's now at Leiston. He's the group flight surgeon."

She hesitated as if trying to put together her thoughts.

"Hank, why are you here?" Her question was said softly, without emotion, but her eyes showed the pain she felt.

"I had to see you."

"Did you get my letter?"

He nodded.

"I tried to tell you how I felt. It was hard to say the things I did. But I knew I couldn't spend each day wondering if that was the day you would die. Hank, I just can't do that. God help me, because I do love you. I just can't go through that again."

He saw tears on her cheeks.

"Kate, I'm sorry. I don't want to do anything to hurt you."

"Then leave, please leave and don't try to see me again." She was looking at him now, tears streaming down her face, the anguish evident.

Hank stood up. "Kate, I......"

"Please, Hank, just go."

Grabbing his coat, Hank brushed past her.

As the bell over the door tinkled, Kate put her head down on her folded arms and sobbed.


Hank's head still pounded from one of the worst hangovers he could remember. All he wanted to do was crawl into his bed and sleep. Opening the door to his room, he reached over and turned on the small desk lamp. In the middle of his desk a single envelope waited for him.

Through the fog of his headache he saw it was from Margo Van Whiting. He slipped his finger under the flap and ripped the envelope open, the flimsy paper tearing easily.

She expressed her sorrow over his "dreadful accident" and knew he would "Come back strong as ever." But the last paragraph told the whole story. "I met someone......never intended to......I know you will understand." He crumpled the letter and tossed it into the trash can.

"Christ, dumped by two women in the same day."

He lay down on his bed, still wearing his uniform and overcoat. In five minutes he was asleep.


"Captain Mitchell, wake up."

Light came from the hallway, enough for Hank to see Corporal Wanamaker.

"What time is it?" he asked, feeling confused and sick.

"About 1900, sir. Colonel Gogan wants to see you ASAP."

Hank sat up in bed.

"Gogan? What the hell's going on?"

"Captain, I'm just the messenger, nobody tells me nothing."

Swinging his legs to the floor, he rubbed his eyes. His head pounded and his mouth tasted terrible. But why would Gogan want to see him?

"Christ," he said, pain piercing his head. "Tell him I'm on my way."


Colonel Max Gogan sat behind his desk looking at several 8 x 10" black and white photos.

"Captain Mitchell, reporting as ordered, sir."

Gogan looked up, focusing on Hank's face.

"You look like hell."

"Yes, sir, feel the same way."

"What'd you do, drink your way through London?"

"Something like that, sir."

Gogan took a deep breath.

"Robin Cunning went down today. KIA."

Hank felt a wave of nausea.

"He was leading a flight against Bruchaven. Apparently the Krauts set up a flak trap, those quad 20's were waiting. They got him and Simmons." He paused while he rubbed his eyes, the fatigue obvious. "Shit.....Robin was one of the best squadron commanders I've ever seen. It always happens to the good guys. Anyway, you're the senior captain in the squadron and the most experienced. You're in command for now. A spot promotion to Major goes with the job. Any questions?"

"Any change in our tactics?"

"I want to take a breather on attacking the airfields. I still think it's a good idea. But we need to review it. For now we'll stick with escort, but I'm gonna let the 952nd stay with loose escort. That's unofficial by the way."

"Is that written in stone, Colonel?"

Gogan looked at Hank. "No. You're the CO now, use your own discretion."

"Yes, sir." Hank turned to leave the room.

"But, you better have a damn good reason for whatever you're doing out there, you read me?"

"Loud and clear, sir."


Walking back to his room, Hank felt anger over the loss of Robin. He'd been a good friend and smart pilot. Never underestimate those kraut sons of bitches, he thought.

So now I'm the 'skipper.' He remembered when skippers were all old guys who'd forgotten everything important. Now that's how the rest of the pilots were going to look at him.

After shaving and brushing his teeth, Hank walked down to the squadron office. He opened the door and went in to find Lieutenant McGowan sitting at the duty desk. The official squadron logbook sat in front of him.

McGowan looked up, a powerfully built officer, the two had been friendly, but not real friends.

"Hey, Hank. You hear about the skipper?"

"Yeah, just found out."

"Want me to log you in from your pass?"

"Yeah, and make a note in the logbook, I'm the new CO."

"No shit?" McGowan looked very surprised.

"Yeah, no shit. Now go find the Ops boss, I need to go over the flight assignments."

"Okay. I mean, yes, sir."

Hank watched him leave. The new commanding officer felt very tired.


Two hours later, Hank returned to his room, ready for sleep and thankful tomorrow was a stand down day for the group. His stop at Gogan's office confirmed they would be back in action the following day, a major push by the bombers against industrial plants in the Ruhr Valley. Fighter opposition was expected to be heavy and the 952nd was scheduled to launch twelve Mustangs for the mission. Hank would lead one flight, putting Chris in charge of the second and Dan, now the squadron Operations Officer, leading the third.

Wilskie had gone over the pilot list with Hank, the two reorganizing the squadron flight for tomorrow's mission. Hank trusted Dan's judgment on each pilot's strengths and weaknesses. It was time to move Clem up from wingman to section leader, but Hank wanted to keep him in his flight. When the question of a wingman for Hank came up, he selected Lieutenant Sam Tesore. He was going to make or break the little prick.

There was a knock at the door.

"Come in, it's open."

Chris opened the door and stepped inside.

"I heard the news from Wilskie. For what it's worth, I think you'll be a good CO. You just gotta realize most of these guys aren't as fanatic as you are."

Hank said, "All I want is for them to kill as many Germans as they can, no holds barred."

Chris looked at his friend. "Just cut 'em a little slack. You've gotten a reputation as an asshole and they don't need that right now."

"What they need right now is to start putting up some numbers. When we start painting kills on aircraft after every mission, then they'll be doing their job."

"Whatever you say. After all, you're the Skipper."

# Chapter Fourteen

USAAF Station 373
Leiston
Suffolk, England
6 May, 1944

"If I get my ass chewed one more time by that son of a bitch, I'm gonna deck him." First Lieutenant Ted Slater flopped down on his bunk, swinging his still boot clad feet up and on the blanket. "We haven't lost a bomber in over six weeks and he's still a damned raving lunatic if you make any mistakes. Christ, he needs to give us a little credit for what we've done."

"You finished?" Farley Jones, his roommate asked.

"Yeah."

"You got penciled in for the Dortmund mission tomorrow. I guess one of Mitchell's guys came down with the flu or something."

Slater looked at his friend with a pained expression. "You mean I'm in Doctor Death's flight?"

"That's about it, little buddy."

"Wonderful, fucking wonderful."

"You're going to do what?"

"Hank, I've been the Group flight surgeon for almost two months. It's time I saw what it's like up there."

Roger Hanson stood with his arms crossed in front of Hank Mitchell's desk. "It's been approved by Eighth Air Force Headquarters in accordance with all applicable directives. Besides, Gogan approved it too."

"That doesn't mean it's a good idea. You have any idea what you're getting into?"

"No, I don't. That's why I'm doing it. How can I be an effective flight surgeon if I don't understand what my patients are going through day after day?"

Hank was concerned for his friend's life. In the months since his accident and during his time as the Commanding Officer of the 952nd, Hank had come to rely on Roger. Although the Luftwaffe had been hurt, they were still deadly adversaries. Bombers and fighters continued to go down over Europe despite the increasing numerical superiority of the allies. Hank knew Roger might not return.

"Well I think it's a damned dumb idea."

"Hank, I'm going in the Wing Commander's aircraft. I've been told he has a hand-picked crew that has over twenty missions under their belts."

"So we'll be providing the escort?"

Roger nodded. "That's what Gogan said. I'll be in the lead aircraft in the lead division. Colonel Thomas has been here from almost the start of offensive operations. I couldn't be in better hands."

"You know what I do anytime we run into the Krauts?"

"No, I guess I don't," Roger replied.

"I try to shoot down the leader. You know, cut off the head? What makes you think the Germans don't do the same thing?"

"If they do, I'll just have to deal with it."

"Christ."


A high pressure system over the European Continent had produced clear skies from Scotland to Italy. Across the expanse of blue, hundreds of white contrails gave evidence of another maximum effort by the Eight Air Force against the German war machine.

Adjusting his mixture slightly, Hank tried to coax as much range out of his fuel as possible, knowing weather like this always brought out more fighters to oppose the bombers. So far the skies had been clear of Germans, but they had only been over the continent for thirty minutes. Every mile he could keep burning fuel from his drop tanks was money in the bank if the Germans attacked. Hank had positioned his flights about four miles on either side of the main bomber stream, leaving the specific altitudes up to Chris and Dan.

The two flight leaders had proved to be exactly what the squadron needed after the death of Robin Cunning. Their quiet professionalism and no nonsense attitudes brought cohesion to the squadron pilots and had allowed Hank to focus on tactics for fighting the Luftwaffe.

This was a different German Air Force. Gone were the veterans of 1940 and '41, chewed up in the skies over Africa, Germany and Russia. Today, many enemy fighters were flown by inexperienced pilots thrown into the breach without significant flight time. That didn't make the enemy any less dangerous. The Germans had still been able to put significant opposition in the air, using a more coordinated command structure and greater use of electronic warfare. There were still some of the "old boys" leading the wings and squadrons and any encounter with the old guard could become lethal in short order.

The tactics pioneered by the 952nd had begun to be adopted by many of the fighter groups. As the invasion drew closer, American fighters took any opportunity to attack the roads, railroads or airfields on the continent.

To his left, Gogan and the rest of the Mustangs flew protectively around the boxes of B-17's. Looking toward the front of the formation he saw the olive drab B-17G carrying Roger. Soon after the initial rendezvous, Hank moved his flight close enough to see the name "Alabama Queen" on the nose. His concerns for Roger's safety were heightened by today's target, Dortmund. The Germans would pull out all the stops to protect the aircraft engine production plant which was their primary target.

Flying a loose wing, Ted Slater maintained his position. Hank had to admit, the young pilot appeared to be competent. When Clem had been grounded by the flu, he decided to see first hand how Slater was doing and had him assigned to his flight.

In their brief, Hank had been very direct with him, telling him he expected tight formation flying if they engaged, a minimum of chatter on the radio and good firing discipline. He remembered Slater's response, "Can do, Skipper."

Roger Hanson knelt just behind the pilot and co-pilot's seats. Surprisingly, he found that he was actually enjoying himself. The fur lined flying pants and coat kept the frigid temperature bearable and once he adjusted his oxygen mask correctly, he almost forgot he was wearing it. The crew had welcomed him at the brief with friendly smiles. His participation on what was considered a dangerous mission gave him immediate acceptance by the crew. In particular, the Wing Commander, Colonel Andy Thomas, went out of his way to keep an eye on Roger during the pre-flight and start, despite being in overall command of the mission and the thirty six B-17's assigned. Thomas spoke with a thick southern drawl, his quiet and friendly nature masking his experience as one of the best bomber pilots in the Eighth Air Force.

Over the intercom, Roger listened to the crew chatter and he could also hear the radio, which was set to the main strike frequency. The complexity of the mission impressed him, all of the aircraft from many different bases coming together as a giant force to fight their way into the hostile skies of Germany.

"Bandits, one o'clock high," came the metallic transmission over the strike frequency.

Thomas leaned forward, surveying the sky, an anxious expression telling Roger that things were about to get busy.

In the distance Hank saw a brief flash. Focusing hard on that piece of sky, he saw black specks begin to materialize. There must be two squadrons of enemy fighters, he estimated.

Drop tanks began to fall from the fighters as flight leads turned to intercept the Germans. Hank watched the closest enemy formation head directly for the lead bomber box and the Alabama Queen. The Focke Wulf 190's sported bright blue noses, their sleek shapes accelerating as they dove from above. Hank knew he couldn't intercept the fighters before they would reach the lead bombers. In a high speed ballet, five Germans

114

closed in on the four B-17's. Hank projected where his flight path would cross the Germans and planned his attack to begin firing at maximum range. With almost a 90 degree angle off, the deflection shooting by the Americans would be a long shot, but should distract the krauts.

The gunners in the lead box began to take the blue nosed Germans under fire, ten .50 caliber machine guns firing from each. Tracers arced out, providing a spider's web of fire the Germans had to negotiate if they were to press their attack. Flashes from the wings of the FW's were interspersed with tracers. The 190 carried two machine guns, which were primarily for aiming their more lethal cannons. While machine gun bullets could kill and cripple, the much more devastating detonation of a cannon shell could rip an aluminum bomber to pieces.


On the intercom Andy Thomas said steadily, "There they are, at least a squadron coming in from one o'clock."

Captain Jerry Smith, the pilot in the left seat, keyed his intercom, "All right, here they come. Make your shots count and keep the chatter down."

Roger jumped as the top turret's twin .50 caliber machine guns opened up, the sound echoing in the cockpit, the smell of cordite filling the air. An instant later, the cockpit seemed to come apart and Roger felt himself falling down the ladder to the lower compartment. Pain shot through his body as he hit the metal ladder then careened into the aft bulkhead. Crumpled on the lower deck, he tried to get up, but immediately fell back, his arm unable to support his weight, the pain piercing into his left shoulder, taking his breath away. A thin fog seemed to cover his eyes, pain running back from his forehead to his neck. My God, he thought, painfully rolling to one side and desperately grabbing the ladder hold with his right hand. Pulling himself upright, his head began to pound, the pain almost blinding. Reaching up he felt pain as he touched his forehead. Lowering his hand, he saw the glove was covered in blood.

In what initially seemed to be slow motion, the German fighters converged on the bombers, now flashing by at incredible speed as they crossed in front of the American fighters.

Hank began his pull to follow the Germans, but his attention was drawn momentarily to the lead B-17. Smoke trailed from the number four engine and pieces of the olive drab skin were missing, blown into the slip stream. In Hank's experience the "Alabama Queen" had been struck a potentially lethal blow. He thought only for a brief instant of Roger Hanson as he pulled the nose of the Mustang around viciously toward the Germans.

Slowly pulling himself up to the cockpit of the Queen, Roger heard the howl of the air stream from a shattered windscreen. Carefully he moved forward and knelt down to check Colonel Thomas, knowing already he was dead. Blood and bits of flesh covered the back bulkhead and circuit breaker panel. One of the German cannon shells had gone off just outside where the Group Commander sat, the fragments tearing through the thin skin and shredding his face. Roger pushed the dead weight of Thomas back against the seat and locked the harness. Removing his glove, he felt the Thomas's neck for a pulse, the man's blood flowing down over Roger's bare hand and soaking into his flight suit sleeve. He wasn't surprised there was no pulse. Thomas's eyes stared straight ahead, the spark of life gone forever. Looking left, he saw Jerry Smith leaning forward, trying to see the right wing. Their eyes met and Roger yelled, "He's dead."

Smith just nodded then reached down to his throat mike.

"Okay guys, the Colonel's dead, how bad is it back there?"

Over the interphone came a series of urgent calls.

"Jones is hit......."

"This is Brown, I need help with Reed."

"Number four's smoking bad, skipper."

Smith grabbed Roger by the arm and yelled, "Reed's the bombardier. Down in the nose. Go help him."

Roger nodded slowly, the pain in his head making him nauseous. He reached for the field medical kit he'd brought along and turned for the ladder.


A mass of turning and twisting aircraft fought to gain the advantage four miles south of the stricken "Alabama Queen." Realizing the yellow wing-tipped Mustangs were after them, four Focke Wulf's had turned to do battle. Hank's fury was unabated as he slid behind one German who must have been looking elsewhere. From only fifty yards, Hank opened fire, the .50 cals shredding the German's fuselage. The stricken fighter's canopy flew off as the pilot began to climb out, only to be torn apart by Hank's continued fire.

With a quick glance to make sure Slater was with him, Hank pulled back toward the fight. One German stood out, his nose painted not only bright blue, but with white flashes on each side of the fuselage. He pulled his nose down as the German simultaneously pitched up toward him. The two aircraft passed each other no more that fifty feet apart, both immediately turning left, trying to gain the advantage. Checking left and right, Hank saw only this German was still in the fight. The rest must have fled or gone down. Pulling hard toward the horizon, Hank kept his Mustang out of phase from the German. Looking for his opponent to make a mistake, he realized this pilot must be one of the old guard. Every trick Hank tried, the German countered. This was going to be a duel to the death. Sweat filled his oxygen mask as he strained to gain the advantage over the German, his muscles aching as the fight continued.


Roger found the navigator, Lieutenant Lloyd Thorne, kneeling over the prone figure of the bombardier. Multiple holes in the front Plexiglas allowed the frigid air to stream into the small compartment, dropping the temperature to below zero. Slipping on frozen blood, Hanson pulled himself alongside Thorne. He removed his own oxygen mask.

"Where's he hit?" Roger yelled over the roar.

"In...his....stomach...I...think," Thorne said, trying to make himself heard over the roar.

Roger leaned over and grabbed the shoulders of Lieutenant Francis Reed, who had both hands clasped over his midsection as he rocked from side to side.

"Look at me.....LOOK at me," he yelled at Reed, who did stop rocking and open his eyes. "I need to check you out....."

They felt the aircraft bank left and heard the power come back on the engines. Thorne looked up toward the flight deck as he keyed his intercom.

"What's going on, Jerry?"

"Turning for home, we've got one engine out and may be losing fuel."

Unzipping Reed's flight suit, Roger found the end of a piece of aircraft skin protruding from the left side of the man's abdomen. The minimal blood flow from the wound prompted him to continue with a quick examination, which revealed no other injuries.

"Lie still, this isn't too bad, but I need you as still as possible. Do you understand me?"

Reed looked at Roger and nodded his understanding. Hanson didn't like what he'd seen. In any other place it would make sense to leave the metal splinter in place until he could get Reed to a hospital. But with the movement of the aircraft, that piece of metal could continue to due further damage. Shit, he thought, there's no good answer.

Roger held up the two pronged end to his communication cord and showed it to Thorne who nodded and pointed to a black box with two openings for line jacks. He inserted the prongs and keyed his throat mike, another wave of pain shooting through his head.

"This is Hanson," he said after the pain subsided, "Is someone hit back aft?"

"Yeah, can you get back here?"

"On my way." But he knew that to get to the rear compartment, he would have to negotiate the bomb bay crawl space. Kneeling on the hard metal deck, Roger took a deep breath and struggled to his feet using his good right hand. Taking two steps up the ladder he leaned against the steps and using his right hand, raised his left hand to the ladder hand hold. Forcing his left hand around the stanchion, he took another deep breath and let himself fall. His hand involuntarily released the hand hold as he fell, but not before the dislocated shoulder popped back into the socket. He lay on the deck for a minute, allowing the nausea to pass, then got to his hands and knees to move aft on the catwalk.


As the "g" forces increased on his body during another turn with the German, Hank realized he needed to distract his adversary.

"Pitch out and try to get opposite turn from this guy," he said over the radio, his voice distorted by the exertion of pulling in the turn.

"Roger."

As he reached the bottom of the loop, he smoothly pulled back, banking slightly to keep the German lined up on the Mustang's canopy supports. Upside down, the Focke Wulf began to move its nose toward Hank, then suddenly rolled right, aiming behind him. He must have seen Slater, he thought. Hank immediately slammed full left rudder and pulled the Mustang left, trying to conserve as much airspeed as possible. Looking left he saw the German pointed toward Slater as he continued to work his nose around toward the enemy fighter.

This is going to work, he thought as Slater and the German converged nose to nose. Then he saw tracers from the German. He was attacking head on and his shots were striking Slater's aircraft. As they passed, smoke began to pour from the Mustang, the stricken aircraft slowly rolling over, its nose heading for the ground. Realizing he now only had one chance, Hank pitched up, rolling inverted and squeezing the trigger as the German slid into his gunsight. Now under 100 yards from his opponent, Hank knew his guns would be lethal. Smoke trailed from the German and Hank ceased fire, watching the enemy fighter roll 90 degrees as pieces began to detach from the fuselage. Suddenly the pilot leaped free, the parachute opening almost instantly.

Hank leveled his wings, his breath coming in hard gasps, sweat streaming down from his forehead, despite the cold cockpit.

"Blackbird Two, come in......"

Maybe he was only damaged, Hank thought knowing the odds were slim. Turning left he noted his altitude now at 9,000 feet. He had no idea where he was and he quickly tried to orient himself. Looking around he noticed a cloud of black smoke rising from one of the hillsides and knew it had to be Slater. He gritted his teeth and turned in the direction of home. Starting his climb he saw the German's white canopy descending, a thousand feet below him.

Before he knew it, he'd turned toward the white shape, now highlighted against the green hills. He checked his guns, knowing there was still ammunition in the cans. I'm going to kill that son of a bitch, he thought, lowering the nose so his gunsight moved over the descending canopy. Suspended beneath the parachute, he could see the pilot and adjusted the nose to put the reticles over the small figure. This is what it's all about, Hank thought, his hand starting to depress the firing trigger. Kill every one of them, don't let anyone survive to ever do this again.

"HANK......HANK, break off, break off......"

Chris's voice snapped him out of his trance and he instantly let go of the trigger, pulling the nose up and rolling over the canopy which continued its descent. *Christ.* Hank took several deep breaths.

Three Mustangs joined on his right wing, Chris in "Glorious Ginny" leading the trio.

"Lead, there's a single Fort at your nine o'clock."


Spent .50 caliber shell casings rolled back and forth across the floor, some stopping as they hit the outstretched legs of Roger Hanson. His back against the port bulkhead, he sat with his eyes closed, trying to rest. The two waist gunners had both taken shell fragments, but the injuries were not life threatening despite the large amount of blood on their flight suits. Bandages and sulfa powder took care of their immediate needs. Now he knew he had to get back to the nose compartment and check on Reed, but fatigue was starting to overwhelm him. Rummaging in his medical bag he found a bottle of codeine pills. Unscrewing the top he shook four tablets into his hand knowing that two was the normal dosage. Looking around he saw a standard issue canteen under the radio table. Slowly he reached over and picked it up, hoping to feel some weight indicating water inside. He was in luck and unscrewed the top, popping the pills in his mouth and washing them down with the cold water. One more minute of rest, he thought, and then I'll go forward.

Joining on the crippled Fortress, Hank realized half a mile out that it was the "Alabama Queen." Her number four engine was stopped, the propeller in the feathered position. Smoke trailed from number three, but it still ran. The right side of the fuselage was peppered with multiple holes and torn skin.

Checking the mission card, he checked the radio callsign for the bomber.

"Ajax Zero One, this is Blackbird Lead."

"Go ahead, Blackbird."

"Four friendlies joining on your right side. Like some company on the way home?"

"Thanks, we'd love some company. And Blackbird, it looks like we're losing fuel, could you check us out?"

"Wilco," Hank said and banked slightly to slide under the Fortress's wing.

"Ajax, you've got fuel venting from multiple holes in the underside of the wing. There's also a lot of oil streaming out of number three."

There was no answer for a moment, and Hank slid back out to the right side.

"Thanks, Blackbird," a weary voice said.

Hank looked over to Chris, held up two fingers and pointed to the left. Christiansen nodded and in a minute his number two and three pulled up and moved over to fly cover on the port side of the "Queen." Hank liked having Chris back on his wing.

Captain Jerry Smith watched as the oil pressure on number three continued to drop. He'd flown the B-17 long enough to know the engine was on its last legs. Grimly he laughed to himself, don't need as much power, the weight of the fuel is going down fast. Then he remembered he was still carrying 8,000 pounds of bombs in the bomb bay.

"Nav, pilot. We've got to jettison the ordnance."

Lloyd Thorne acknowledged on the intercom and reached over Reed to move the "Bomb Bay Doors" switch to open.

"Ready to jettison," Thorne said.

"Nothing below us but trees."

"Roger," Thorne said. He pushed the jettison button, feeling the aircraft shudder as the bombs released from their shackles falling clear of the aircraft.

"Check to make sure they're all gone, Nav."

Thorne moved aft to the bomb bay crawl space, the light from the open doors filling the normally dark bay. The wind whipped past him from the damaged nose compartment, plunging down and out the bay. Sticking his head into the space he couldn't believe his eyes. Clinging desperately to the platform with his right arm, Roger Hanson lay across the catwalk, his feet dangling over open bomb bay.

"HOLD ON," Thorne yelled. He ran forward, reaching the nose compartment and flipping the switch that would close the doors. Turning he plunged back to the crawl space reaching down to help Hanson.

"You okay?" he yelled.

Roger was on his knees, staring at Thorne.

"Doc, you alright?"

Slowly he nodded, getting to his feet and brushing past the Navigator.

"Son of a bitch," Thorne said and followed Roger forward.

Five minutes later, Roger had made his decision. Reed seemed to be stable, with no additional bleeding from his abdomen. Looking at the option of removing the metal and possibly making the patient's condition worse, he decided to keep him warm and as stable as possible. He could only hope they wouldn't have to bail out or crash land as the violence of either might kill Reed. Roger's intense headache told him he must have a concussion, one more reason he couldn't attempt any type of procedure. Whatever was going to happen now, he'd done everything he could. But that was the way medicine often played out, you did your best then left it to a higher power. Roger leaned his head against the aluminum bulkhead and closed his eyes.

A bright red flare arced up from the B-17 on final to runway 09. Seeing the universal signal for wounded on board, the tower already had ambulances and fire trucks rolling.

Escorted by four Leiston P-51's, the decision was made to land at the fighter base as it was the closest field with immediate medical response available.

Two small smoke puffs came off both main tires as the "Alabama Queen touched down and began to decelerate. Trailing the bomber, four fighters flew overhead and entered the downwind circuit for the runway.

"Tower, this is Blackbird 01, I'm going to park and shut down by the Fort, let my ground crew know."

Hank taxied past the squadron parking area toward the B-17 which had just secured its two remaining engines. Fire trucks and two ambulances parked in a semi circle in front of the bomber. Opening the cockpit, Hank saw a parking spot 50 yards from the B-17, which had ground crewmen approaching it carrying wheel chocks, fire extinguishers and two stretchers.

Quickly shutting down his own engine, Hank jumped to the ground and ran toward the Alabama Queen as the forward hatch opened.

From the far side of the aircraft, a fire extinguisher discharged with a loud hiss as a cloud of $CO_2$ was directed into the engine compartment by one of the crash crew.

Lloyd Thorne dropped to the concrete and motioned to one of the stretcher teams.

"Over here, we need to get the bombardier out."

Hank moved to the small group surrounding Thorne.

"The Doc says we gotta take him out through the nose. We need to get a stretcher in and lift him out."

Looking around, Hank saw one of the crash crew.

"Back the crash truck up to the nose compartment. You'll have to get him out through the nose."

The man knew what Hank meant and ran toward the red fire truck.

Jerry Smith dropped to the ground, his feet unsteady for a moment as he regained his balance.

"Where's the Doc," Hank asked seeing blood spatters on the man's flight jacket.

"Up there with Reed.......the Colonel's body is still in the seat." He took a deep breath. "Gotta go check on the waist gunners."

Smith turned and walked toward the group standing around the rear hatch.

Reaching up for the hand holds, Hank pulled himself up and threw his feet inside the hatch. Twisting, he turned to see Roger looking toward him without recognition.

Blood stained Roger's khaki flying cap and caked blood covered his forehead.

Hank reached out and put his hand on Roger's arm.

"Roger, you okay?"

Hanson turned to stare straight ahead and nodded.

"We have to be very careful with the patient. He's got a bad splinter in the abdomen." Roger's voice was steady but surprisingly soft, as if he was in a quiet operating room.

"They're gonna take him out through the nose." Hank looked at Roger who continued to act as if he was in a trance. "Are you hurt?"

Roger shook his head slowly and said, "Just roughed up a bit." He reached up and rubbed his eyes. "Heck of a headache though."

They heard the crash crew slide a crash bar into the largest cannon hole in the Plexiglas. A loud cracking sound followed as the bar ripped open the thin acrylic. In another minute there was a hole large enough to slide a metal basket stretcher into the compartment. Hank grabbed one end, lifting it over the gunsight assembly and guided it alongside Lieutenant Reed.

"Okay, how do we do this?" Hank asked.

Roger seemed to return to the present, as though he had just ended a long sleep. "Get a couple people up here, I think my shoulder's dislocated. I can't help you lift him."

Ten minutes later Lieutenant Francis Reed was on his way to the base hospital, still conscious and in great pain, but alive.

Jerry Smith and a ground crewman, who had joined them to lift Reed onto the stretcher, now helped Hank assist Roger out the lower hatch to the waiting arms of the ground crew. Using a fireman's carry, two burly mechanics carried Roger to the open rear compartment of an olive drab ambulance, where a corpsman motioned them to set him down.

Hank walked over and watched the corpsman carefully remove the blood soaked cap and examine the side of Roger's head.

"They need to get the Colonel out of the aircraft," Roger said, not looking at either Hank or the corpsman, his voice again showing no emotion.

Kneeling down in front of his friend, Hank said, "They'll take care of him, don't worry."

"Doctor, you're going to need stitches. Let's get you up to the hospital."

Roger nodded. "I'll ride up front." He stood up and turned to walk around the ambulance, but stopped to look back at Hank.

"I'm glad I went....I never realized what it was like." Hanson turned around and opened the door, sliding into the front seat.

Hank stood on the tarmac watching the ambulance pull away. His friend was safe, but something was different.


Staring out the window, Hank leaned back in his swivel chair thinking about today's mission. He was tired as usual, but for the first time in a very long while, he felt relaxed.

"Would you have really done it?"

Hank turned to see Chris standing in the door of his office in the admin building. The tall pilot leaned against the door jam, his arms crossed on his chest.

Remembering the rage he felt at losing his wingman and the sight of the German pilot under his gunsight, Hank said, "Honestly, Chris, I don't know."

"Damn it, Hank, what the hell's the matter with you. Can you hate so much that you're willing to forget what makes us different from those bastards?"

"I think I did for awhile."

Chris walked in and sat down in one of the two chairs in front of the desk. "We may win this war, but at what cost?"

Hank rubbed his face, the skin still marked with the impression of his oxygen mask, the scars livid on the side of his face. "Don't have an answer to that one, my friend and I suspect no one does."

"But every day we do this, it takes a toll. It has to. So we press on and either die in an airplane or come out mentally unbalanced for the rest of our lives."

"You know, Chris, I decided it didn't matter anymore. A Brit pilot once told me not to worry about the future because we don't have a future. Go out there everyday and kill. That's all that matters."

"Are you serious?"

"I don't know anymore. It made sense to me at the time." Hank paused. "I just know that I'm glad you were there today. I don't think I was ready to kill someone under a chute, even a Kraut."

"Then maybe there's hope for all of us,"

Hank remembered the Arado he had shot down last month.

"Christ, maybe I'm around the bend. But I hate the bastards. How can I stop that?"

"I don't know. If there's a dozen pilots on a mission, there're probably a dozen different reasons for being there. I guess all any of us can do is get by and try to keep some sense of right and wrong."

"Thanks for sticking by me."

"Hell, Doctor Death has to have at least one friend."

"Is that what they call me?"

"You didn't know?"

Hank shook his head.

Chris got up. "I'm going to the club. Can I buy you a drink?"

"Thanks, I'm heading over to the hospital to see Roger. They told me they're going to keep him overnight."

"Well don't take too long, Dan told me we're on alert for tomorrow's mission on Frankfurt. Should be about a 0830 takeoff and he thought we were escorting a Liberator group."

Hank nodded, his mind already going down the list of things he needed to do to get the squadron ready to go back into battle tomorrow. How many missions did this make for him? Must be close to a hundred he thought, I need to check my logbook. But what the hell does it matter anyway, it's just a number. Picking up the phone he dialed both the Maintenance Officer and Operations Officer, asking them both to come down to go over tomorrow's mission. It shouldn't take more than an hour to get things rolling, then I'll go see Roger.

Reading down the first copies of today's debriefs, he heard a knock on the door frame.

"You busy?"

Hank looked up to see Roger standing in the doorway, a white bandage covering part of his head, his arm in a sling.

"What're you doing out of the hospital? Come in and sit down."

Roger sat down carefully on one of the chairs in front of the desk. "I wasn't going to take up a bed or anyone's time taking care of me."

"Physician heal thyself or something like that?"

"There's nothing wrong with me that needs a hospital bed and I'm a doctor, I should know."

"Okay, I believe you. I'm glad you seem to be back in this world. You were pretty out of it when I first saw you."

Roger hesitated, then said, "I think it was the let down after knowing we had landed. It seemed like I'd been on that plane and that mission for my whole life. Plus I do have a bump on my head that allows me to act strangely for at least 24 hours."

Hank laughed. "At least your sense of humor is back."

"I think I need to fly a couple more missions," Roger said with no humor in his voice.

Nodding, Hank said, "That doesn't surprise me."

"It doesn't?"

"No, you went into the fight and got busted up. It's like getting back on a horse that's thrown you. You need to prove something to yourself."

"That's stupid. I've studied psychology, I understand motivation and need. This is just a desire to see more of the mission. We never made it to the target. I want to be exposed to every facet so I can understand what the aircrews have to deal with."

"When I got back in a Mustang for the first time after I was shot down, it was real simple. I wanted to see if I could still do it. The first air combat was the same thing. Would I chicken out or could I get back in the fight? Roger, you may be a flight surgeon, but you're a person too. You need to see the beast again to make sure you are who you think you are."

"Maybe you're right."

"Just do me a favor. If you go again, make sure we're flying escort. I'd like to make sure you come home in one piece. Now, I'm gonna have a drink to celebrate being alive one more day, how about you?"

"I probably shouldn't, but the hell with it, a drink might help me sleep."

Hank found a bottle in his lower drawer and put it on the table with two water glasses.

"Scotch okay?"

Roger nodded.

"I'm a little short of ice."

"That's fine."

Handing Roger a glass half full, Hank raised his own glass. "To another day."

Roger echoed, "Another day."

The two men sipped their scotch, neither talking.

"There is great medicinal effect in a glass of scotch, one of my primary prescriptions for what ails aviators."

Hank didn't respond to Roger's joke, instead he put his glass on the table and took a deep breath.

"I almost gunned a Kraut coming down in a chute today."

"What?"

"Actually he was the leader of the group that shot the Queen up. I was able to bag him and as he was coming down, I lined up to kill him."

Roger put his own glass down and looked at his friend. "What stopped you?"

Hank shook his head. "A radio call from Chris. If it hadn't been for that I think I might have done it."

"That's very much against the rules as I understand them."

"Roger, that's the point, I don't think there are or should be any rules. My intent has been to kill every German pilot and aircraft I can until there aren't any left."

"We never did have that talk I promised when I got here did we?

Hank shook his head no.

"That's my fault. I thought you had those demons under control. Other than the odd name on your aircraft and the skulls under your name, you seemed to be flying right."

"And generally with a hangover," Hank said, pouring more scotch into his glass.

"So where do you go from here?" Roger asked.

"I think I stay here and do what I've been doing, just go at it a bit differently. Chris said something that really hit home."

"What's that?"

Pausing to take a drink, Hank said, "He said I was willing to forget what made us different from the Krauts."

"You think he was right?"

"Yeah, he was right. It's just too easy to go down that road."

"If you know that, it'll make turning around a lot easier."

"Roger, with you and Chris to keep me honest, I just might make it."

The young physician smiled, then winced as the bandage pulled against his head.

"Ouch."

# Chapter Fifteen

Bourdon Street
Mayfair
London, England
20 December, 1944

The single concession the Dorchester Club appeared to have made to the war was criss-crosses of masking tape on all exterior windows. Hank stood on the steps looking up at the ornately polished wood door. A tasteful sign told passers by that this was indeed the Dorchester Club, but did not tell them it had been in this very spot since 1832. A private club with the most stringent of selection criteria, prominent Londoners had been known to wait a decade for their application to be approved.

Right now Major Hank Mitchell didn't much care for London or any private clubs. He was scheduled to meet Ambassador Winant for lunch precisely at noon. Hank liked John Winant, he always had. But today, Hank's squadron was airborne and he was here being social. When the invitation had been forwarded from General Doolittle's headquarters to Colonel Gogan, there had been no question about Hank's attendance.

Opening one of the large doors, Hank saw an older man sitting at a large desk reading a copy of the Times. Dressed like he remembered Neville Chamberlin in the newsreels, this man was clearly the door guard.

"May I help you," the man said, his tone barely civil.

Probably wondered how a bloody Yank found his way into the Dorchester, Hank thought.

"Major Henry Mitchell to see Ambassador Winant."

The man stood up, straightening his long dress coat. "Just a moment....sir, I will see if the Ambassador is available." He turned without another word and disappeared down the hallway.

Hank looked around the ante room. Portraits of several men he didn't recognize adorned the walls, next to a recent addition, the air raid procedures for the Dorchester Club.

"Please follow me, Major." The man's tone was distinctly more hospitable, his mouth even showing a slight smile which might have been a grimace.

"Hank, good to see you," John Winant said, standing up and coming around the table to shake Hank's hand.

"Nice to see you, sir. Thanks for inviting me."

The two men chatted about mutual acquaintances until their lunch order was taken. Winant turned serious.

"Hank, your parents are worried about you. It's none of my business, I know. But your Dad and I go way back. He asked me to talk to you and find out what's wrong."

Ready to lash out, Hank saw the look on the Ambassador's face and knew he was simply trying to help out his college roommate. Hell, the Ambassador of the United States to the Court of St. James had better things to do with his time than find out why Hank had stopped writing home.

"The letters?"

"Hank, they said you simply won't write, even to answer their own letters to you. Parents worry about their children. Your injuries had them very worried and then you didn't come home for treatment and went back to flying combat. Someone had told your mother you wouldn't be in combat again. She counted on that, almost felt your injuries served a greater purpose, to save your life. Then the picture arrived for Margo, which she promptly showed your parents and pardon my French, the shit hit the fan." Winant reached over for his water glass, taking a long drink. "You're a grown man and a squadron commander. I'd never stick my nose into this, but your folks are hurt and worried."

"Sir, I appreciate you taking the time to talk to me. There's no excuse for how I've been acting and now I know it. I got so wrapped up in the squadron and the big push for the invasion, I didn't think anything else mattered."

"According to your Group Commander, you've turned out to be his best squadron commander. That's important, but I'm glad you've realized there are people back in the states that still matter."

Hank thought about his parents. Always very correct, they didn't show their emotions easily. But he knew they both loved him and he'd taken that for granted.

"Things are pretty quiet right now with this weather, I'll write them and try to make amends."

"I've got a better idea. After lunch we'll walk back to my office and give them a call. We should be able to catch them at the breakfast table."


"Tyler, it's John from London......I am well, and yourself?" His voice raised to carry over the long connection to New York.

The ambassador motioned to Hank to come over and take the phone.

"Tyler, I have someone here who would like to talk to you."

Winant handed Hank the phone and walked out the open office door, closing it carefully.

"Dad? Dad, it's Hank."

"My God, son, are you all right?"

"Dad, I'm fine."

The delay on the trans-Atlantic cable required a slow pattern of responses, but the two men quickly developed a rhythm.

"Hank, we've been worried since you stopped writing."

"Dad, I've had to deal with some things. But I realize it's no excuse to stop writing."

"We thought you'd come home last year and then you didn't. That hit your mother pretty hard."

Hank didn't say anything for a moment. "I'm sorry for that, I should have written her."

"Are you doing okay now?"

"Doing fine, Dad. I'm a Major and have been commanding my squadron since March.....they're a good group."

"I've always been proud of you, Hank. Watch out for yourself."

Hank knew much of his success as a squadron commander had been because of his total disregard for his own safety.

"Don't worry, Dad. Is Mom there?"

"She's in D.C. visiting Iris and doesn't get back until tomorrow."

"Tell her I miss her and will send her a long letter right away."

Suddenly the connection was broken, leaving Hank listening to a scratchy dial tone. Replacing the phone in its cradle he sat down in the ambassador's chair, knowing he'd been selfish for the last year. Now he realized how it had hurt his parents.

Despite Mr. Thompson's objections, Hank sat in the left front seat of the ambassador's 1937 Bentley as they made their way south from London on the Eastbourne Road.

"I appreciate your time, Mr. Thompson."

The grey haired chauffer smiled, but kept his eyes on the road.

"My pleasure, Major. Haven't been south of the city for some time, it's quite enjoyable, actually."

"How long have you been driving for the Ambassador?"

"Oh, ever since he arrived, guess that would have been '41. Drove Mr. Kennedy before that."

Hank sat back in the seat and tried to relax, but kept asking himself why he was making this trip, what did he expect to find?

The winter countryside passed quickly and Eastbourne Road turned into London Road, the buildings of East Grinstead beginning to look familiar.

"There it is, the book store," Hank said, pointing as Mr. Thompson slowed the car and turned into the small parking area.

An elderly well dressed woman looked up as Hank opened the door, the bell jangling to announce him. Quickly she returned to searching the book shelves.

"Can I help you?"

Hank turned to see George Hunnicutt standing behind the counter, wiping his hands on a tea towel.

"Captain Mitchell, it's been a long time."

Hank tried to gauge the man's reaction, but the older man's features were impassive.

"Hello Mr. Hunnicutt. I was hoping to see Kate."

Hunnicutt tossed the towel on the counter and said, "She's not here just now," his tone not unfriendly but also not warm.

"I just wanted to find out how's she's doing, sir."

He paused then said, "If you go down to the hospital, you might catch her. Her shift ends in an hour. I think she was working on Ward Three today."


Parking just off Hollye Road, Mr. Thompson assured Hank he would be perfectly happy reading his paper and that the Major should take as much time as he needed. His instructions were to then take Hank back to Leiston whenever the Major desired.

The hospital looked unchanged to Hank as he walked under the covered walkway to the Ward Three door. Remembering his last visit to see Kate, he suddenly wondered if this was such a good idea after all. Then he saw her through the window of the day room. She turned, her expression unchanging as her eyes met his. Hank remained where he was as she walked away from the window toward the door.

"Hello," she said evenly.

"Hello, Kate." She looks tired, he thought, probably working too much.

The two walked toward each other and stopped a foot apart.

"You can tell me to leave and I will. But I hope you won't," he said.

She shook her head.

A cold wind blew leaves across the walkway and Kate folded her arms across her chest.

"It's cold, let's go inside," she said, raising her hand to her mouth and coughing.

The two sat at a small table in a hallway alcove off Ward Three. She'd been able to get two cups of hot coffee from the lounge and now they sat facing each other.

"Kate, I know what you said the last time we met. I understand how you feel. But I've thought about you a lot over the last year and had to see you."

"I haven't forgotten my Yank either." Her eyes were sad, perhaps weary.

"I don't know what's going to happen. But this war's going to end soon, I'm sure of it. Maybe there's still a chance for us."

Kate picked up her cup, cradling it with both hands but not drinking. "We come from different worlds, Hank. Our futures are going to go in different directions. The time we spent together was wonderful, but it was in a different time. When the war ends, everything will change. I'm an English girl who lives in a small town and works in a book store. You come from a different world and need to go back to that world. It would never work."

Hank sensed she had thought about this many times. Her tone sincere and sad at the same time, making her words powerful and final. "Kate, we don't know that. Anything is possible if you give it a chance."

"You've changed," she said, more a question than a statement.

"I don't know, maybe I have. I did realize that there was life after the war and the good guys need to act like it."

"That's a rather odd comment."

He saw a brief sparkle in her eye, the sparkle I remember, he thought.

"I guess I figured a few things out, seems I had stopped thinking real straight for awhile. It took a couple of my friends to set me right."

Impulsively she leaned across the table putting her hand lightly on the side of his face.

"My dear Yank."

Hank took her wrist and lightly kissed the top of her hand.

"I couldn't push you out of my mind, no matter how hard I tried. Now I never will," he said.

"You will, you have to. Hank, there's no future for us. You must accept that. Please, do it for me." Kate's eyes were misty, her voice soft.

"Kate, I love you. I know it now, I guess I always did. I won't let you go, not now."

She stood up, tears now streaking her face. "Hank, you have to," she said and stood up turning for the corridor. At the entryway, Kate turned and looked back at Hank who now stood next to the table.

"Good bye."

Confused by Kate's reaction, Hank had asked Mr. Thompson to drive him back to Leiston. There was little conversation during the drive, Hank's thoughts kept returning to Kate. Was there someone else and she didn't want to tell me? Or did she really believe there was no place for her in his world? It couldn't be his face. She, more than anyone else, understood and accepted his scars. Somehow he must get through to her and find out what is really wrong. He was finally ready to finish this war and get on with the rest of his life, but now he wanted that life to include Kate.

Hank found Chris in the squadron admin office. Now the Executive Officer, he and Hank collaborated on every aspect of running the squadron. As he came through the door, Hank sensed something was wrong.

Chris looked up, his face grim. "We lost Wilskie."

Throwing his coat on the chair, Hank waited for the details he knew were coming.

"His flight mixed it up with some 190's just north of Regensburg. Four of them, five Krauts, but there must have been some of the old guys flying the FW's. Taylor was flying wing for Dan and said these guys were good. Two of them went after Dan and Tails couldn't get a shot at either one. He thinks Dan bailed out, but he had two Krauts after him and couldn't confirm."

"Shit. Gogan know?"

"Yeah, I told him as soon as I got the word."

The reality of a shooting war where men get killed everyday returned to Hank, pushing any thoughts of after the war out of his mind. He thought of Dan, with them from the start back in the States, a solid pilot and good friend. The familiar pain of loss was with him again. It seemed the cost of this war would never end. That would be a tough letter to write to his folks back in Washington State. He had never understood why Robin Cunning seemed to carry the weight of the world on his back. Now he knew.

"Are we alerted for tomorrow?"

Chris nodded, "Berlin." One word that told the whole story, the mission would be long and hard. Even with the German air defense network breaking down, Berlin still enjoyed the best of what remained. Anytime you flew against the capital, the enemy would do everything in his power to stop you. That had always translated to downed aircraft and dead or missing aircrew. Tomorrow would be no different.

Hank thought for a moment. "I want Clem slid in to replace Dan as the flight lead."

"I don't disagree. He may be junior to some of them, but he has seven kills and I think everyone respects him as a pilot."

"Send the Corporal to run him down, I want to talk to him before tomorrow."

"Can do," Chris said, then as an afterthought, "How'd it go in London."

"Wasted trip," Hank said, picking up his coat and walking out the door.


"Blackbird, bandits 12 o'clock high."

Less than 50 miles from Berlin, the 90th Bombardment Group showed the result of multiple attacks by the Luftwaffe over the last two hours. Several aircraft had dropped out of the formation to try and make it back to either England or a safe landing in France. Of those remaining, several aircraft flew with one of their four engines feathered, the aftermath of the attacks pressed home by the Messerschmitts and Focke Wulf's.

Hank's squadron had engaged several times, driving the attackers off, without loss while downing at least two enemy fighters. Checking his own fuel, Hank felt comfortable taking the bombers to the flak belt and then picking them up as they emerged on the return track. With Allied armies taking more territory every day, running low on fuel could be handled with a fuel stop at several fields now designated as enroute diverts.

Clem Dunmire's flight had performed well, his natural skill now sharpened with over eight months of flying combat in the Mustang. Hank looked over his shoulder, seeing Clem's Mustang, the wingtips still painted yellow from the old flight. Ahead, hostile aircraft split left and right intent on attacking both sides of the formation. With drop tanks long empty and jettisoned, the Mustang literally snapped left as Hank pulled toward the group of Germans attacking from the east.

Lining up on the lead German, Hank saw a large group of bandits on his left coming at the bombers from the northeast. Estimating twenty plus fighters in the second group, half had split off and were converging on his four Mustangs. Firing a quick long range burst at the first leader, he pulled left hard to meet the new group, his wingman hanging on through the turn.

Loud cracks filled Hank's cockpit followed by a searing pain in his right leg. He knew instantly he'd been hit. Taking deep breaths from his oxygen mask, he tried to focus on the German fighters now flashing past him toward the bombers. *Son of a bitch.* He felt nauseous, the urge to vomit strong. Maintaining a climbing left turn back toward the bombers, he glanced around looking for Germans. With no immediate threat looming, Hank looked down to see blood oozing from above his knee, soaking his flight suit. Trying to push on the right rudder, a massive pain shot through his leg, making him gasp.

The Germans had vanished, their slashing attacks completed, probably to regroup for another attack before the bombers entered the flak belt around Berlin.

"Blackbird Two, Blackbird One is returning to base. You've got it, Chris." Hank began to turn to the northwest, adding power to climb.

"Blackbird One, you got a problem?" Chris replied.

"Airplane's busted up, need to get it home," Hank lied.

"You need an escort?"

Hank knew one more Mustang to escort him to England would cut down on protection for the bombers, who still had a longer trip with Berlin still in front of them. "I'm fine. See you at the club."

"Roger," came Chris's reply, the skepticism obvious in his voice.

Trimming the Mustang for a slow climb, Hank pulled out the large bandana he always carried in his flight suit. Trying to push the cloth under his leg hurt like hell, but he had to stop the bleeding. He found the small first aid packet taped to the side of his seat. Finding a gauze bandage wrapped in waxed paper, he tore it open and pressed it against the bullet hole above his knee. Next he pulled the bandana as tight as he could and tied the knot securely. That's all I can do, he thought, looking at his blood soaked flight suit and wondering if it was enough.

Now at 30,000 feet, he pulled power to the most economical setting and checked his course. After confirming a good compass heading and trimming the aircraft, he checked his leg. The blood flow had almost stopped, but the pain remained, now a constant ache that ran the length of his right leg. At least none of those sons of bitches will be attacking from above me, he thought.

The increased altitude would make him less of a target, but the colder temperature began to take its toll. Moisture from sweat and blood helped to accelerate his heat loss. He guessed the cockpit temperature at near freezing, and he found himself shivering.

Hank could see the hole in the aircraft skin where a single machine gun bullet had entered before hitting his leg. The lack of an exit wound or any other holes in the cockpit told him the bullet must still be in his leg.

Trying to ignore the pain from his leg, Hank pulled out his aerial chart and looked for his approximate position. He guessed the large town to his north must be Perleburg, which made it about 400 miles to Leiston. The formation had been fighting a headwind before the German fighters showed up, so he should have a tailwind now. Maybe an hour and 15, he thought, knowing he could update that estimate as he recognized landmarks enroute. Other than the Luftwaffe base at Salzwedel, this route would take him between the large defensive areas around Bremen to the north and Hannover to the south. He hoped one lone fighter flying at 30,000 feet wouldn't bother anyone enough to come after him.

The cold had stiffened his fingers, making it necessary to keep exercising and squeezing his hands. Thank God for these lined gloves and boots, otherwise I'd be done. Flexing his left hand, he remembered bailing out the last time. Not again, he thought.

Hank checked the oxygen pressure gauge, which registered 310 psi in the system, plenty, even at this altitude. One more check of the compass, now steady on 255 degrees, and he told himself he'd done everything he could. Now it's a matter of getting home.

As he put another 100 miles behind him, the drone of his Merlin engine began to put Hank to sleep. He caught himself as his head dropped, the oxygen mask hose hitting his chest. *Christ, I can't stay awake.* Initially the flood of adrenaline kept him on top of everything, but now he found it hard to concentrate. The pain in his leg had subsided to a dull ache as long as he didn't move.

Thirty minutes later, Hank realized the cold and loss of blood had taken its toll. His entire body ached and he felt nauseous as he looked at the altimeter which now showed 31,000 feet. *What I'd give for one of those autopilots the bomber crews have,* he told himself as he tried to hold his altitude. *How long can this take?*

Alone in his freezing cockpit and fighting to stay alert, Hank didn't see the distinctive pattern of Amsterdam until he was almost on top of it. The sight of the coast raised his spirits, but now he'd lost his ability to think clearly. Trying to remember the heading to Leiston from over the city center, he came up with 243 degrees. *That must be it,* he hoped, turning sloppily to the left and over shooting the heading. *Gotta start down,* he said to himself and pulled the power back. Checking the fuel mixture set to the auto rich position, he couldn't remember when he'd selected it. *Okay, thirty minutes to go, you can do this Mitchell. Get lower, warmer, air's thicker, I'll take off this damned oxygen mask, it'll be okay.*

Crossing over the coastline, the single Mustang descended through 22,000 feet over the grey North Sea. Something made Hank think of his identification code and he found the switch, flipping it on. *Concentrate,* he told himself, *don't forget anything.* Looking around the cockpit, he saw the small piece of cardboard glued on the instrument panel listing the radio frequencies for Leiston Approach and Leiston Tower.

Fumbling with the radio selector he sensed the aircraft picking up a rate of descent and pulled back on the stick as he passed 11,000 feet.   Shit, fly the airplane, Mitchell.   He unfastened one side of his mask, gratefully removing the rubber sealing ring from his face and breathing in the cockpit air.   The lower altitude seemed to help clear his mind.

"Leiston Approach, mayday, mayday, do you read?"

No reply came back from his radio.

Taking a deep breath, Hank checked his heading.

"Any aircraft, any aircraft, this is Blackbird One, mayday, mayday."

The frequency remained silent.

Ahead the coast appeared through the light haze.   Have to find a land mark, he thought, maybe Lowestoft, then head south down the coast.   Passing through 6,000 feet over the white capped water, he estimated ten miles to the coast.   His leg felt numb and lifeless, he tried to move his foot up to the rudder pedal, but couldn't make it move.   Shit, I'll never be able to use the rudder or brakes on roll out.   Now what, he wondered?   Land gear up?   That's one way to stop.   It's also a good way to wreck a perfectly good aircraft with only one bullet hole in the side.

Glancing down, he could make out the harbor at Lowestoft, the lake running inland.   He knew Leiston lay less than twenty miles farther down the coast.   Banking left, he turned south, now watching for the River Alde.   Holding his altitude at 2,000 feet, Hank switched his radio to the tower frequency for Leiston.   A wave of nausea overcame him, his head now pounding, a cold sweat breaking out on his face.

Now flying by instinct and practice, he lined up on the field, the runway pattern very distinct from the surrounding farm fields.

"Tower, Tower, this is Blackbird One, five miles north, single for landing...declaring an emergency."   Hank found himself out of breath after the transmission, the wave of nausea returning.   Mechanically he started the landing checklist, checking the boost pump to "normal."   Setting the RPM to 2600, he put the landing gear handle to the "down" position and flaps to "full."

Ahead he saw the runway 18 almost on heading.   Only 4200 feet long, he knew he couldn't make the arc, his vision starting to blur.

"On final to one eight, won't be able to stop....."

"Winds are light and variable, you are cleared to any runway. Emergency equipment is standing by."

Hank's focus now became the touchdown point at the end of the runway, his hours in the Mustang allowing him to maintain his rate of descent.   Unable to push on his right rudder, he tried to align his course slightly left of centerline, grateful he didn't have winds to fight.

Right on the end, he told himself, the Mustang now only 100 feet above the ground.  The green from the grass and black tarmac rose up as the Mustang's tires touched, throwing up puffs of smoke.  The pain in his leg shot up to his groin as he tried out of habit to use his rudder/brake pedals.  Holding his tail off, he tried to use his ailerons to keep on center line, knowing when the tail hit all bets were off.

Seeing the runway intersection coming with his speed still over 80 knots, he pulled the mixture to the idle cutoff, turned the ignition switch off and closed the fuel shutoff valve. The aircraft now began to drift right toward the runway edge as Hank pushed on the left brake, feeling the tail drop and aircraft decelerate.   Suddenly the Mustang swerved left across the centerline and plowed into the grass toward the aircraft parked on the ramp.  With one final push Hank locked the left brake, swinging the aircraft hard and stopping with a violent crash.

# Chapter Sixteen

American Field Hospital Acton
Sudbury
Suffolk, England
December 22, 1944

Through a grey fog the sound of music made Hank Mitchell open his eyes slowly and look around. He saw a metal frame above him supporting ropes and pulleys. *What the hell?* His right leg was elevated and he could feel a pressure pulling on it. Past his leg, he saw a partially opened door. Hospital, he thought, remembering waking up at Portsmouth after his last smash up. Slowly he took stock of his body, moving one part at a time until he tried to move his right leg. God, that's not going to work, he thought. Everything began to come back to him. He remembered being in and out of consciousness as the ground crew pulled him out of his aircraft. Roger had been there, he remembered, but not much else.

The door swung open, a nurse in a white uniform entered and walked to his bedside.

"Good morning, Major. How are you feeling?" Her nametag said "1st Lt Coleman."

"You tell me," he said thickly. "God, I need a glass of water."

She reached for a metal carafe and poured him a glass. "Here, drink this."

Nothing had tasted that good in a long time, Hank thought.

"That's better, thanks."

"Now tell me how you feel?" she asked.

"First tell me where I am?"

"You're in the field hospital at Acton. We're about twenty five miles from Leiston."

"What time is it? And what day?"

She looked at her watch.

"It's 0825 and they brought you in late yesterday."

"So what's the diagnosis?"

Nurse Coleman smiled. "That's the doctor's job. Let me go get him. You must be pretty special, you brought your own."


Three minutes later, the door swung open as Roger Hanson entered, followed by Nurse Coleman.

"Are you gonna get yourself busted up every Christmas?" Roger asked, grinning at his friend.

"As long as you're around to fix me up."

Roger stepped aside as Nurse Coleman began to take Hank's pulse, blood pressure and temperature.

"What happened?" he asked Roger, who held up his hand.

"Let the Lieutenant get your vitals and then I'll fill you in."

Five minutes later, the chart filled out, Nurse Coleman left Hank and Roger alone.

"Okay, what's the story?"

Roger stood next to the bed, his hands in his pockets.

"We removed one bullet from your right thigh. According to the manual, it's from a 7.62 mm German machine gun. That bullet hit your femur and fractured it in addition to embedding itself in the bone. You were damn lucky it missed any major blood vessels or you would have bled to death before you even got close to Leiston. The good news is the fracture is minor. According to the x-rays, it's a hairline fracture that only runs about half way across the bone. That little fact will make the difference between two months and six months to recover. By the way, why didn't you divert to any of the forward fields in France?"

"Hell, I wanted to see you.......and sleep in my own bed."

"Right," Roger said and continued, "We cleaned out the wound, applied a cast and pumped two pints of blood into you. In case you want a souvenir, I kept this for you." Roger held up a misshapen piece of metal.

"Something to show them back at the club? By the way, when do I get out of here? And what the hell is this Rube Goldberg contraption holding my leg?"

"You're not going anywhere for four to five weeks. We have to make sure that bone heals correctly. Right now, if we didn't have that traction splint pulling on those big muscles in the leg, they would be pulling the bone and not allowing that fracture to knit together correctly. You get to lay here until we're comfortable the bone can support your weight."

"You've got to be kidding me."

"Hank, there's no way around it. And after four weeks in traction, you'll be spending another four to five weeks in a wheelchair. At your age, the bone should heal just fine and it'll be good as new."

Hank Mitchell lay back on the pillow and closed his eyes.


Colonel Gogan's arrival at the hospital caught Hank by surprise as he finished morning exercises in his wheelchair. Carefully balancing on his left foot, Hank moved to the bed and sat down heavily, very conscious that Gogan was watching him.

"So how's the leg feeling, Major?"

"Still sore from the bullet wound, but getting better," Hank answered.

"Can we smoke in here?" Gogan asked.

"Yes, sir. There's an ashtray on that side table."

Gogan pulled out a pack of Lucky Strikes and lit one.

"They're sending me back to the states next week. The new group commander is coming down from headquarters, Larry Weller, you might remember him from Wendover. Anyway, I'm going back to form a new group to take overseas as part of the new 20th Air Force for the last big push on Japan."

"I guess Europe's winding down, sir."

"Still lots to do over here. But we still have to invade the Jap home islands. Christ, I don't even want to think about it.

The Doc tells me you're out of the airplane flying business for at least two months. After that, you should be fine."

Hank tried not to show any surprise, but that was the first he'd heard of a long range prognosis. He assumed Roger had provided his best estimate.

"Yes, sir."

"I need experienced combat aviators to whip this new group into shape. Most of the pilots are right out of advanced training, no combat experience. I'd like you to come with me when you heal up. You can either have one of the squadrons or the deputy group commander job, your choice. We'll form the new group at Langley. The first people and airplanes start showing up next month. What do you say?"

The evident surprise in Hank's expression prompted Gogan to raise one hand.

"Before you say no, let me be straight with you. When you first got over here, I thought you were a smart ass who was going to get himself killed in short order. Everyone knew you could fly the aircraft and when you got your first kills we knew you could fight. But you were still a cocky son of a bitch, almost more trouble than you were worth. After you got shot down, something changed. I'll admit I thought you might have gone a bit flak happy for a while, but you got results. You showed me you could lead a squadron in combat and not everyone can do that. The air corps still needs you and the greatest need is going to be in the Pacific."

"Can you get Christiansen on the same set of orders?"

Gogan laughed and put out his cigarette.

"He's slated to be one of the other squadron commanders. He's been running your outfit for the last month and been doing a damn good job. Unfortunately people are starting to punch tickets over here and with you medically down, headquarters sent down a new Major to take over the squadron."

What the hell, Hank thought, I'm ready for some sunshine.

"You got a deal, Colonel."

Gogan walked over and offered his hand.

"Hanson said they were releasing you next week. Come on back and help out with the group until you leave for the states."

When Roger found Hank the next morning, he was half way through his morning exercise, briskly moving his wheelchair down the inner corridor.

Stopping himself from making a smart remark, Hank saw a serious look on his friend's face.

"Everything all right?" he asked Roger.

"Have you put any weight on it?"

Roger's express direction had been to keep all weight off his leg when he began moving himself from bed to wheelchair.

"Maybe once or twice."

"Knowing you, I figured you would. How'd it feel?"

"Well I didn't lean on it. But it felt....not too bad."

"Let's head back to your room."

The two started back down toward Hank's door, Roger pushing the wheelchair down the linoleum hall.

"Hey, Gogan was here yesterday and said you thought I could get back on flying status soon."

"Maybe that's a little optimistic. But if you work hard and do what you're supposed to, it could happen."

They arrived at his door.

"So where the hell were you, anyway?" Hank asked turning back to look at his friend.

Roger hesitated. "I had a call from Duncan Frazier at East Grinstead. He asked me to come down and see him." He pushed Hank's chair over near the window and sat down in the opposite chair.

Hank wiped a film of light sweat off his forehead. "The exercise feels good," he said, stretching his arms and moving his hands. "You said you visited Doc Frazier, how's he doing?"

"Hank, he's fine. But the reason he called me to come down has to do with you."

"How so?" Hank asked, wondering what the connection could be.

"He knew you and Kate Murray had become close when you were there."

At the mention of Kate's name, a cold feeling went through Hank.

"Is something wrong with Kate?"

Roger nodded. "I'm afraid so..."

Roger looked down then at Hank.

"She's very ill. Apparently she'd been feeling tired for some time and then started coughing. Initially they thought it might have been asthma, but finally Frazier made her get a checkup. They found a mass in her chest."

"What the hell's a mass?" The conversation began to feel like a nightmare to Hank.

"There's a form of cancer that spawns rapid cell growth, often in the form of a tumor. We don't know what triggers it. But once the growth has started, it can accelerate and in some cases spread throughout the body. The medical term is Non-Hodgkins Lymphoma. "

"So what can they do?"

"Unfortunately this is one of those areas of medicine that has eluded any real cure. The normal treatment is to remove as much of the mass as possible then expose the area to radiation using a cobalt device."

Hank sat in silence. He had to see her.

"How quick can you get me down there?"

"Wait a minute. You're not exactly the picture of health yourself. You'll be spending the next three weeks in that wheelchair – if the leg can take your weight, maybe then."

"I want to go tomorrow."

"That's crazy. Your leg hasn't fully healed yet."

"You're the doctor, but you're also my friend. You know what this means to me. I've got to see her and I don't give a shit what it takes."

Roger didn't reply.

"Whatever it takes," Hank added.

"You've always been a hard headed son of a bitch," Roger said as he got up. "I'll be back in a minute."


"Slowly and carefully, and I mean it, damn it. I looked at your latest x-rays and your leg might be ready to start adding weight. Let me say that again, might be. Okay, let's try it. Remember the cane is your weight bearing structure. Hold the cane close alongside your leg and move it in conjunction with your leg motion."

Hank grasped the cane, and pushed himself up on his left foot, holding the cane alongside his right leg.

"All right, slowly and carefully add a little weight, supporting the rest with your cane. Then take a small step." Roger had positioned himself on Hank's right side, ready to provide support.

Taking small steps, Hank moved five paces across the floor, carefully turning and retracing his steps to the bed.

"So far, so good."

"No pain, particularly anything sharp?" Roger asked.

Hank shook his head no, not wanting to lie to his friend.

"Good, let's take a few more steps. Then you can rest."

The two sat in chairs facing each other, Hank's cane over his left knee.

"No reason not to release you if you can get around all right. You look like you're getting the hang of walking with a cane," Roger said.

"So you can get me out of here and down there?"

The doctor nodded. "You're still a hard headed son of a bitch, but we'll figure something out. And I'll be with you to keep you from doing anything stupid – which we know from experience you have a knack for."

During the drive south, Hank sat sideways in the back of the Ford sedan while Roger drove, the leg supported by the wide seat. Under his uniform pants, Hank wore a small brace that provided some additional support. Doctor Frazier would meet them and take them to see Kate's doctor. His leg hurt like hell. But he had to see her.

He remembered that last meeting. Her insistence there was no future for the two of them. Did she know she was sick then, he wondered?

"Any idea how long Kate has known about this?"

Roger kept his eyes on the road as he replied.

"Duncan Frazier told me she found out in mid December. They told her they wanted to operate on the mass immediately, but she made them wait until after Christmas. I guess she wanted to spend the time with her father."

Looking out at the bare branches of the trees, Hank wanted to see Kate, but was afraid of what he might find.

Doctor Richard Montague Adams II knocked on Duncan Frazier's door frame and peered into the room where Hank and Roger sat with the doctor.

"Dicky, please come in," Frazier said as he stood up, the other two following suit.

Adams was a pleasant looking fellow, in his late 40's, slightly overweight with thinning hair.

"You've met Roger Hanson before, and this is Major Hank Mitchell."

Handshakes were exchanged as they all returned to their seats.

"Thank you for traveling down to see Kate," Adams said. "We hope it will help."

"Doctor Adams, I only shared the basics with Major Mitchell, not knowing how things have progressed," Roger said, not looking at Hank.

"Right. I was hoping things would have improved since we talked. I'm afraid that's not the case."

"Why do I feel like I'm the only one in the dark here?" Hank asked.

Adams looked at Roger who nodded.

"Major, we removed as much of the mass in her chest as we could, ten days ago. At first everything looked very favorable and we intended to transfer her to London for the follow-up cobalt treatments." The doctor paused then continued, "Unfortunately she developed an infection and we've been fighting that for the last week. Her system has been under stress from the disease and the effect of a major operation. It was too much and her immune system was overwhelmed. We've got to beat this infection or I'm afraid things don't look very good."

"What exactly does that mean?" Hank asked, afraid what the man might answer.

"She could die before we could get her to London."

"Is there anything we can do?" he asked Adams, "Anything at all?"

Adams looked at Hanson who opened his briefcase and handed Adams a small cardboard box.

"Thank you, Doctor. Time is of the essence, please excuse me." Adams stood and walked swiftly out of the room.

Hank looked at Roger questioningly.

"Am I missing something?"

"It's just as well that you don't know, Hank. That way you can't get in trouble."

"Since when have I worried about getting in trouble?"

Roger stood up and turned to Duncan Frazier.

"Give me five minutes, then bring him down," he said and followed Adams.

Duncan Frazier stood up and closed his door.

"Okay, Doc, what's going on?"

The tall doctor remained standing and walked to the window.

"Have you heard of penicillin?" he asked Hank.

"Yeah, supposed to be the new cure-all after sulfa powder."

"Quite so. However production of the drug is currently only sufficient for dispensing to active duty military personnel. It'll be available to the public at some point, but not in the near future. Your friend Roger has pinched some of the penicillin for Kate. We hope it will do the trick."


Kate Murray lay on a hospital bed behind a white linen curtain suspended from small metal hangers. Hank saw her eyes were closed. She seemed very serene, her breathing shallow but steady.

Sitting down carefully, making sure he didn't hit her bed with the cane, Hank leaned back and looked around the small space. An intravenous bottle hung upside down from a thin stand, the rubber tube extending down to the bed where it attached to a bandaged area on the inside of Kate's left arm. A small vase holding a branch of holly sat on the small storage cabinet by her bed. On the bed stand by Kate's head, a metal thermos and water glass sat next to a small jar with a thermometer immersed in alcohol.

Doctor Adams had told Hank that Kate was lightly sedated to allow her to rest. He'd administered the first dose of penicillin and they would monitor her vital signs every hour. If the new drug was going to have any effect, he felt they would know within four to six hours. Hank was welcome to wait in her room or in the lounge at the end of the corridor.

"But then you must know your way around the hospital," Adams had said, glancing at the scars on Hank's face.

As he sat watching Kate, Hank remembered the days when he had desperately needed help and support. And she'd been there. Those days seemed so long ago, he thought, and God I'm tired. He should be angry about what had happened to Kate or his own leg, but the spirit wasn't there. It was as if he had reached a point of peace with himself and everything else.

This quiet hospital and this woman gave him what he needed to make it through, he reflected. What would have happened if he'd never come to East Grinstead or met Kate? He knew there were no answers to those questions and perhaps that was just as well.

"I found us two rooms here at the hospital. That will save some money since we aren't on official travel orders." Roger sat down next to Hank in the small lounge near Kate's room.

"So we're AWOL?" Hank asked.

"Not exactly. We're officially on leave. I've got more days on the books than I could ever take and you earned 30 days convalescent leave on top of what you already have – which I'm guessing is a lot."

"Never really took any leave, just passes here and there." Hank reflected that he hadn't really seen much of England, just the base, the hospitals and London a couple of times. Someday he'd come back and take it all in the right way. "Hey, I know of a great hotel not far from here, the Excelsior. Let's run over and get two rooms, but I'm paying."

"You don't have to do that," Roger protested.

"I guess I never got very specific about my family, did I?"

"The Ambassador told me they were a very prominent family in New York."

Hank laughed. "What he meant was they have more money than most small countries and I'm an only child. So I'm writing the checks and you're keeping me honest."

The staff at the Excelsior remembered Major Mitchell and were very pleased to offer rooms to both American officers. Hank's last visit had resulted in gratuities that significantly dwarfed any tips the staff had ever received in East Grinstead. Hank's request for 'two of your best rooms' told the clerk they were in store for a repeat of his generosity.

After a quick shave and tea in the dining room, they drove back to check on Kate.

"Still too early to tell. Certainly there's been no deterioration from this morning, just no progress. She's awake now if you would like to see her," Doctor Adams said, his expression very friendly.

Hank nodded and turned to his friend.

"You go in and see her," Roger said.

Adams turned and led Hank down the corridor to Kate's room. The doctor turned as they entered the door. "Ten minutes, she needs to rest." He pulled the screen back and stood out of the way for Hank to enter.

Kate looked up from the pillow and smiled. She lay with both arms on top of the blanket, the intravenous tube still attached to her left arm.

Hank kept his eyes on hers and walked to the edge of her bed.

"Hello, Kate," he said and gently took her left hand in his as he leaned over and softly kissed her forehead.

"Hank," was her only word in response.

He sat down as gracefully as possible, ignoring the sharp pain and hanging the cane over one arm of the chair.

"I missed you, Kate Murray,"

"You're hurt," she replied, her eyes leaving his and moving to the cane.

"I'm okay. But the big question is how do you feel?"

"A bit punk, I'm afraid. Did they tell you what happened?"

Hank nodded.

"It's all so overwhelming. I've never been really sick before and I'm scared."

He reached over and took her hand again.

153

She continued, "My father has told me it will be all right. But working around this hospital for several years, I know a little bit about what has happened to people who have cancer. There's not much they can do." Her voice trailed off.

"You let me worry about that. For now we've got to beat this infection."

"Doctor Adams told me what your friend Roger did for me....."

"Let's not spread that around, I don't want to see Roger sent to prison," he said, trying to make her laugh.

Doctor Adams appeared at the sliding curtain.

"Major, it's time."

"I've got to go for now. We're staying at the Excelsior. I'll be here for you."

Hank leaned over and kissed her forehead.

"Thank you," she said softly as he rose.


"If she can beat this infection, we'll work on getting her transferred to London," Doctor Adams said. "There are several hospitals doing the cobalt therapy and I'm hoping we can get her in one of the programs."

Hank wasn't sure he'd heard the doctor correctly. "What does that mean? Is there some problem getting her the treatment she needs?"

"Major, not only is this new technology, but priority for all treatment still goes to the military. I'm sure we can work something out in time."

Roger interrupted, "Doctor, you and I both know that time is critical in cases like this. What kind of delay do you expect?"

Adams shook his head. "I'm afraid it's too hard to say. Each case is taken on its own merits and then worked in based on outside requirements."

Hank sat back and tried to absorb the doctor's words.


Later that evening, Roger and Hank sat in the main lounge at the Excelsior with a bottle of port on the table between them.

"You've been remarkably quiet tonight," Roger said.

Hank looked up from his glass.

"I've been thinking about what kind of options we have here."

"What do you mean?"

"Suppose we decided to take things into our own hands?" Hank asked.

Roger put down his glass and looked at his friend.

"Why do I think I'm not going to like where this is going?"

# Chapter Seventeen

The Causerie
Claridge's Hotel
Brook Street, Mayfair
London, England
February 4, 1945

"You do know how to do things up right when you set your mind to it," Roger said as he sipped a double martini and watched the crowd in the restaurant.

"My dear doctor, we've paid our dues and the least we can do is enjoy the fruits of the land." Hank lifted a toothpick piercing three large olives and proceeded to pull one off with his teeth, returning the remaining two to his drink. "We needed some place to stay in London. Claridge's is comfortable and located right where we need to be."

"And the only reason we're here is the Ambassador called in a favor."

"Not really. This is where my father always stays when he's in London and he knows the owners."

Roger laughed. "In any case it beats living in a Quonset hut and eating in the mess hall."

"I'll drink to that," Hank said, draining his martini. "So what was this great idea you mentioned?"

"I know you want to make something happen for Kate. I was thinking about something that might help."

"I'm all ears," Hank said.

"When doctors come on active duty, they send them to indoctrination training for six weeks to learn how to be an officer. My roommate from indoc and I hit it off. We've stayed in contact."

"I'm not sure where this is going, but I trust you."

Roger held up his hand. "Jason Russell is assigned to the Edgewood Arsenal, just north of Baltimore. It's a research facility. That made sense because Jason's background was more theoretical than clinical. We used to talk all the time about how the war's huge effort in mobilizing so many people to work on problems would bear benefits to the world of medicine. The kinds of things that might take years to develop on a shoestring budget were happening in just months."

"Still not sure where you're going, but it sounds promising," Hank said, indicating to the waiter they needed two more drinks.

"Jason dropped me a line four months ago and was talking about an investigation they had been conducting that showed promise for combating cancer."

Hank nodded at the waiter as he put the full glasses down and removed the empties.

"Until now, the primary method for battling some cancers has been surgery and radiation. The idea is to kill the bad cells and that will allow the normal cells to flourish. Radiation tends to kill most everything and there's a limit to what you can expect to achieve. But now they are starting to see the emergence of chemicals that target specific types of cells, killing only the bad ones."

"Why didn't Adams mention that?"

Roger shook his head. "I doubt he knows. Hank this is the very tip of current research. Who knows how long it will take to make it through all the trials and then be released for general use."

"There's got to be a way we can use that info to help Kate."


"Sir, the ambassador will see you now."

A middle aged woman ushered Hank and Roger into the second floor office of John Winant.

The ambassador stood up and came around his desk to shake hands with the two officers.

"Hank, good to see you. And Major Hanson, how have you been?"

"Very well, sir," Roger said as he and Hank sat down in the two chairs facing Winant's desk.

"How's the leg?"

"Healing. Still sore, but I've got Roger to administer secret potions to make it better." Hank felt the sharp pain he'd gotten used to feeling when sitting down.

The three all smiled.

"So you're out of the line of fire for now?"

Hank nodded. "Yes, sir. Actually I think I'll be heading back to the states to help stand up a new fighter group. I guess my European flying days are over."

"It does bring the reality home. Even with the Germans on the run, the Japanese home islands still stand there waiting for us."

"Yes, sir."

Winant sat back in his chair and smiled. "Now what can I do to help the cause."

"Sir, that's exactly why we're here.

The ambassador looked mildly surprised, not expecting any real business to be discussed.

"Please go on," Winant said, his tone now that of the Ambassador of the United States to the Court of St. James.

"Sir, I need to get a young British woman back to the states." Hank waited for his response.

"You've taken me a bit by surprise, Hank. Is there a relationship between you and this young woman?"

"Well yes...and no. I met her while I was in East Grinstead for treatment. We became friends, but nothing else. Roger and I have discovered she's very ill and can't get the treatment she needs here in England. I want to take her back to New York so she can get what she needs."

The ambassador said nothing for a moment, then turned to Roger.

"And you think there's merit to this plan from a medical viewpoint?"

"Yes, sir. The resources here in England are stretched so thin her treatment could be delayed to the point where it would do no good. Hank has talked with his father and they've arranged for her to be treated at New York Memorial. But we have to get her there as soon as possible."

Hank jumped in, "We're aware of the red tape involved in getting a civilian, particularly one with an illness, from here to there. I know I'm going around the system, but we don't have time to wait."

John Winant looked at the serious expression on Hank's face and remembered that same expression on his father's face over the years. The two men had been friends for many years and Winant had known Hank for his entire life. Now he was being asked to bend or possibly break the rules for a friend.

"This has problems all over it, Hank, but I'm willing to try." Winant's expression had changed from genial to serious. "I can certainly arrange for travel permits and any paperwork. But how do you intend her to travel?"

Roger spoke up, "Mr. Ambassador, I've checked with our transportation office and there's a hospital ship sailing from Portsmouth in four days. The young woman is able to travel, but will need some level of care, which the St. Olaf can provide."

"Is there any precedence for a civilian, an English civilian no less, to take passage as a patient on one of our hospital ships?" Winant asked.

"Sir, the ships are configured to accommodate female patients. There normally aren't many, so she wouldn't be taking the bed away from a wounded GI. It would be just like one of your female staff going back to the States on orders."

Winant thought for a moment. "Does she have a passport?" he asked. "Perhaps we could simply issue a set of permissive travel orders."

Hank had no idea.


"Actually Kate does have a passport. She traveled to the continent in 1937 and toured for a bit." George Hunnicutt stood behind the counter at his bookstore, the second stop for Hank and Roger after leaving London.

"If you can find it, we have a plan. But if it's to work, we need to move fast."

The older man looked confused. "What do you mean a plan? For Kate?"

"Sorry, we should have told you the plan first," Hank said. "Because of the lack of capacity in England, Kate's radiation therapy may be delayed until it does no good. I want to take her to the States where we've arranged for her to be treated at one of the best hospitals in America."

"America?"

Roger held up his hand to cut off any argument from Kate's father. "Sir, I've talked this over with Doctor Adams and Doctor Frazier at the hospital and they agree completely. It's the only way."

"But she's still sick in her bed. How can she travel?"

"There's an Army Hospital Service ship, the St. Olaf, sailing from Portsmouth in four days. We think we can get her on the ship, and that will put her in New York City in less than two weeks, undergoing the best medical treatment in the country. Doctor Adams gave his approval for her to travel."

George Hunnicutt sat down slowly on a stool behind the counter. "My God, New York City.....that's so bloody far away. How can I let her go?"

"This could be her only chance, Mr. Hunnicutt. You've got to let her go."

"Does she know about this plan?"

Hank shook his head. "She was asleep when we stopped to talk with Doctor Frazier."

Turning to Roger, George Hunnicutt asked, "Can this save her?"

He replied, "I don't know. But I do think it will give her the best possible chance."

"Then she must go," he said, his eyes betraying his fear.


Kate lay propped up in her bed, a magazine open beside her.

"I'm not sure I understand, Hank."

"We want to take you to New York City, to one of the best hospitals in the States for your follow on treatment."

Roger stood on the opposite side of the hospital bed. "Kate, your treatment here could be delayed too long. This way you'll not only get treated earlier, but you will be seen by some of the best and brightest cancer specialists in the world. This is a good hospital, but it simply can't compare to New York Memorial."

Kate took a deep breath. "I believe you, Roger. It's just such a big step."

"I know it's a big step. But it's the only way."

Alice Tinsley reached behind her desk to the large credenza which was stacked with files.

"Here it is."

She opened the large manila envelope and took out a thick packet of papers.

Hank Mitchell sat in a chair beside her desk, watching her separate the different files. Once she had them in different piles she began handing them to him one at a time.

"This is a set of permissive travel orders for Katherine Murray issued for the convenience of the government, no travel funding or per diem authorized. Here are your orders from Eighth Air Force putting you on temporary additional duty as an official courier for the Department of State. The ambassador decided he couldn't wait for the normal courier and asked General Doolittle if he could borrow you. You'll be taking a locked briefcase from here to the State Department office in New York City, where you will turn it over to the individual listed in your orders. Doctor Hanson, I have a set of orders for you directing you to accompany Major Mitchell for medical purposes, which also authorizes you to travel to such places as necessary in conduct of these orders. We have the appropriate endorsements for all, which should get you on board the St. Olaf well before sailing." Alice stopped talking and looked at him. "And if anyone ever takes a close look, Major, we'll all go to jail." Then she smiled.

"Is there anyway I can personally thank the ambassador?"

"Actually he had to travel north for several days. He told me to say God speed and good luck.

"I know this would have never come together without your help. But I don't know how to thank you."

Alice looked surprised. "It was my pleasure. Now before you get on your way, here's a letter for you from the ambassador. He told me you should use his phone line for your call."

Hank took the envelope from her.

Kate Murray sat in the rear seat of the olive drab sedan as it made its way south toward Portsmouth Harbor. The car's heater did a good job keeping the damp chill out of the car, but Kate still kept a wool scarf snug around her neck. She wore a plain black wool coat which she had described as "her only nice coat." As tired as she felt, she couldn't doze off, her mind trying to deal with where she was and where this journey might take her. Her fear about the disease had been joined with apprehension of the journey to America. Everything seemed to be happening so fast. She knew this trip might be her best chance, but leaving England and her father scared her terribly. Looking over at Hank, she knew whatever her fears, he would be there.

Roger sat in the front seat, next to an Army driver. Despite the last hectic days, he was awake, watching the landscape out the window. He could see the first buds on the trees as winter began to give way to spring. He carried a letter from Colonel Ridgeley to be delivered to an old friend of his who now ran the Edgewood Arsenal research program. The program being conducted jointly by Yale University and the Office of Scientific Research had made some real progress in developing drugs that might treat cancer. This letter might help him to find out what was happening in Maryland.

As they moved into the outskirts of Portsmouth, Kate could catch glimpses of the Channel. The only time she had ever been aboard any kind of boat had been her trip to France in 1937. She could still remember her fascination with the constantly moving seascape during that four hour trip. Now the Atlantic Ocean lay in front of her and that was difficult to comprehend. She knew German U-boats still sank ships as they crossed to and from America, something she had only seen in newsreels, never imagining she would be there herself.

Evidence of earlier German air attacks could be seen in several boarded up buildings as they entered Portsmouth. The road swung down near the shore and she could see rows of barbed wire that ran parallel to the shore, perhaps left over from the invasion preparations in 1940. Traffic picked up as they worked their way down to the harbor, large trucks moving away from the docks toward London.

Their car pulled off the main street and stopped at one of the entrances to the docks. Several older men in British Army uniforms stood guard, their Enfield rifles leaning against a wooden guard shack. The driver rolled down his window as one of the soldiers leaned over to look in the car. Seeing Roger's oak leaves, he saluted and asked for their identity cards.

"Your destination, sir?"

Roger leaned toward the window and replied, "The hospital ship St. Olaf. Can you tell us how to get there?"

The guard handed their identity cards back and pointed to his right. "Turn right at that green warehouse, then straight ahead to pier six. You'll find the St. Olaf there." He saluted.

"Thank you, Corporal."

The pungent smell of creosote lingered in the car, telling them they were in a working dock area. Trucks and forklifts moved down the roadways that ran between the large warehouses. Behind the wooden structures several small cranes were moving material off the ships alongside the piers. The scene reminded Kate of an anthill, movement everywhere, but everyone seemed to know what they were doing.


Moored at the end of a long wooden pier, the Army Hospital Ship St. Olaf was a center of activity. Cars and trucks of all description stood parked next to the ship as the Army personnel and Portsmouth dock workers prepared her to sail. Several large access hatches in the ships side were open. At the first hatch a long line of men were passing cardboard cartons up from a large truck. At the other, two stretchers were being loaded on the ship, an ambulance parked directly below the opening. High above the pier, lines of white lifeboats hung ready in their davits. A large red stripe ran the length of the white hull, highlighted in the center with a vertical stripe that gave the illusion of a large cross.

Roger looked at the forward accommodation ladder. It ran up at a steep angle and was fifty feet long.

"You two think you can get up the ladder, or do you want to go in through that lower door?" he asked.

Kate had always been fit and athletic, but now she felt weak from the operation and time in bed. She looked out the window, her eyes following the grey ladder that stood out against the white hull. Hank leaned over and looked up at the steep climb that awaited them.

"I think discretion is the better part of valor," Hank said softly.

"I take it you'd rather pass on the ladder?" Kate asked.

"Not sure I could get to the top. But if I did, I bet I'd be back in bed and in traction."

"What would the pilots of your squadron say if they knew you snuck aboard the ship next to the cartons of food?"

"Come on, young lady, let me escort you aboard. I think we'll use that lower hatch."


Checking in with the medical administration department took forty minutes and they were lucky Roger was with them. Rank seemed to smooth the procedure, but when Roger identified himself as a physician everyone immediately got very interested in helping them. Eventually Kate was assigned to one of two small female wards on the ship. Hank was able to get a stateroom with Roger near Kate's ward. The ship carried over 500 patients, mostly Army wounded from the continent who had been evacuated to England as their first step home. Roger told Hank there were over 100 medical staff traveling with the wounded, including nine doctors. The ship, while primarily designed to move injured back home, did have two operating rooms and could deal with most emergencies that might arise as they crossed the Atlantic.

They would be sailing in the morning, as part of a medium sized convoy enroute to New York. Escorted by Navy destroyers and two British ASW trawlers, there would also be long range aviation flying over them to search out any U-boats that might be lurking in their path. While protected by international convention, everyone knew that torpedoes fired in the haste of a night attack in the stormy Atlantic could hit any ship. The nightmare that haunted everyone on St. Olaf would be the inability to move many of the non-ambulatory wounded to lifeboats in the event the ship suffered fatal damage in an attack.

On the main deck, with almost everyone in some type of uniform, Kate's civilian clothes received some interested stares as she and Hank slowly walked toward the stern. After the hectic events of the last two days they had decided not to join Roger, who left earlier with an Army friend to have dinner ashore. The two doctors had known each other back in the states and Roger thought it good to have a contact among the ship's staff. Returning with several bottles of booze for the trip provided additional impetus for the "run ashore" as the British Navy called it.

Wrapped up against the cool breeze that came off the harbor, the two had not spoken much, both happy to take in the strange sights and sounds. As someone who had always reconsidered and rethought any major decision, Hank found himself surprised that this unusual plan seemed totally natural to him. To be walking with an English girl on the deck of an American hospital ship, headed across the Atlantic to try and save her life. He turned to watch Kate as she stopped and took hold of the life line, looking back toward Portsmouth.

"I wonder if I'll ever see England again?" she asked, almost to herself.

Hank put his hand over hers. "Of course you will. You have the word of two very knowledgeable Americans who always get their way."

She smiled as she continued to look out toward the far hills.

"I've always wanted to see America," she said, her voice now wistful. "I've read so much about the history and famous places. They seemed so exotic and different from England. Cowboys and mountains, the Mississippi River, and the Statue of Liberty, it's all so exciting."

Kate had turned to him, her eyes showing that old sparkle.

"And you'll see them all, I promise. But if we don't go inside pretty soon, we'll both freeze to death before we get there."

She followed him back toward the main deck hatchway, casting a last look at Portsmouth before she ducked into the hatch.

# Chapter Eighteen

The English Channel
February 10, 1945

On the morning tide, six ships of Convoy ON 287 slipped their moorings.  They were enroute to rendezvous with the other convoy ships and escorts for the westbound transit.  Aboard the St. Olaf a mood of relief, not joy, seemed to settle around the wards and lounges.  Men and a few women, wounded and now recovering, were finally headed toward home and loved ones.

By noon, six ships had become fifteen as the Isle of Wight disappeared behind them.

Land was still visible on their starboard side as the first lifeboat drill was called away.  Dark clouds scudded across the sky, adding the threat of inclement weather to the already challenging task of acclimating landsmen to shipboard life.  The resulting confusion didn't surprise anyone as soldiers and airmen struggled to find their stations and don their bulky kapok life preservers.  Roger had told Hank that about five percent of the patients were considered non-ambulatory and medical staff had been assigned to assist them in any emergency.  Hank watched the proceedings and imagined what it would be like at night or in bad weather with the ship actually going down.

The loudspeaker blared, "All hands secure from drill." Most people moved inside to get away from the cold wind coming up the channel. A reminder it was still winter in the Atlantic.

Hank saw Kate coming toward him and he waved her out of the line to where he stood in the lee of a large lifeboat. Kate wore a dark blue preserver that she had now untied, but it still hung over her shoulders.

"You look like quite the experienced hand, Miss Murray."

She looked behind her at the large white boat. "Out of the wind, it's rather pleasant."

"For now anyway. Let the crowd go first." He turned to look outboard, where a destroyer, it's hull painted in alternating patterns, sailed as convoy escort.

"Looks rather small from here," Kate said.

"Hard to imagine they take on the worst the Atlantic has to offer and come back for more. I remember my trip over, we hit a major storm and those destroyers would almost disappear under the waves. I don't think I'd ever make it as a sailor."

"It's hard to believe we're actually on our way to America," she said, slipping her arm through his.

"I think it's time I told you a little bit about my family."

Kate didn't reply. Her questions since their first meeting had always resulted in very vague answers. While she'd been curious, she didn't feel she had any right to push him.

"You've never been very forthcoming about them. All I know is they live in New York and your father works for a bank."

"Actually he owns a bank, several banks and a lot of other things," Hank said, his tone slightly apologetic.

"So, he is rich?" Kate asked, now looking at him.

Hank nodded.

"I see." Kate turned back to watch the sea. "Not the kind of family that looks forward to their son bringing home a girl from England who works in a bookstore and has cancer to boot. Am I right?"

"No, that's not it at all. My parents are good people. It's just that my future had been written in stone before I ever left for overseas. That future included an engagement and wedding on my return."

"An engagement?" she asked, turning back to him. "Hank, why didn't you ever tell me?"

"I didn't think it mattered, I got a 'Dear John' letter after being burned and figured that was it," he said.

"So what has changed?" Kate asked.

"The ambassador left me a note to call New York. I'd asked my father to set up a consult at New York Memorial for a friend of mine who was traveling with me to New York. I didn't get any more specific and he didn't ask. Anyway, he wanted to tell me it was all set and also that my former girlfriend Margo couldn't wait to see me, which made my parents very happy."

"I see." Kate turned back toward the water.

"It's just a misunderstanding. I'll set everything straight when we get in to New York."

"I guess that makes me quite the odd duck."

Hank reached out and slowly turned her to face him.

"Kate, I love you. Don't ever forget that." He pulled her toward him and they embraced. He couldn't see the tears in her eyes.


Hank waited at the door to Ward 4A, where Kate had spent the transit across the Atlantic. In the background he could hear whistles from outbound ships greeting the ships from the convoy entering New York harbor. It had been thirty minutes since the announcement had come over the announcing system, "All hands to station for entering port." He found himself slightly apprehensive to see his family, more concerned about how they would react to Kate than his own scars. You can get used to anything, he thought. At one time his face seemed the end of the world to him. Now, he couldn't care less.

"I'm ready," he heard Kate say and turned to see her in her best coat, a wool scarf nestled around her neck.

"You look great," he said. "Let's go on deck."

Stepping through the hatch, they joined several hundred of the patients, all watching the same sight.

"My goodness, Hank. I've seen pictures, but I never imagined."

In the distance, against a bright blue sky, the figure of Liberty stood with her arm outstretched, welcoming the St. Olaf home.

Hank felt strangely moved, finding he couldn't reply. Standing next to him was a young woman who was looking at

Liberty with the same hope so many have had before.....give me a chance at life.

A line of tugs moved out toward the ships, each looking for its assigned charge. On bridges of the ships, Captains prepared for the final step of the journey, the bad weather and U-boats behind them one more time. The occasional whistle blast broke the morning air as other ships sounded a welcome.

Thirty minutes later, two large tugs warped the St. Olaf alongside pier 86 on the west side of Manhattan. Large covered buildings ran the length of the quay, their opened access doors showing a fleet of ambulances lined up to receive the non-ambulatory patients. Down on the pier a small crane stood ready with an accommodation ladder hanging in mid air, ready to swing into place. Line handlers waited on the pier for the large mooring cables to be passed down from the ship. A whistle blew and simultaneously coiled messenger lines were thrown to the line handlers. The larger cables were slowly pulled down to the pier where they were attached to the bollards. "Now hear this, the ship is moored. Welcome home." A band which had been playing at one end of the pier suddenly broke into "When The Saints Come Marching Home." A cheer went up from the men on deck, many wiping tears from their eyes.

"Wards One through Four prepare to disembark. Form a single line at the after gangway."

"Come on," Hank said to Kate. "Let's introduce you to New York."

After checking out with the ward, retrieving the briefcase from the ship's safe and passing the debarkation desk, Hank, Roger and Kate walked down the gangway to the pier. Their travel orders allowed them to bypass the in-processing desk and Hank led them toward the chain link fence at the end of the pier, the briefcase handcuffed to his left wrist, his right hand holding the cane that had become second nature to him. Roger carried both his and Hank's Valpak bags and Kate had a small case of her own. The air was brisk and their breath steamed in the noonday sun.

"This is a great city," Hank said "We don't have to be anywhere or do anything until the day after tomorrow, for now we can..." He slowed his walk and stopped thirty feet from the exit gate to the pier.

Roger and Kate stepped past him, then turned back questioningly.

"There's my father."

Hank began walking again, his companions matching his speed.

On the far side of the fence, a tall man in a wool overcoat and fedora stood by himself, his hands clasped in front of him. As they exited the gate, the man walked toward Hank extending his hand.

Wordlessly they shook hands.

Tyler Mitchell was the first to speak, his eyes watering in the cool breeze. "Welcome home, son."

"Thanks, Dad."

His father paused for just an instant as his eyes took in Hank's scars, then he turned to Roger and Kate.

"Dad, this is Roger Hanson, my partner in crime."

"Doctor, Tyler Mitchell, it is a pleasure to finally meet you."

"Nice to meet you, sir," Roger replied.

Kate stood to one side, still holding her small suitcase.

"And this is Kate Murray. Kate, my father."

Tyler Mitchell smiled at Kate and offered his hand. "Ah, you must be the friend Hank told me about. Welcome to New York." He quickly said, "Here, let me take your case."

"Thank you," Kate said, unsure how to take Tyler Mitchell's welcome.

"Now come on, Hank, there's a few more people here to meet you. They're trying to stay warm in the car."

As the group approached a large Rolls Royce touring car, the driver's door opened and a uniformed chauffeur stepped out and opened the rear door.

Hank saw his mother step out, her expression expectant and hesitant at the same time. She walked toward them as a beautiful younger woman exited the car behind her.

Susan Mitchell approached her son, her eyes fixed on his face.

"Hi, Mom," he said, putting his right arm around her, the briefcase still at his side.

"Hank," she said quietly, "You're finally home."

Standing behind his mother, Hank saw Margo Van Whiting standing with a broad smile on her face.

Susan stood to one side as Margo took two steps and put her arms around Hank.

"Welcome home," she said and stepped back politely awaiting introductions.

Tyler Mitchell inserted himself, introducing both Roger and Kate, who shook hands with Susan Mitchell and Margo.

"Now let's get back to a warm house and cold drinks," Tyler said as Henry Gadsen, their chauffeur, put their bags in the trunk.

Kate would always remember the drive to the Mitchell's three story townhouse which looked out on Central Park. She sat in the rear facing middle seat with Hank and Roger. The Mitchells were on each side of Margo in the wide back seat.

The flood of small talk left her and Roger sitting quietly and smiling politely. The traffic was light as they rounded Columbus Circle and turned north on Central Park West.

In many ways, the winter scene reminded her of London before the war, the ordered buildings and then Central Park itself, much like Hyde Park, only larger. London was now a bit shabby compared to this gleaming city, much like herself compared to the young woman sitting across from her. When Hank told her about his family she simply hadn't understood the chasm between Manhattan and East Grinstead. Now she felt very out of place, her plain wool coat and simple shoes in stark contrast to the beautiful clothes of Margo and Mrs. Mitchell. What must they think of me?

"Hank, you'll be in your room, of course. Miss Murray, I'll have Henry put your luggage in the Rose Room." Mrs. Mitchell turned to Roger. "Major, I believe you would be most comfortable in the Blue Room."

Neither Roger or Kate had ever been in a home where the rooms had their own names.

Climbing the wide front steps to the carved wooden double door, they all followed Mr. Mitchell into the front sitting room. Larger than her father's entire shop back home, the room was complete with a piano and a heavy wooden bar with a selection of liquor bottles sitting on top. To one side two sterling silver stands held crushed ice and two bottles of champagne. A tall man with silver hair stood behind the bar, his face a mask of calm.

"I think a toast would be in order," Tyler Mitchell said, nodding to the man.

With a smooth motion the man removed the first cork, pouring the liquid into stemmed glasses that were arranged on the bar. As he opened the second bottle, the elder Mitchell began to hand the glasses around.

Susan Mitchell had slipped her hand through Hank's arm and was standing next to him, a glass now in her hand.

Looking around, Tyler raised his glass.

"To those home from the war, we rejoice at having them safe."

Everyone took a sip and then looked to Mr. Mitchell.

"Let's sit down and catch up. Lunch will be served shortly." He gestured to a large couch with several arm chairs in front of it. Margo sat down next to Tyler Mitchell, leaving a space next to Susan.

"Here, Hank, sit next to your mother," Margo said, smiling at him.

Roger and Kate each slid into an arm chair.

"Where do you call home, Major?" Tyler asked.

Finishing his drink, Roger set it down on a side table. "I grew up just north of Seattle." The tall man, whom Susan had called Dexter, topped off his champagne glass and returned to the bar.

"We always talked about a trip to see that part of the country. There never was enough time and now the war makes travel too hard," Susan Mitchell said.

"And you, Miss Murray?"

"Please ma'am, just call me Kate," she said.

"Is that short for Katherine?"

"Yes, ma'am."

"Kate's from East Grinstead. It's about two hours from London."

"You don't say," Tyler added.

"I loved London," Margo inserted. "So much history. I'd love to go back."

"I'm afraid it will take many years to repair the bomb damage," Roger said, "The Luftwaffe did quite a job."

There was an uncomfortable silence.

"So tell me, Major, have you ever been to New York Memorial?" Tyler asked.

"No sir, I'm looking forward to it. The word around medicine is that they've been making some important strides in fighting consumptive diseases."

"Quite right, although I'm just a layman, the doctors do brief us on their activities during our board meetings. In fact there will be an institute dedicated to research, opening next to Memorial. It will be called Sloan Kettering. We expect great things." Tyler sipped his champagne. "Hank, we have the consult set up with Doctor Bill Glenn at nine, Wednesday morning. Henry will drive you."

"Thanks, Dad."

Tyler turned to Kate. "Don't let Bill's southern drawl fool you. He's as sharp as they come. Georgia Tech pre-med, Harvard Medical School, summa cum laude."

"Thank you," she replied, the reality of her illness returning after the distraction of meeting the Mitchells.

"Hank, if you're up to it, there's an engagement party tonight at the Plaza for Austin Dunning and Margie Hollister. You could wear your uniform and you'd be able to see all our friends. Wouldn't that be fun?" Margo said.

"I can't imagine what I'd have in common with any of those people anymore, Margo," Hank said, his voice sounding vaguely threatening.

"Luncheon is served." Dexter's voice came from behind them, breaking the unpleasant silence.

"Exactly what's going on here," Tyler Mitchell asked his son behind the closed doors of the second story library.

"What do you mean?" Hank said, pouring himself a drink from the small side bar.

"First of all you show up with a woman in tow. Why didn't you tell me about her when we talked? Then you make that comment about not having anything in common with our friends anymore. What's going on?"

Hank took a drink. "Okay, I should have told you. But it wouldn't have changed anything. I'll do whatever I can to help her beat this disease. And I don't have anything in common with our friends anymore. Unless any of them have killed young men with .50 caliber machine guns lately."

"This is crazy. My son goes off to war and comes home a different person." Tyler stood by the window, facing his son.

"War does that, Dad. Getting your face burned does too."

"Hank, I'm sorry for your injuries. But you can't wear them like a hair shirt for the rest of your life."

"Who said I'm going to? But what happened over there changed me. And since I haven't taken the time to tell you, you need to know the only reason I was able to fight my way back was because of that woman, Roger Hanson and Chris Christiansen. And if you think I'm not going to do everything I can for any of them, you're wrong." Hank drained his glass and started for the door.

"Wait a minute, damn it," Tyler said harshly.

Hank stopped and faced his father.

"I'm sorry, this took me by surprise and I clearly don't understand everything that's happened. Give us a chance to sort this out. You're home now and we can get everything back on track. Let me help you."

"Thanks. I guess I've kept you and Mom in the dark. It seemed the only way I could get through was to do it my way. I should have thought about you."

Tyler walked over and poured himself a drink, motioning with the bottle to Hank, who nodded. He handed the glass to his son and raised his own."

"Pax?"

"Pax."

Tyler sat down in the couch. "Do you love her?"

Hank nodded.

"You sure? It's not some overseas infatuation?"

"I don't think so. When she knew she was ill, she tried to hide it from me and walk away. I guess she thought she was protecting me. She's a wonderful woman, Dad. And she didn't have a clue about the family fortune until we were on the boat coming home."

"I'll be damned," Tyler said, taking a drink.

"Now she's fighting this disease and I've got to do everything I can to help her."

"Fair enough."

"And I'm going to ask you to help me."

"Of course I'll help you. But you could make taking care of her your full time job if you want to."

Hank shook his head. "War's not over. I'm slated to be the Deputy Group Commander for a new unit standing up at Langley. We're getting ready to go to the Pacific."

"What?" Tyler exclaimed. "You've done enough. Hell you can't even walk right. I can certainly fix this, Hank."

"Dad, I don't want you to fix it. I'll go and do my job. I need you to help Kate get better while I'm gone."

Tyler looked at his son, proud and concerned at the same time.

A cold north wind blew across the observation deck of the Empire State Building. The small group of visitors took shelter from the frigid air on the southern side of the building. Kate stood next to Hank as he pointed out some of the landmarks. She wasn't cold, a new, very expensive wool coat with matching leather gloves and scarf kept her warm.

Hank had insisted when they started their sightseeing that she had to be protected to keep up her strength. Susan Mitchell sent them to Bergdorf's on 5th Avenue and gave them the name of her favorite saleswoman.

Kate had never seen prices for clothes like she saw in the exclusive store. Three different woman had waited on them, mentioning that Mrs. Mitchell called ahead to set up the shopping session.

"There's Ellis Island, probably the biggest gateway for immigrants coming to the States from Europe." Hank stood behind her, pointing so she could follow his arm to whatever location he was talking about. "Of course you probably still think of us as 'the colonies,' don't you?"

She turned to smile at him. "I think there will always be a special bond between our countries."

Hank put both his arms around her and stood watching the harbor.

Kate kept thinking back to that morning at breakfast. She had come down early and found Tyler Mitchell reading his paper and drinking a cup of coffee.

"Kate, good morning. I hope you slept well."

"Yes, quite well thank you. I'm afraid I was rather tired." She sat down next to Tyler who had stood up and pulled out her chair for her.

175

"Coffee?"

"Yes, please."

Margaret, whom she recognized as the Mitchell's cook from the night before, stepped into the dining room. "What can I bring you for breakfast, Miss?"

"She makes a mean barley cake if you like them," Tyler said.

"I'm not really sure what they are, but I would love to try one."

Laughing as she left the room, Margaret said, "One stack, coming up."

Tyler put down his cup of coffee.

"This must seem like a long way from home."

Kate nodded. "I try not to think about it. It is so far and I do miss my father."

"I think I can feel a little of what you must feel. When Hank was in England he seemed very far away. Then when he was hurt, we felt totally helpless.

"Those were difficult times for him. But he's a strong person and I think it made him stronger."

"Thank you for what you did for Hank. It means a great deal to his mother and I. And please think of this as your home for as long as you're here. We're very happy you're with us." His earnest demeanor touched Kate deeply.

Now, as she leaned back against Hank and stared out across the harbor, she felt secure and hopeful.

# Chapter Nineteen

New York Memorial Hospital
1275 York Avenue
New York City, New York
February 22, 1945

Doctor William Glenn closed the manila file that had been delivered by courier from Tyler Mitchell. The two men had been friends for many years and Mitchell's position on the Board of Directors had been strongly encouraged by Glenn, then the Director of Surgical Services.

"Damnation," he said quietly and looked at his watch. The subject of the closed medical file on his desk had a nine o'clock appointment. The diagnosis and treatment history from Queen Victoria Hospital were not unusual. Bill Glenn had seen the same situation many times over his thirty-two years practicing medicine and specializing in trying to treat human cancers. His sense of hope had not been diminished, but the lethality of the disease continued to frustrate him. He knew that it was only a matter of time for science to find a cure. But how many people would lose their lives in the interim.

"Tyler, my friend," he said to himself, "I only hope I can do some good."

The case he had just read had a very predictable outcome. In ninety five percent of the cases, the patient would not survive past three years. A smaller amount would last a period longer, always hard to predict. An even smaller number would beat the disease due to early discovery and a great deal of luck. Well, he would meet the young woman and do his very best. Perhaps this would be one of the happy endings.


Hank had always liked Bill Glenn. A friend of the family for as long as he could remember, Glenn had a superb reputation as a clinician. Hank was thankful he was able to see Kate.

What Tyler had not told Kate was that Bill was also one of the most expensive and exclusive physicians in the entire city. Hank knew that his father had called in a favor.

"My gosh, a frontal attack," Bill said as the trio of Hank, Kate and Roger entered his third floor office.

Bill stood up and came around his desk to shake Hank's hand. "Your father told me you'd been beat up a bit over there," he said, seeing Hank's scars. "Welcome home, Hank."

"Thanks, Doc. I'd like you to meet Doctor Roger Hanson, our Group Flight Surgeon and my good friend. And this is Kate Murray."

Bill shook hands with them, motioning to chairs sitting around a small table.

"I read your file, Miss Murray. It's hard to get an accurate picture from a file, but the basic information I needed was there. The first step here is for us to do a complete analysis, which will include a full physical exam. I'd like to get started right now if that meets with your approval."

Kate nodded. "Certainly, Doctor. And please call me Kate. I do appreciate you taking time to see me. I'm ready to begin right now."

"Good. I have one of my assistants outside who will take you down to the lab for a few basic tests. Once you've finished there, she'll bring you back up here and we'll get started."

When Kate had gone, Bill returned to his desk.

"Hank, I'm going to be honest with you, as I will with Kate. And this is probably exactly what Doctor Hanson has told you. This is a difficult case in that historically it does not have a positive outcome."

"That's why we're here, sir," Hank said. "Her care in England would have been very much pro forma and wouldn't have even commenced by now. I knew that she would have a better chance over here."

The older man looked very serious. "We'll do everything we can for her. But you have to go into this with your eyes open. This is a long shot."

"Yes, sir," Hank said, "I understand that. But what else can we do?"

"That's the question everyone asks. There's only one answer. Try to beat the odds."

"Sir, Roger has a friend in the Army Medical Corps who is stationed at Edgewood Arsenal in Maryland. According to his friend, they've been looking at using drugs to combat cancer. Have you heard anything?"

The older man shook his head. "No, but probably no reason I would. The services are notorious for keeping things close to the chest. I have a friend at Edgewood myself, one of the best pharma guys I've ever met, Alfred Gilman. They pulled him out of Yale when the war started."

"I'm going to take a trip down there to see my friend and find out what's going on, maybe it can help Kate," Roger said.

"One thing about wars, we seem to always make huge strides ahead in science. Too bad most of the time that effort starts with better ways to kill human beings."

Hank and Roger stood up to leave.

"Kate will be here until around 2:00 pm, so there's no reason for you to stick around."

"Thanks, Doc. We'll be at the house if anything comes up. You've got the number."


"You feel like heading south to check out Edgewood?" Hank asked Roger as they climbed the front steps to the townhouse.

"Probably better to get going. Then we can figure out how to get back to England," Roger replied.

The two men went inside, leaving their hats on the entryway table and going into the study.

"I think we can get something out of Dover, either replacement bombers heading over or a regular MATS flight."

Roger unbuttoned his blouse and sat down. "Sure don't have time for a boat ride back."

Hank laughed.

"Let's get you on the train to Baltimore. I'll have one of the associates from the local office pick you up and run you out to Edgewood."

Roger said, "You don't have to do that. I am capable of taking care of myself."

"Hey, my ball, my bat, my rules, I win. We've also got a permanent suite at the Grant Hotel which we save for visiting bigwigs. You'll stay there, no arguments."

"Okay, I know when I'm in over my head," Roger said.

Susan Mitchell came down the staircase and walked into the study. Both men saw she was carrying a manila envelope.

"This came by courier while you were gone, Hank." She handed the package to her son and watched him inspect the return address.

"War Department, that's interesting." Hank slid his finger under the flap, ripping the paper with one movement. He withdrew a stack of papers which were stapled together. Reading them carefully he raised his eyebrows in surprise. "My orders," he said as he continued to read down the page. "Report not later than 1200 7 March, 1945 to the Group Commander, 321st Fighter Group, Langley Field." He continued to read, flipping one page over, "This is considered official notification of overseas movement within sixty days."

"That solves your trip to England," Roger said.

Hank tried to think of all the things that would be affected by these orders. Only two weeks away, how would Kate's treatment be progressing by the time he left? "This is going to make everything a lot tougher."

Susan Mitchell put her hand on Hank's arm. "Your father said you'd be going back to flying. But so soon?"

"I guess so. We'll just have to get everything sorted out before hand."

Hank checked his watch as he walked up the stairs to the main entrance of New York Memorial. Roger had stayed at the townhouse, getting his plans in line for his trip south. The two had agreed that Roger would leave tomorrow on the New York Central Railroad Express that left in the morning from Penn Station. He would be in Baltimore by noon and arrive at Edgewood mid afternoon. Roger was trying to find his friend Jason Russell through a mutual acquaintance in Washington D.C.

Opening the door to Doctor Glenn's outer office, he saw Kate sitting at one end of the couch, her eyes closed. The receptionist's desk was empty. The only sound in the room was the rhythmic click of the overhead fan.

Reaching down to touch her arm, he said, "Hi."

Kate opened her eyes, looking momentarily disoriented. She smiled at him, and took a deep breath. "I dozed off."

He sat down next to her, taking her hand in his. "Long day?"

"Everyone was very nice," she said. "I'm waiting to talk with Doctor Glenn now."

"Well, there's a hot bath and nice dinner waiting for you at the house. As soon as you finish we can head home or go anywhere you would like."

The door to the inner office opened. Bill Glenn still wore his white lab coat. "Kate, sorry for the wait. It took a while to get your x-rays developed. Come in and we can talk."

Kate stood up and turned back to Hank. "Will you come in with me?"

Hank nodded and followed her into the room.

"I know today was long. It was very important that we establish where you are in your treatment cycle. I saw some indications in your blood test that made me want to get the series of x-rays done right away. What both the blood workup and radiology indicates is a second tumor that either has grown since the surgery or was so small they didn't detect it at the time."


Roger closed his eyes and leaned back. On the seat next to him the New York Times headlines described the continuing battle on the Pacific island of Iwo Jima, General Patton's push through the Siegfried Line and the capture of Posen by the Red Army. Funny, he thought, with the exception of lighter traffic and a few more uniforms, New York City didn't appear any different to him than before the war. Penn Station had been busy, but that was normal. He noted that at least half of the people in his car were wearing some type of uniform.

He couldn't shake his thoughts of last night when Kate and Hank returned from the hospital. There was no way around the requirement for another surgery to remove the new tumor. Despite Hank and Roger's efforts to be as encouraging as possible, she had been terribly discouraged. Her memories of the infection and post operative pain still fresh in her mind, the tears came readily as they told Roger the news.

Opening his eyes, Roger knew that dozing off wasn't in the cards. His thoughts returned to Kate. If her tumor had grown that much in one month, the cancer must be particularly aggressive. He knew that Bill Glenn must have felt the same way, but apparently hadn't told Kate. Glenn did lay out a very intense radiation therapy designed to kill the cancerous cells. Killing both healthy and diseased cells, the hope was the healthy cells would regenerate and remain dominant. The more aggressive the cancer, the less likely radiation therapy would be successful.

A feeling of weariness came over him. Sometimes it seemed so pointless. He could ensure the pilots of the group were as healthy as possible, so they could go out and sometimes get killed. Now he sat here in what most likely would be a futile attempt to save the life of a young woman who didn't deserve the hand she'd been dealt. Careful Hanson, he told himself, you're going to get philosophical and that doesn't make you a better doctor.

The call from Hank had resulted in a Mr. Phillip Jamerson standing on the platform with a cardboard sign which read, "Major Hanson."

Carrying only a small valise borrowed from the Mitchell's, they avoided the crowd waiting for their baggage and were quickly on the road north toward the arsenal.

A pleasant young man, Phillip quickly made sure Roger knew he'd been rejected by the military due to a knee injury, which still made him limp. The young man now worked in the credit appraisal department of First Street Bank of Baltimore, one of the banks owned by the Mitchell family.

Roger had never spent much time in this area and the drive turned out to be very pleasant. Phillip, a native Marylander, extolled the virtues of the area in general and the Chesapeake Bay in particular. The two men ended up in a heated discussion over the merits of seafood of Puget Sound versus the Bay. Both agreed that tonight they would attempt to sample the fare of the western shore, although Phillip insisted the eastern shore of the bay hosted the best seafood restaurants in the area.

The gate guard directed them to a large building next to the main entrance of the arsenal. Dreading the administrative process it seemed was always necessary to gain access to a base for the first time, he was pleasantly surprised after talking to a Sergeant at the pass and decal desk.

"Sir, there's the base phone book. All you need to do is call your friend and he can come out to escort you on board."

"I'll wait here until you finish," Phillip said.

Thirty minutes later Roger and Major Jason Russell pulled into the parking lot of the Medical Division's Pharmacology Section. The two friends had not seen each other in almost three years and both were animated as they caught up with each other. Once inside they climbed a set of stairs to Jason's office on the second floor.

Roger accepted his offer of coffee and the two continued to tell each other about their work over the last three years.

"I decided I had to find out what those aircrews were going through, so I flew four missions with the B-17's."

"So how was it?" Russell asked.

Shaking his head, he said, "Worse than I could have ever imagined. There's nothing glorious about it. The air war is bloody, ugly and terrifying. I think this war will leave a lot of men scarred for life from what they've seen and had to do. I just hope the rest of America realizes it. But I'm more interested in what you've been doing. And I've got to be honest. I've got an ulterior motive."

Looking quizzically at Roger, he asked, "And what would that be?"

Relating the story of Kate's illness, Roger watched his friend get more attentive as he brought him up to the most recent events in New York.

"So what I told you in the last letter was enough to get you down here sniffing around?"

"I realize it's a long shot. But if she stays with conventional protocols, it's only a matter of time."

"How old did you say she was?"

"Twenty seven."

"Otherwise in good health?"

Roger nodded. "As far as I know this was the first time she was ever in a hospital."

Jason stood up and walked to the window. In a moment he turned back to Roger. "Sit tight, I need to go talk to someone."


Ten minutes later Russell returned with a second man who followed him into the room.

"Roger Hanson, meet Lieutenant Colonel Gilman, my boss."

The two men shook hands and Gilman sat down behind Jason's desk.

His pleasant features were grim, his eyes betraying the long hours working in the lab.

"Major, it's probably a good thing that we're all reserve officers and not too rigid about security. Jason's letter to you probably crossed the line concerning what he told you. But there's nothing we can do about that now. So in for a penny, in for a pound. When he mentioned that you had met and were working with Bill Glenn an idea occurred to me." Gilman stopped talking and put his fingertips together as he considered his words.

"What I'm about to tell you is classified. I guess we can justify that you have a need to know. If not, we'll all be in Leavenworth in the near future. In December of '43, an American ship carrying mustard gas shells was sunk by the Germans in the harbor of Bari, Italy. In treating the survivors, one of the physicians with a knowledge of chemical warfare noted the remarkable effect on the white blood cell count of the men who were rescued from that ship. He remembered that a theory had been advanced after the gas attacks in World War One exploring the potential use of nitrogen mustard as a treatment for lymphomas. So we've been working hard on developing a derivative of nitrogen mustard as a chemical treatment for lymphoma."

Gilman got up and began to pace back and forth behind Jason's desk.

"We're ready to start human testing and have a good sample of men, different ages, backgrounds and race. A good sample. What we don't have is a significant number of women. Right now only six of the sixty subjects are female. Do you think your patient would be willing to take part in the test?"

"Doctor Glenn told me that with normal protocols, her chances are extremely slim. This might be her only chance," Roger said. "He's operating on her tomorrow to remove a second tumor he discovered on his initial exam. That will give him the opportunity to check her thoroughly before starting radiation treatments and now this."

"The test was going to take place here. But I think it would be possible to have Bill administer the medication and document the results. In fact I'd like to have someone with Bill's experience involved in this." Gilman returned to the chair. "All we have to do is figure out how to conduct the test in New York."

"I've already thought about that," Jason said. "If we go with the planned dosages, Roger could take enough for the full cycle with him when he goes back to New York. Then we contact Doctor Glenn to go over the test procedures."

"One thing I don't think I mentioned," Roger said, the thought just occurring to him. "Kate Murray is a British citizen. Any issues there?"

Gilman looked at Jason who shook his head no.

"Then I'm at your disposal. I can return to New York tomorrow or wait a week, whatever's necessary. She should be ready to start any protocol at the end of the week."

"Well, gentlemen, it appears we have consensus. Why don't you two work out the final details and I'll try to get Bill on the phone." The Colonel stood up and walked to the door. "She must be quite a lady."

Roger had never thought of her quite like that, but she was quite a lady.


"Nervous?" Bill Glenn asked.

Kate nodded her head.

Laying on the gurney, she was covered from the neck down in a white sheet. The room was cool and she felt detached from her body.

Hank stood next to her, holding her hand, the concern obvious on his face.

"We'll take good care of you," Bill said. "But I wanted to give you some very exciting news. I had a call late last night from a friend of mine. He has been working on a new treatment for lymphoma. Your Doctor Hanson talked with him in Maryland and they've invited you to take part in the initial trial of the new drug."

Hank squeezed Kate's hand softly. Roger had come through for her. "That's great, Doc."

Kate smiled at them, not sure what it all meant, but encouraged by their words.

"I couldn't be more pleased," Bill said. He reached down and put his hand softly on her arm. "Now, young lady, I'm going to get scrubbed and I'll see you in a few minutes." He winked at Hank. "We'll take good care of her."

They were alone and the only sound was a soft hissing in the radiator.

"That's great news," he said.

"It really is."

"You ready for this?" Hank asked.

"Yes and no," Kate said. "Last time I was blissfully ignorant, now I know what to expect."

"This time you've got me with you. It will go swell."

"The supremely confident fighter pilot. I guess that's why I fell for you."

"Why not one of the RAF chaps? There were lots of them at Victoria."

Kate smiled. "I think it was your accent."

"What accent?"

The door opened and two white coated orderlies entered.


Colonel Max Gogan threw the official message on his desk and called to his adjutant, "Hey, Smitty, see if you can get me a phone number for Major Mitchell. I know he's in New York City. The address is in the folder labeled "Leiston."

He went over the logistics in his mind. The new group, now officially the 321st Fighter Group, had been scheduled to be ready for overseas movement on 7 May. Now headquarters had moved that date forward one month. The B-29's flying out of the Marianas Islands against the home islands of Japan were taking losses that long range escort could reduce. Almost like Europe he thought, the bombers take the fight to the enemy alone until we figure out how to protect them. In Europe we actually needed the P-47's and P-51's for their range. Now we need a landing strip. That's why a bunch of young Marines are fighting their way across a piece of volcanic rock in the Pacific.

Son of a bitch, he thought. They had to be headed west in little more than a month. Most of the pilots were already here at Langley and by and large up to speed. But there hadn't been any opportunity to work on large formation tactics. Well, we'll just have to move things up and fly our asses off, he thought. But I need Mitchell and Christiansen here to whip these guys into shape.

The Group would be equipped with brand new Mustangs right off the production line in El Segundo, California. Flown directly to the Naval Air Station in Alameda, they would be loaded on an escort carrier for the trip to Iwo Jima. The ground maintenance crews would leave Langley in two weeks for the cross country train journey to meet a Navy transport for the trip to the island. I'll be ready for this war to end, he decided, but I wouldn't have missed it for anything.


Roger put his bag down in the entryway and walked into the front sitting room.

"Welcome back," Hank said, getting up from an armchair.

"Is it always this cold in New York?"

"Come back in August."

"How's Kate?" Roger asked, his tone serious.

The two sat down.

"Doc Glenn told me it went very well. He can explain all the technical stuff to you. He did remove a second tumor and now feels that she is clear," Hank explained.

"That's great. How did she come out of the operation?"

"So far, so good. It's only been two days, but the pain is much less. There's no sign of any infection. So I've got my fingers crossed. Now tell me about this new program."

Roger explained the background of the research and how the team at Edgewood was using their research to field a drug which would target the cancerous cells of lymphoma.

"So it was an accident that they found out mustard gas has a beneficial effect."

"Some of the biggest breakthroughs in the history of medicine have come from accidents. Luckily, accidents that someone was curious enough to pursue or smart enough to recognize the significance."

"Almost like some of the trial and error at East Grinstead."

"Very much like that. And the effort will continue as long as medicine exists. There's still a lot to discover out there."

Hank stood up and walked to the bar.

"This is enough for me right now. Drink?"

"You having one?"

"I'm still a fighter pilot, right?"

"Make mine scotch, very expensive scotch."

Hank ignored the ringing phone as he poured the dark amber liquid into a tumbler. "Ice?"

Roger shook his head. "Too much time in England. Straight up for me."

Hank handed Roger the glass.

"Sir, there is a Colonel Gogan calling for you. Are you available?"

They turned to see Dexter in the doorway.

Hank looked with surprise to Roger.

"Wonder what that's all about?" Hank asked.

Roger shrugged.

"I'll take it in here, thanks."

He walked to the desk, picking up the receiver.

"Major Mitchell, sir"

"Hank, it's Max Gogan from Langley."

"Yes, sir. I'm surprised you tracked me down."

"I wouldn't be interrupting your leave if it wasn't important."

"Yes, sir."

"Hank, they moved our schedule up by thirty days. I need you here right away."

The news hit Hank like a sledgehammer, the reality of having to leave Kate at this critical time.

"I understand, sir."

"Good, we need you and Christiansen here pronto. These guys are solid sticks, but we need you to get them ready for combat."

An idea occurred to Hank. "Yes, sir." He paused then said, "Colonel, do we have a group flight surgeon?"

"No, I've been trying to get one, but no luck."

"Sir, Roger Hanson is available as long as we don't need him for another month or so."

Roger looked at Hank with a very quizzical look.

"We just need him prior to heading overseas."

"Colonel, if you work your end, I'll see what I can do from here – but I'd like to think we can make this happen."

"So when do you think you can get down here."

Hank thought for a moment. "I'll be there in four days, sir. Is that all right?"

"See you then."

Roger walked over to the desk.

"What was that all about?" he asked Hank.

"Here, let me top that drink off."

Roger moved his glass out of the reach of Hank who was trying to pour scotch.

"You want to tell me what that was all about?"

"As I recall, you were dreading the return trip to England."

"Yeah."

"The 321st Fighter Group is currently without the services of a flight surgeon. It struck me you might like the job. The beautiful Pacific, palm trees, sunshine, blue water...."

Roger held out his glass, which Hank topped off.

"You're not kidding?"

"They really do need a flight surgeon. But I also need you to stay here and watch out for Kate. I have to be at Langley in four days."

"You can't get in a Mustang. You're still healing!" Roger exclaimed.

189

"I'm getting better every day. I promise I won't overdo it. Just give me an up check and I'll ease into it slowly."

Roger shook his head. "I should be locked up for agreeing to this. But I'll do it for Kate. And you will listen to my instructions carefully and follow them explicitly. If you don't, you'll be in a hospital when the Group goes overseas. Agreed?"

Hank nodded. "Thanks."


Two hours later, the two men arrived at Kate's room and knocked lightly on the closed door.

Pushing the door open, Hank quietly said, "Kate?"

"It's all right, I'm awake."

Hank pushed the door open and went in. "Our wandering miracle worker is back."

"Hi, Kate," Roger said walking to the side of her bed. "I understand this time has gone a bit easier than the last."

She smiled, the brightness in her eyes telling the story of a successful operation.

"I'm still sore, but I feel so much better than before."

"We'll just have to make sure it stays that way," Hank said. "Can I get you anything?"

"No, thanks, they just gave me my medication."

Roger said, "I'll leave you two alone while I to go find Doctor Glenn."

"He brought the medicine for you from Maryland."

"Can you tell me more about it?"

"I'll let Roger explain. He'll be helping with the test and keeping an eye on you for me."

She looked hard at him.

"Gogan called today from Langley. I have to leave. We're going to arrange for Roger to stay here and keep a close eye on you. I'll be back as often as I can, it's not that far. Once I get back in the cockpit, I can even fly up here, land right at Floyd Bennett Field. So don't worry, it'll be fine."

Kate said nothing.

"This took me by surprise too. I wish it hadn't turned out this way, but we can handle it. You'll have Roger and my family, it'll be okay."

She wiped her eyes.

"Hank, I know what you have to do. As much as I want you here, I can do this. It's just that I've gotten quite used to having you around."

He took her hand and bent over to kiss her lightly on the forehead.


Hank Mitchell walked into his father's study after returning to the house.

"There you are," Tyler said. "How's Kate doing?"

"Very well."

"Did you tell her about leaving for Langley?"

Hank nodded. "She took it pretty well."

"Better than I would in her position," his father added. "Sorry, that was a cheap shot. I guess I'm not ready to have you go back to war either."

"This time's different. We're going over there to finish this thing. I don't even remember what I was thinking when I went to England."

"You've changed. More than I would have ever imagined."

"I guess I finally had to grow up. It wasn't a very pleasant experience. But without it I would have never met Kate."

Tyler laughed. "And all along we saw a big wedding in the Hamptons with all the trimmings. You know I think Margo's a good girl, but watching you with Kate tells me this is the real thing."

"I think so. And that makes it hard to think about going back to war."

"I can still fix that." Tyler's eyes were serious.

Hank shook his head.

"I've never asked you to pull any strings until now, with Roger. That's all I need."

"That should be taken care of within the next day or so. There's no guarantee. But if there's a valid billet in the group, my friend told me it shouldn't be a problem. Now let's go down and try to break the news to your mother."

# Chapter Twenty

Langley Field
Norfolk, Virginia
March 2, 1945

Climbing the stairs to the upper level of Hangar Six, Hank ran a critical eye over the three Mustangs parked inside. They looked like they'd seen a lot of flight time, the faded paint and oil stains told the story. Mechanics crawled over the aircraft, all of which had panels open and work stands positioned around them. Hank took a deep breath. There was a unique smell around high performance machines like these. It immediately brought back memories of days past.

"I'm Major Mitchell, reporting in to Colonel Gogan."

"Yes, sir." A Corporal sitting behind a typewriter stood up, his eye momentarily flicking to the scars on Hank's face. "I'll let the Colonel know you're here."

"Corporal," Hank said, stopping the young man in his tracks.

"Yes, sir?"

"What's your name?"

The man looked momentarily confused and a little apprehensive.

"Uh, Thomas, sir."

"Nice to meet you, Corporal Thomas."

The Corporal now looked surprised.

"Yes, sir, thank you, sir."

Max Gogan got up from his desk and came around the desk.

"Welcome aboard," Gogan said, offering his hand.

"Thanks, sir."

"By the way, you're out of uniform." He handed Hank a carbon copy of a letter from the Department of War. "Deputy Commander of a fighter group is a Lieutenant Colonel's job. Here's a set of my old oak leaves. Congratulations, Colonel."

Hank held the two silver devices in his palm. "Thanks, that means a lot to me."

Gogan seemed embarrassed by Hank's comment and reached across his desk. "I don't know what you did. But as soon as I called about Hanson, they came right back and said his orders were in the works."

"He's a good man. I'm glad it worked out."

Gogan sat back and said, "Sit down. Coffee?"

"Thanks."

"Thomas," he called through the open door. "A cup of coffee for Colonel Mitchell."

"Is Thomas one of ours?"

Gogan nodded. "He'll go with the aircrews when we head out. The rest of the support stays here at Langley along with these tired old airframes."

"I know you couldn't tell me on the phone. Where are we going?"

Thomas walked in with a steaming cup of coffee, setting it on the edge of Gogan's desk.

"Iwo Jima."

"That's something I didn't expect."

"Curtis LeMay wants fighter escort for the B-29's that are hitting Japan from the Marianas. The only place we can really stage from is Iwo."

"They're still fighting on the island," Hank said.

"The airfield is already capable as an emergency divert. As quick as they can put the support in place, Twentieth Air Force wants Mustangs operating out of there."

"How far is it from the island to Japan?" Hank asked.

"About 600 miles to Tokyo as the crow flies. Most of the targets are within 200 miles of Tokyo, but they expect some missions farther up north."

"That's a hundred miles farther than Berlin."

"Yeah, lots of sore butts before we're done."

Hank's thoughts returned to those long missions across Europe. These would be totally over water.

"Any word on Christiansen?"

"He got in late last night. I think he's sleeping off a hangover from his first night back. He'll be in transient billeting. They put all of us in the same wing."

"I think I'll go check in and look him up," Hank said as he got up from the chair carefully.

Gogan's eyes narrowed slightly. "How's the leg?"

"Just a little stiff, nothing to worry about. Hanson gave me an up check. I'm ready to start flying right away."

"Good."


Hank stepped into the open hangar area after leaving Gogan's office. His leg was bothering him, but he decided to ignore it. It would take at least two days for his pre-flight screening to be completed and gear issued. By then he hoped the pain would be better.


Doctor Bill Glenn read aloud from the two page brief which Roger had delivered to him along with Kate's drugs.

"This seems pretty straightforward. One CC administered with a saline solution each morning for seven days. Then a five day break, followed with another seven day cycle. We'll administer the cobalt treatment concurrently. That pattern continues for six weeks, then we evaluate. Is that how you read this?"

"Yes, sir. We talked about the dosage protocol at Edgewood. This is one of six different cycles they're going to test. Hopefully they'll quickly get a feel for the effectiveness and the side effects," Roger answered.

Bill shook his head. "Radiation is tough enough. This is going to be the old one-two punch. Did they say what they expected?"

"They hope the side effects will be limited to nausea, weakness and fatigue. This really is unknown territory."

"That young woman up there seems to be pretty tough. I hope the results are worth all of the pain she's gone through and what she's about to endure."

Roger didn't reply, but his hopes echoed Doctor Glenn's. Last night, sitting with Kate, he realized how much he wanted to help her. Maybe it was his reaction to the carnage of the air war and loss of so many young men. Perhaps this was the first step to get his world of healing back on track. Roger hadn't studied medicine to patch up flesh torn apart by machine gun bullets and flak. Sitting in this famous hospital and taking part in what might be a breakthrough treatment reminded him why he loved medicine.

"Well Doctor, let's get this treatment started," Glenn said as he rose from his chair.


Kate Murray lay propped up on two pillows. A book lay on the bed by her hand. Here eyes were closed, but she wasn't asleep. The quiet room had become a haven for her in the hectic world of New York Memorial Hospital. She missed Hank, but now looked forward to each day, her hope building as she regained her strength. Roger's support had been very important. While Doctor Glenn gave her great confidence in the treatment, he didn't explain things the way Roger did. She appreciated the hours that Roger had spent with her, talking and running her few errands.

Last night Hank had been able to get a long distance call through. Hearing his voice made all the difference in the world. He was scheduled for his first flight and so far he felt good. They both laughed about his promotion to Lieutenant Colonel. He'd told her he would always be a Captain at heart. He couldn't talk about the schedule, but for her not to worry, he'd be able to fly up soon.

The door opened and Bill Glenn entered followed by Roger.

"Good morning, young lady," Glenn said. He reached for the clipboard hanging on the foot of her bed.

"Hi," Roger said, walking over to the bed. "Looks like you were able to get some reading done," he said looking at the book on the bed.

"What are you reading, Kate?" Glenn asked, returning the clipboard to its hangar.

"A Tale of Two Cities". Roger picked it up for me yesterday."

"Always one of my favorites," he said and moved down to Kate's side. "Your chart looks very good. So good in fact that we think it's time to start with the next phase of your treatment."

A chill came over her, the reality of her disease never far from her thoughts.

Glenn covered the radiation procedures then went over the plan for introducing the drug, which he called Mechlorethamine. "You understand this is what we call a clinical trial? There are almost seventy people who will be participating over the next six weeks. Kate, we don't know exactly what the results will be or even what side effects you might encounter. This is one of those leaps of faith we have to make in medicine to try and move forward. This new drug might even make things worse. But I'll tell you upfront I don't think that's the case. I just want you to go into it with your eyes wide open."

Kate, whose eyes were now very wide open asked only one question. "Roger explained a lot about this last night, Doctor. Do you think that with only the normal radiation therapy I would have any chance of beating this?"

Bill Glenn sighed. "No, Kate. In my experience the radiation might delay the inevitable. But a favorable outcome based on all other factors is very unlikely."

"Then, I'm ready."


Hank sat on the bench in the pilot's locker room after putting on his flight gear. His locker sat next to Gogan's and had a small amount of privacy from the main locker rows. He looked around to ensure no one was watching and raised his right foot up and placed it against the wall. Slowly he began to apply pressure, trying to simulate the force he knew would be required for the rudder pedal and brakes of the Mustang. It hurt, but not too bad, he thought. Still wearing the brace that Roger had fashioned, he felt he could justify climbing into a cockpit.

An hour later, RU 23, an early model P51D sat idling in the hold short area of runway Zero Eight. Looking to the east, the high clouds told Hank he'd have plenty of airspace to work the cobwebs out of his flying skills.

"Langley Tower, Romeo Uniform Two Three for takeoff."

"Army Two Three, you are cleared number one for takeoff, runway Zero Eight, winds 060 at ten."

"Two Three, roger."

Pulling on the runway, Hank finished his takeoff checks and took a deep breath. So far, he'd been able to cycle the rudder pedals and brakes with some pain, but certainly tolerable. Now it was time to see if he could handle the takeoff torque of the Merlin.

"Two Three's rolling."

Running up to 54 inches of manifold pressure, Hank released the brakes and began to feed in right rudder. At sixty knots the tail came up and he could see the end of the runway. Pulling back slightly at 110 knots, the Mustang left the runway and began to climb away. Turning right he could see pine trees flashing under his wing as he continued toward the Atlantic and the working area.

"Langley Tower, Romeo Uniform Two Three is departing to the east."

After switching to the operational frequency for the acrobatic area off the Virginia Capes, Hank began to work through his checklist of maneuvers. Slow flight and stalls were followed by mild acrobatics and finally overheads and barrel rolls. A feeling of confidence began to return as he finessed his moves, putting the Mustang right where he wanted it. With one hour of fuel remaining, he enthusiastically headed back to Langley for practice landings.

Later, after wheel chocks had been put in place, he pulled the throttle to idle cutoff and secured the ignition and fuel control. The big prop slowly wound to a stop and Hank unstrapped from the seat. The 321st Fighter Group now had a real Deputy Commander.

"Hey, you remember how to fly that thing?"

Hank turned to see Chris Christiansen in the driver's seat of a jeep.

"Just barely."

"Well, hop in. The boss wants us up at the ops building.

Since he'd checked into the Group, he and Chris had spent most of their time together whenever Chris wasn't in Washington D.C. visiting his long time girlfriend Ginny. If he was going back into combat with the Japs, he was glad to have his old friend by his side.

"Here's the final movement order for our aircrew contingent. We've got three weeks before we board air transport for the west coast. I confirmed the maintenance group is at sea with the Navy and the aircraft are also. It looks like we'll be using Military Air Transport from San Francisco to Pearl. From there we transfer to Naval Air Transport Command for the rest of the trip to Iwo. We should be on the island five days after leaving Langley." Gogan put down the message he'd been referring to and looked at his staff. Besides Hank as the Deputy Commander and Chris as the squadron commander for the 327th, the other two squadron skippers, Majors Dee Raines and Fred Goodrum were present. Major Johnny Major, the Group Operations Officer completed the group.

"Besides flying our asses off for the next three weeks, does anyone have any major problems at this point?"

"I'm still waiting on two pilots," Chris said, "But that's it for me."

No one else raised any issues.

"We're starting to get some direction from LeMay on how he wants us to escort the B-29's. They've been learning a lot from the operations out of China and now the Marianas. The good news is that the Jap pilots are not the same caliber we saw in Germany. For a lot of reasons, they haven't been able to keep up with their aircrew attrition. Most of the pilots that are now defending the home islands are inexperienced, low time aviators. The bad news is that these sons of bitches don't think twice about ramming our bombers. Sort of airborne Kamikaze's. The other thing that we have to rethink is that, at altitude, the B-29 is just as fast as the Mustang. Depending on upper level winds, the entire intercept problem is different from anything we saw in Europe with the B-17's and 24's." He turned to his squadron commanders. "I want you to work hard on unit tactics with Colonel Mitchell. He had a lot of success out of England adapting the best tactics for dealing with the Krauts. This is a

198

different kettle of fish. But I want you to use his experience as we work on building the divisions into a coordinated team in the air."

Hank stood up and lifted the cloth cover over a movable chalk board. Underneath a very ambitious schedule showed the squadrons, and launch times for the next three week's training schedule.

"We don't have much time, so we'll skip right to simulated large formation escort practice. One of the keys is to make sure we have plenty of ground training and discussion on procedures before we ever get in the air. The Brits are proud of their hero Horatio Nelson. He figured out that in the confusion of battle his captains needed to know how he thought so they could react without orders. We're going to try to do the same thing. I want everyone from the squadron commander to the most junior wingman to understand what we're doing and why we're doing it. We've got one more issue in the Pacific that none of us has dealt with before. England might be an island, but it's a hell of a lot bigger than Iwo Jima. And the English Channel is not 600 miles wide. We need to emphasize to every pilot that he's a navigator at all times. Understanding the weather and good dead reckoning may be the only thing that gets some of these kids home. More later on the B-29 lead nav ship program they've started using, but for now, test your guys and sharpen their skills with a compass and a watch."

"Okay, first brief tomorrow at 0430. We've got a service squadron to simulate the bomber formation. You'll see we're starting with each squadron flying alone. We'll do that for two days then combine for full group operations. You'll notice all flying is daytime. They've pulled the escorts from any of the night B-29 missions. Apparently there's been almost no response by Jap night fighters."

"No complaints here," Goodrum said.

"Almost makes it sound like a cake walk," Raines added.

Gogan stood up. "Far from it. The flak they've seen is just as effective as we saw over Berlin. The other problem is the long over water distances. You get shot up over Japan and it's a damn long way home. At least now they can divert into Iwo. But they still lose aircraft that can't make it back to one of the islands. They've lost a lot of them over the last several months. The Navy has helped with an umbrella of Catalina's they send out from Iwo to provide search and rescue. Rumor has it they are even adapting several B-29's for the same role. They obviously wouldn't land on the water like the PBY's, but could drop rafts and accurately pinpoint the survivor's position. Then the Navy shows up with either the seaplane or in some cases submarines."

A different war, Hank thought. But if this is what it takes to end this part, so be it.

"Another thing we'll have to deal with is flying a lot higher than we normally did in Europe," Gogan continued. "Right now the Superforts are routinely dropping from over 30 grand. Those altitudes will affect our aircraft and people. Our new flight surgeon, Roger Hanson, will be making sure everyone is familiar with all aspects of altitude sickness and proper use of oxygen. The B-29's are pressurized in the crew compartments. Because their guns are remotely controlled, they don't have to have their gunners standing in the open."

"But we're sitting in our little frozen cockpits for six hours watching them drink coffee and eat donuts," Chris said sarcastically.

"The price you pay for being a swashbuckling fighter pilot," Hank answered.

"All right, gentlemen, get the word out to your pilots and be ready to fly tomorrow."


"You're sure I can't have them get you some dinner?" Tyler Mitchell asked.

"No, sir, but thanks. I grabbed a sandwich while Kate was taking a nap."

Tyler handed Roger a glass of scotch and sat down in the chair next to him. "Is she doing better?"

He took a drink and put the glass on the table. "I guess it depends on what you call better. She's getting sick less, but still is nauseated most of the time. It's bad enough that we're worried about her nutrition at this point. She's lost most of her hair, which is discouraging and embarrassing. I would say she's simply hanging on."

Mrs. Mitchell had walked in and heard Roger's comments about Kate. "Can we go see her yet?"

"I did ask Bill Glenn and he said yes. Let me ask Kate, though. She might not want to see anyone right now, it's hard to say."

Tyler asked, "Have you heard when Hank will be able to make it up here?"

"That's the one good piece of news. He's flying a Mustang up here the day after tomorrow. Gogan's given him a two day leave." Roger didn't tell the Mitchells that he'd called the group commander and briefed him on the situation. Gogan had immediately told Hank to take an aircraft for a cross country training flight.

"Thank goodness," Susan Mitchell said. "They need to see each other."

Roger Hanson agreed.

A cold March wind blew off Jamaica Bay as the lone Mustang rolled onto final approach at Floyd Bennett field. While the war spread military aircraft around the entire 48 states, it was still unusual to see a Mustang fighter flying over Brooklyn. Roger stood on the ramp in front of base operations and blew on his hands to keep warm. The duty officer inside had told him that transient aircraft parked just off to the right and he was welcome to walk out and meet the fighter after it shut down. When he had arrived at the main gate in the limousine, the duty sentry immediately produced a visitor's pass, probably thinking Roger was meeting some VIP.

Roger had talked with Hank several times over the last three weeks keeping him updated on Kate's condition. He sensed his friend's frustration hearing of her condition while not being able to be there for her. Now we both need to return to Langley, Roger thought, what's that going to do to Kate? With about two and a half weeks to go on her course of treatment, she was fighting hard to stick with it. The constant nausea, weakness and lack of appetite had taken a terrible toll.

As they pulled out of the base operations parking lot Hank began to ask Roger questions.

"Is it getting any easier for her?"

"Hank, there's nothing easy about it. It's as tough a course of treatment as I've ever seen. Jason told me they had several people pull out down south, they just couldn't take the side effects."

"Shit."

"My sentiments exactly. And you better be ready for how she looks. She's lost over twenty pounds and all her hair. Most of the time she has a little cap on that your mother sent her. She doesn't feel good and knows how bad she looks. It's tough anyway you look at it."

"But is it working?"

"We don't know and won't for some time. Without opening her up again, the only way we have of monitoring tumor growth is to see something on the x-ray or detect something with lab abnormalities."

Hank looked out at the passing streets, he felt lost in the city he called home.

"You go in, I'll wait down the hall," Roger said.

Hank nodded, took a deep breath and opened Kate's door.

The noise of the door opening caused Kate to open her eyes. She turned her head slightly, the fogginess of sleep still holding her. A smile came to her lips as she realized who was there.

Hank walked across the room, his eyes on hers. He didn't say a word, but leaned down and kissed her forehead then her lips.

"I missed you," she said quietly.

He nodded, afraid to speak, his emotions overwhelming him. She seemed so small lying in the bed, the stocking cap slightly askew. He knew this illness wasn't his fault, but he felt helpless to do anything to help her.

"Sorry it took me so long to get back."

"At least you're here now."

"And I wouldn't want to be anywhere else."

"I know I look a sight.....this has been harder than I expected."

Hank pulled a chair over to the bedside and sat down, taking her hand.

"Roger told me." Hank knew his words were inadequate. "If it's my only chance, then I've got to take it."

The two of them looked at each other, the terrible reality something they had never discussed directly.

An hour later Roger looked around the door to see Hank still holding her hand while Kate slept quietly. Pointing to his watch, Roger made a motion indicating they needed to leave.

Hank gently put Kate's hand down on the blanket, rose and kissed her lightly on the forehead.

Driving back to the townhouse in the evening traffic, the two sat in silence in the back of the limousine.

Roger had known Hank Mitchell for over a year. During that time he had watched the aviator react to almost every possible emotional test. But this was a different mood than Roger had ever seen before. His friend seemed empty and lost.

"I got my orders," Roger finally said, trying to get Hank to respond. "The report date is the beginning of next week. I suppose you could get that adjusted to let me keep my eye on Kate."

"We're getting ready to stage for overseas. I, we, need you with the group now. Not only do we need to do the overseas screening on all pilots, but I need you to educate everyone on high altitude flying."

Hank's comment took Roger by surprise. "Why high altitude flying?" He had expected the overseas screenings, it was standard procedure.

"The 29's fly a lot higher than the Forts. We don't want any physical problems from the pilots not understanding the rules and effects of low pressure exposure during the missions. And the flights will be longer than we ever saw in Europe."

"I can take care of that. But how about Kate?"

Hank turned to look at his friend. "That's what I've been trying to figure out for the last hour."

The driver turned off Central Park North and stopped at the curb in front of the Mitchell's house.

"Let's have a drink and see what our options are," Hank said, opening the door. Throughout his adult life, Hank had been very successful in maintaining control in any situation. His time spent at Queen Victoria Hospital was one of the few situations where he found himself at the mercy of outside forces. Kate had helped him make it through that time. Perhaps his bloodlust when he returned to Leiston had been driven as much by his hatred of the Nazis as his own need to regain control of the world around him. He only felt comfortable when he enjoyed control of his life. Now he found himself trying to deal with Kate's illness where every aspect seemed to be driven by things he couldn't control. Now the imminent departure of the group for the Pacific brought all of his frustrations home. Somehow he would make all this work.

"I thought I heard you come in," Susan Mitchell said.

# Chapter Twenty One

Iwo Jima
Bonin Islands
April 16, 1945


The harsh sunlight assaulted the eyes of the 321st Fighter Group pilots as they stepped out the door of the R-5D Navy transport. The final long overwater flight from Guam had taken three hours and culminated a seven thousand mile journey from Langley Field.

A stiff breeze blew from offshore lifting a hazy dust from the volcanic soil of the island. In the distance, Mt. Suribachi stood starkly black against the blue sky. Their final briefing from the Navy intelligence unit on Guam detailed the last desperate counterattack by the Japanese defenders of the island on the 25th of March. The young intelligence officer noted the island had been declared secure the next day, but several suicide attacks had taken place by the isolated defenders still not mopped up by the Marines.

"You've got to be kidding me," Chris said and they walked across the ramp toward several Marine trucks waiting on the perimeter road.

"Leiston wasn't a half bad place, now that I have something to compare it with." Hank threw his Valpak into the rear of the truck and climbed over the tailgate, moving forward to the wooden seats on the side.

Today's arrival brought the 321st up to full strength. Colonel Gogan had arrived the day prior with half of the pilots and support staff. Now the challenge for the group would be to inspect each of their new aircraft and prepare to commence operational flights.

The island looked like Hank imagined the surface of the moon must be like. Almost a total lack of vegetation helped to accentuate the craters which covered almost every piece of ground not resurfaced for use as a runway or road. The debris from the assault and battle for the island still lay strewn everywhere, the evidence of the ferocity of the struggle which intelligence estimated cost the Japanese over 20,000 troops.

There were the first signs that the island was being transformed from a defensive bastion to an offensive air base. Sign posts stood at most road intersections providing direction to units or services as more support troops came ashore.

The three trucks pulled to a stop next to a large olive drab tent. A small hill provided some amount of shade for the tent which had two of its four canvas sides pulled up, showing several tables on its twenty foot by twenty foot wooden floor. Outside the tent a small sign hung from a wooden post: "321st Fighter Group."

As the pilots climbed down from the trucks, Hank saw Colonel Gogan exit the tent and walk toward them. Behind Gogan, the largest Master Sergeant Hank had ever seen walked in step.

"Welcome to Iwo Jima, gentlemen," Gogan called loudly. "Master Sergeant Hawkins has your billet assignments." Seeing Hank, the group commander walked over, extending his hand. "Okay trip?"

"Yes, sir. Although it seemed it would never end sometimes."

"A taste of what we're about to get into," Gogan said, laughing. "The Marines put us in a small troop support area behind that hill. The area has tents, a small mess hall and latrines, all the comforts of home. We have to keep it policed up and they'll provide all logistics support like food, water and toilet paper. It's tolerable, but it ain't the Ritz. Why don't you go get settled then come back here." He pointed toward a dirt path. "Follow that trail around the hill and you'll run right into it. But stay on the marked paths, they've been finding some Jap anti-personnel mines in the area. And I want all the pilots to carry their forty fives. There's still Japs in the caves around here."

A little different from England, Hank thought. "Have you seen the aircraft?" Hank asked.

"They're here, made the trip without incident. Our maintenance group got here two days before the aircraft arrived. Master Sergeant Hawkins is the senior maintenance chief and one of the toughest sons of bitches I've ever run across. Right now he's got the mechs down at field number two working on the acceptance inspections."

The Master Sergeant stood watching the pilots as they walked down the path to billeting.

"I'll introduce you in a minute. Hawkins is really something." The two men turned and began to walk toward the big admin tent. Gogan continued, "Seventh Fighter Command is our immediate boss. They work for 20th Air Force. So far they seem pretty level headed. They've given us two days to be ready to start flying missions. The plan is for us to fly as divisions under the guys who've been here. We do that for a week or so, then go fully operational."

"I guess the sooner we get started, the sooner we go home," Hank said.

Despite the imminent return to combat, most of his thoughts on the long trip from Virginia had been about Kate. He kept remembering saying good bye to her that last day. She'd worked through the weakness and nausea to get out of bed and put on a green dress that Susan had brought her. A beautiful emerald green silk scarf covered her head and she even wore light makeup. It helped Hank to see her up and looking better than she had in weeks. But they both knew they couldn't escape the reality of separation.

"How long do you think?" Kate had asked.

He shook his head. "I think the phrase is '...for the duration.' All we can hope is that it's over as quickly as possible."

"Will you have to be there until the end?"

Hank knew the answer, but couldn't make himself tell Kate.

"You look good in green," he said, changing the subject.

She laughed. "You're a terrible liar, Colonel Mitchell. But your mother was so sweet bringing me this dress and helping me get ready."

"They like you a lot. Let them help you get through this."

Kate's expression changed, her illness never far from her thoughts.

"We haven't really talked about the future."

"Seems like we tend to get too involved in the here and now," Hank said.

"After the treatments, Doctor Glenn told me I'd be well enough to travel in about two weeks." She paused. "Maybe it makes sense for me to go home until the war ends."

The thought that Kate would return to England hadn't occurred to Hank. He assumed she would stay in New York for monitoring or more treatments.

"I thought you'd just stay here."

"Hank, this isn't my home. My father is still running his business and counts on me." Her voice was soft, but there was a tone of insistence.

He took her hand. "Would you be willing to adopt this as your home?

"How would I do that?" she asked.

"By marrying me."

Kate didn't reply. She squeezed his hand and looked down for a moment.

"Kate, you changed my life and my world with your love and kindness. I want to share that world with you more than anything else. Neither one of us knows what the future holds. But I think we both need each other to face it."

She looked up, tears welling up in both eyes. "Yes, my love, I'll marry you."

Over the next several days Hank had asked himself if their commitment made it harder or easier to say good bye. He couldn't come up with a good answer, but he did know it made him feel good knowing they were to be married when he returned. And he would return.

"Here's where you and I hang out. Corporal Thomas is getting everything organized. Hell, just like home," Gogan said, motioning to the desks inside the tent.

Not exactly like home, Hank thought.

Susan Mitchell knocked on Kate's door, waiting for her to answer.

"I was just getting ready to come down," Kate said, opening the door.

"Remember, if you don't feel up to it, we can have a tray sent up."

"Actually I've been feeling much better. Once I get some of my old energy back, I'd love to see more of the city."

Smiling, Susan took Kate's hand. "Let me be your guide. I would love to show you the town."

Kate had come to truly care for Susan Mitchell. Her effort and concern over the last several weeks helped Kate make it through the final part of her treatment. Having spent most of her formative years with her father, Kate had missed the relationship between mother and daughter. While neither would have ever said it aloud, both women enjoyed their developing bond.

"I've always heard about the Metropolitan Museum of Art. I'd like to go there if we could."

"Then that's where we'll start," Susan said, "Whenever you're ready."

They walked downstairs to the front sitting room where Tyler stood behind the bar with a martini shaker in his hand.

"Hello, you two," he said coming around the end of the bar. "Kate, please sit down over here."

The Mitchell's sat in chairs on each side of Kate.

"Kate, we're so happy to have you with us. It makes our connection with Hank stronger knowing how he feels about you." Tyler hesitated for a moment as if searching for words. "No one could be more pleased by your engagement. However I must say it did catch us by surprise. Hank had to leave so quickly that he asked us to wrap up a few details for him. It would have been customary for him to give you a ring to symbolize your betrothal." Tyler handed Kate a small square box.

Kate took the box and looked at both of them. "I don't know what to say."

"Open it, my dear," Susan said.

Against the dark blue velvet lining of the box, the sparkle from the ring reflected the lights of the room.

"I've never seen anything so beautiful," Kate said.

"It was my mother's," Susan said. "She loved Hank so much and would have been very happy that he found you. We had always talked that if I had a daughter, she would wear this ring. Now she will."

Kate looked up. There were tears in Susan's eyes and she was smiling.

"Will you allow me to stand in for Hank and put it on your finger?" Tyler asked.

There were now tears in her eyes as Kate nodded. "Yes, please."

Tyler carefully removed the ring from its box, gently took Kate's left hand and slipped the ring on her fourth finger. "We'll let Hank do the wedding band," he said, kissing her cheek.


Hank tried not to think about how far they were from a friendly landing field. Despite his experience in Europe, these long overwater flights against Japan were unlike anything he'd ever seen. The fighters had to join up with the bomber formations for the flight to Japan. Not only did each B-29 carry their own navigator, but the strike also had a command navigator providing overall direction. The B-29's were equipped with additional radios and electronic navigation equipment that made the long flights almost routine.

The Pacific weather patterns presented a new set of challenges from Europe. The large frontal systems created barriers that the strike formations had to force their way through, regardless of the thunderstorms and high winds associated with them. It was critical for the fighter pilots to maintain contact with their nav B-29 as they pressed through the weather. If any of the single piloted fighters became separated from the large formation, they could end up hundreds of miles at sea with only a basic compass to get home. The return flight also required picking up the big Superforts as they passed back out to sea after their bomb runs. If a fighter missed that rendezvous, it was a long lonely trip home.

In the first several weeks since the 321st had started flight operations, they saw minimal reaction from Jap fighters. Hank had flown on almost every mission and had only seen hostile fighters three times, never within range to engage. The

Jap anti-aircraft fire was another story. Every mission the group saw B-29's go down after braving the heavy flak concentrations at targets like Nagoya and Tokyo. Some of the stricken bombers made it back to Iwo for emergency landings. Many others had to ditch in the sea on the long flight back to the Marianas Islands.

Hank turned to look behind him at the staggered divisions of Mustangs flying on each side of the larger B-29 formation. The group had launched 28 fighters to rendezvous with the bombers who had already been airborne for over two hours after departing their base in Saipan. He estimated they were about one hundred miles from their target, the Japanese Imperial Naval Base at Yokosuka. While most of the large warships of the Jap fleet had been sunk, the planners for the invasion wanted to destroy the ability of the enemy to launch small craft or suicide craft to attack the invasion fleet.

The base contained the largest naval construction and repair facilities on Japan's east coast. One hundred and forty eight bombers would be making attacks on the base and port areas in Yokohama. The entire formation would use Suno Point as the IP, turning east after completing their bomb runs to rendezvous with the fighters over the town of Chikura. While the bombers were in their run, Hank would lead his group toward Tokyo to pick up any fighters coming from the northwest.

"Nancy Able, Nancy Able, Point Whiskey, I say again Point Whiskey."

The lead navigator's radio call confirmed Hank's dead reckoning by announcing the formation was twenty minutes from the IP. He checked his armament switches for the tenth time, noting everything looked good. Hank was flying the squadron lead for Dee Raines today. The 325th's squadron commander had a severe sinus infection and Roger put him off flight status for seven days. On the far side of the formation, Chris led ten Mustangs from the 327th.

Cruising at 26,000 feet, scattered cloud layers lay beneath the formation revealing a blue gray sea. In the distance, Hank could now break out the low coastal plain south of Tokyo. The bomber's targets lay beyond the low peninsula and Hank expected the formation leader to begin his swing to the south at any time to line up on his northerly bomb heading. As the fighter element commander, Hank's responsibility was to detach the Mustangs at the appropriate time to make their fighter sweeps and clear the way for the B-29's. Looking at his watch, he decided to detach Chris and his squadron.

Hank thought about how easily Chris had assumed the role of a squadron commander. His pilots respected him as a pilot and an officer. They had reacted well as he pushed them to perfection in the air. The result was an effective, combat ready squadron. He could tell that Chris enjoyed the responsibility to the point that his friend talked about staying in the service after the war. He's come a long way from the green kid who stuck with me over the English Channel, Hank thought.

"Baker Two, this is Baker Lead, you're cleared to detach," Hank transmitted on the raid frequency.

"Roger Lead, Baker Two detaching," Chris replied.

Hank knew Chris would now accelerate toward Tokyo while the bombers turned south. The two courses would provide about a five minute lead for Chris and his ten fighters to sweep ahead of the bombers to pick up any Jap fighter in the area. Hank would lead the remaining Mustangs on a wide sweep to the west, putting themselves between the Jap fighter strips on the Kanto Plain and the Superforts. With the speed and armament of the B-29's, the entire defensive philosophy of escorting bomber formations had evolved. No longer trying to protect lumbering B-17's and 24's as the Luftwaffe flew circles around them, it was more like a football guard throwing a quick block as a fast running back darted into the end zone.

In addition to the increased performance of the B-29's, the difficult problem of the long overwater flight provided additional advantage to the Americans. Japanese land based fighters were seldom found very far out at sea. The reason was not a lack of bravery by the enemy pilots, but a more practical reason. It was simply too hard for them to find the American bombers in the vast area off the coast. Always arriving by slightly different courses, the staggered times of the air strikes also made positioning defensive fighters very difficult. The result had been many hours of long uneventful flights punctuated by ten to twenty minutes of intense combat over the target area. Funny way to fight a war, Hank thought.

As the bombers turned right toward their attack heading, Hank keyed his radio, "Bravo One, Bravo Three, detaching at this time."

"Good hunting," came the reply from the B-29 mission commander.

The two Mustang squadrons, made up of six flights totaling eighteen aircraft rolled out heading almost north toward Tokyo. Spreading out into a wide formation, three flights guided on the two squadron leaders. By plan, Fred Goodrum's aircraft descended three thousand feet and began looking for enemy fighters. Hank turned his squadron ten degrees to the right. He was now paralleling the bomber's track, providing an additional line of defense.

Against the brownish green landscape, Hank's eyes caught a flash that he knew by instinct was a fast moving target.

"Bravo One, bandits on the nose, low, moving left to right. Lead's in." With his drop tanks long since gone, all Hank needed to do was to flip the guard on the gun switch as he rolled smoothly right toward the small specks which had begun to grow in size. The Mustang accelerated and he could now make out six fighters, two painted olive drab and four a dark grey. Still below the Mustangs, the Japanese were climbing toward the bomber formation.

Quickly checking his mirrors, Hank saw his wingmen holding position as he closed in on the hostile fighters. Watching the six Jap fighters, Hank estimated it would be a tough shot at long distance. But they were heading for the bombers and that couldn't be ignored. Maybe if they see us they'll break off their attack and take us on, Hank thought. Squeezing the trigger he watched tracer rounds arc out toward the Jap fighters. The enemy pilots continued on their heading. *Shit!*

Hank had the Mustang at full power now, gaining on the enemy aircraft that were still climbing toward the B-29 formation.

Hank watched the enemy aircraft take individual headings, their flight discipline now sacrificed for individual attack runs on the bombers.

"This is Bravo One, I've got their leader. Everyone else pick a target." Hank fired a quick ranging burst, knowing he was still too far for a kill. The tracers flew slowly behind the aircraft, which Hank could now see was a Shiden fighter, code named "George", the Jap's newest and best aircraft. Hank felt the blood rage building. Destroying that aircraft was the only thing in his world.

Closing fast on the enemy aircraft, Hank knew the speed differential would cause him to overshoot the Jap. Leveling his wings, he pulled the Mustang thirty degrees nose up, bleeding off airspeed as he closed to 200 yards. Kicking the rudder hard, he pulled back violently toward the George, putting his gunsight reticles directly on the cockpit. Allowing the Mustang to stabilize for an instant he pressed the guns switch and saw tracers hitting home. Smoke immediately began to trail from his target, but the pilot continued toward the bombers. Hank continued pouring rounds into the Jap but the aircraft didn't change course. Tracers from the B-29's guns flew past the target and drifted under Hank, the American gunners now adding their defensive fire.

Maintaining course, the Jap pilot was steering directly for the lead B-29 in the western box. With sickening realization, Hank watched the George on a collision course with the big bomber. Disregarding the B-29's fire, Hank desperately tried one last burst. A violent explosion caused Hank to pull back hard on the stick, narrowly avoiding the ugly black smoke left by the exploding Jap fighter.

Just clearing the B-29 he turned back to the left looking for any other targets or Mustangs in trouble. Out of the corner of his eye he saw with horror as an olive drab Zero hit a Superfortress. Debris flew back from the stricken bomber, its upper fuselage now torn open to the atmosphere. The upper defensive turret on the B-29 was gone along with the upper third of the vertical stabilizer.

"Bravo One, rendezvous port side of the bombers." Hank worked his way back on the west side of the bombers as ugly black flack bursts began to fill the sky. The initial anti-aircraft explosions were several thousand feet below the bombers, but Hank knew the Jap gunners would be correcting quickly. He could see several Mustangs joining on him.

Providing close escort, Bravo One and Three rendezvoused and stayed with the bombers as they completed their bomb runs. The flak intensified as they approached Yokohama, the ugly black bursts appearing suddenly among the bombers as they pressed their bomb run.

Just like bomber crews everywhere, holding course despite the anti-aircraft fire, Hank thought as he saw the bomb bay doors opening on the Superforts, indicating a drop was imminent. There was no sign of any hostile fighters, although he continued to search the sky with Mt. Fuji in the background. Bombs began to fall from the Superforts, the individual bombs clearly visible to Hank.

A bright flash coupled with black smoke erupted from the wing root of a bomber in the second box. In terrible slow motion the port wing on the big aircraft folded up, the fuselage beginning a nose down spiral to the left. Hank had seen enough in Europe to know that getting out of that aircraft would be impossible as the g-forces built up in the bomber's death spiral. It was part of the cruel equation of the air war, sometimes there was nothing anyone could do.

Hank noted all his Mustangs were accounted for as the bomber lead turned the formation back toward the sea. He saw the B-29 that had been rammed by the Jap fighter still fighting to stay in formation, having slipped back two boxes. Looking at his strike list, he saw the alternate squadron lead's side number was B-12.

"Bravo One Two, this is Bravo Lead. Take the formation lead, I'm going to take my flight back to cover one of the bombers."

Easing below the rest of the fighters, he pulled his power and began to move back toward the stricken B-29 that had now slipped to the back of the formation. I don't know if that aircraft will hold up for the trip to Iwo, he thought, but I'll be damned if I'll let the Japs pick him off. He could make out the side number, but could also see the artwork on the nose, a voluptuous woman in a bathing suit, labeled "Hi-Jinks Two." He adjusted the power and signaled his number two wingman to move over to the right side of the Superfort. The shiny metal skin of the bomber was shredded with multiple tears. Only wires, and twisted metal spars showed where the large top turret had been. Amazingly all four engines seemed to be turning normally and there was no smoke coming from anywhere.

"Hi-Jinks, want some company?"

"Affirmative. It's getting a little lonely back here." The larger formation was now several miles ahead of them.

"What's your situation?" Hank asked, knowing the bomber's pilot understood the real question was 'can you make it to Iwo?'

"Four good motors. Except for the structural damage we're okay. We do hear pretty heavy vibration." After a brief pause, the pilot transmitted, "We lost one man."

Hank knew he had reached a decision point. If they left now, they could get to Chikura, join up with the main formation and start the return trip. If he stuck with Hi-Jinks and the bomber went down during the long overwater leg, they'd be on their own. He thought about his two wingmen, now flying on the right side, a couple of young kids that he'd gotten to know since they arrived at Iwo.

"You lead the way, Hi-Jinks and we'll keep the bad guys off your back."

"Roger," came the reply, "And thanks."

There is a saying in aviation that God looks out for fools and aviators. Hank shut down almost three hours later, after watching an aircraft that probably would never fly again touch down on the volcanic runway in the middle of the Pacific. He thanked God that the little group had not encountered any bad weather or significant winds during the trip from Japan. A little luck always helps in combat.

Despite the loss of the one Superfort over Yokohama, it had been a good day. Nine young men were safe again and that was something that had become very important to Hank Mitchell.

"Wondered when you'd get back," Chris called up to the cockpit from the Jeep he'd pulled alongside Hank's aircraft.

Standing up for the first time after those long flights had become one of his most anticipated moments. I must be getting old, he thought, this just kills my back. He jumped to the ground as Chris walked up.

"Hop in and I'll run you over to debrief."

The sun, now high in the sky, created waves of heat across the bare terrain as Chris drove toward the Quonset hut that served as the intelligence debriefing office.

"You took a chance sticking with that guy," Chris said.

"Yeah, I know."

"Hard to call sometimes."

"You'd have done the same thing," Hank said.

"Yeah, probably." Chris stopped the jeep. "Hurry up and I'll run you up to admin. The Colonel wanted to talk about tomorrow's meeting."

An hour later, Hank and Max Gogan finished the escort plan for tomorrow's maximum effort mission against Nagoya. There would be two fighter groups flying escort and Gogan would take the lead for the 321st. He wanted Hank to take a break and catch up on some of the administrative tasks that had taken second priority to all of the flying recently.

Corporal Thomas stuck his head into the tent's rear compartment that Hank used as an office. "Sir, there's a Captain Kelly out here. Says he wants to say thanks."

A young man in a sweat stained flight suit stepped into the office, a crumpled baseball cap in his hand. He saluted Hank and said, "My name's Jamie Kelly, sir. I'm the pilot of Hi-Jinks. Down at the flight line they said you were leading the Mustangs that brought us home."

Hank smiled and extended his hand. "You brought them home, Captain. We were just there to provide company. Here, sit down."

He could see the weariness on Captain Kelly's face. Hank estimated the young man might be 24, but looked 44.

"I'm sorry about your crewman."

"Yes, sir," the young man said, pain evident in his eyes. "He'd been with us from the beginning. Wouldn't you know it, he's the only guy in the crew with a wife."

For an instant, Hank thought of Kate. Another young wife was going to get a telegram and her life would change forever.

"What was his name?" Hank asked.

"Sergeant Conrad, Billy Conrad, from Racine, Wisconsin."

The two sat in silence for a moment.

"That was a hell of a job getting that aircraft home in one piece."

Kelly shook his head. "We were lucky. I've known a lot of guys that didn't make it."

"Yeah," Hank said, "me too."

Hank reached down to the lower drawer of the field desk.

"Captain, I need a drink. How about you?" Hank poured bourbon into two glasses and handed one to the young pilot.

Raising his glass to Captain Jamie Kelly, Hank said quietly, "To Sergeant Billy Conrad."

# Chapter Twenty Two

New York Memorial Hospital
York Avenue
New York, N.Y.
May 12, 1945

Susan Mitchell stood at the window overlooking the street below, her arms folded across her chest. In a high backed wooden chair, Kate Murray sat quietly, occasionally checking the large wall clock which read ten minutes after nine.

The door opened and Bill Glenn, wearing a stiffly starched white lab coat walked in carrying a thick folder.

"Good morning, ladies," he said moving slowly behind his large desk and sitting down.

Susan walked over, smiling at Glenn and sat down. "Hello, Bill."

"Sorry I'm late, my last appointment ran over."

Kate said nothing, her expression one of expectancy and concern.

"You look like spring in New York agrees with you, Kate."

She nodded. "I've become very fond of Central Park."

He opened the folder.

"Well, let's go over the results of your last exam. I wanted you to know that I've been in contact with Doctor Gilman in Maryland."

Kate moistened her lips, trying to prepare herself for bad news.

"As they expected, the results varied greatly from patient to patient. If we knew why, that would put us closer to licking this disease. But we don't know why some of the patients responded very well while others showed very little progress," Daniels continued. He opened Kate's folder. "The good news at this point is your results are in the most positive response group." He smiled at Kate. "It seems to be working."

She closed her eyes, the tears already welling up.

"Bill, does that mean she's cured?" Susan asked.

He shook his head. "It's too early to tell anything definitively. Doctor Gilman has laid out an ongoing program of monitoring and we are ready to reinstitute treatment if any signs of the lymphoma return. As long as the disease stays in what we call remission, it's simply a matter of a full exam and lab work up every three months for the first two years, then twice a year after that.

Susan reached across and put her hand on Kate's arm. "Looks like we need to start planning a wedding," she said.


Hank read the flight assignment sheet dated 4 June 1945, noting that Chris was taking two divisions of his squadron on a special photo escort mission. The reconnaissance version of the B-29 had allowed extensive post strike assessment of the damage done by both the high altitude bombers and the new fire raiders that went in much lower to drop their incendiary bombs. Vulnerable to the Jap day fighters, the single aircraft missions always took a heavy escort.

"Corporal Thomas, run over to ops and tell them I'm writing myself into the 327th's recon mission this morning."

Thomas rose, putting a cover over his typewriter. "Yes, sir. Are you taking someone's place?"

"No, have them add me as a fifth aircraft in the first division." Almost a day off, Hank thought, I'll let Chris lead the flight. Most of his flights over the last month, he had been the airborne fighter lead and this was a chance to just enjoy flying for a change, no responsibility for anyone else. Of course by virtue of his rank he was ultimately responsible, but that was a formality and Chris didn't need any help in the air.

He pulled open the drawer and took out the letter he'd received the day before. The medical report that gave Kate a clean bill of health was the best gift anyone could have given him. She'd been so enthusiastic about the time she spent with his mother. They'd become friends and the two of them couldn't wait to plan the wedding whenever a date could be set.

Looking across his desk to the dusty road that led to the airfield, Hank wondered if they would ever wrap up this part of the war. Rumors talked about an invasion in November if the bombing campaign could soften up the home islands. It seemed to Hank that every big city that he'd flown over had been severely damaged. But just like the tenacious Jap soldiers on Iwo that still held out, the Japanese would fight for their homeland with even greater effort. It's going to be a bloodbath, worse than Europe, he decided and their wedding might have to wait for another year or more.

He often imagined how he would enjoy showing her the States. That's what we'll do for a honeymoon, he decided, a tour of all the great cities and sights. Hopefully the luxury Pullmans would be back in service, which would be the best way to show her the vastness of the country.

"You're all set Colonel, the brief is in twenty minutes," Corporal Thomas called, breaking Hank out of his day dream.

Picking up his web belt, Hank buckled it on, adjusting the .45 holster on his hip. "How about running me down to the briefing hut?" he asked Thomas.


The briefing had been professional, short and for the first time in a long time almost enjoyable to Hank. It reminded him of being a wingman again, just fly wing, keep your mouth shut and everything will be fine. The pilot, co-pilot and navigator of the Superfortress nicknamed "Bad Betty" sat quietly as Chris covered the normal fighter brief up to the point of rendezvous, then the navigation route, frequencies and emergency procedures.

The primary purpose of the mission was to photograph two cities which had not been regular targets of the 20th's recent bombing raids. Nagasaki, their first target, was located on the southwestern shore of the southern island of Kyushu. From there, the group would turn northwest and fly about two hundred miles, crossing the inland sea and then photograph the city of Hiroshima, located about 300 miles southwest of Tokyo. The cameras on the modified B-29, official call sign "Lima Baker One Two", would be able to take high altitude, wide area photos for the target analysis experts to plan future missions. The pilot, Captain Kirk Jennison, briefed the flight that the over land portion of the flight would be conducted at 25,000 feet. Weather was expected to be clear and it was a good day for taking pictures.

The closest thing to a milk run since we got here, Hank thought as they left to man up their aircraft. The only thought that nagged at him was the increase in suicide runs by the Jap fighters who would ram the big bombers in a desperate attempt to protect their homeland. Maybe I'd do the same thing if we were defending New York, he thought, but it's still hard to imagine.

"Decided to go with the first team today?" Chris asked as they stepped into the bright sunlight.

"Thought I needed a little break from flying up front," Hank responded, not meaning to sound so serious.

The two fell into step.

"I'll tell ya, my ass has been dragging," Chris said.

"Maybe we're both getting too old for this," Hank said, laughing."

"Speak for yourself, Colonel."

They walked on for a minute.

"Got some great news yesterday."

"What's that?" Chris asked.

Hank had only shared the contents of Kate's letter with Roger. "Kate wrote that all of her tests were good."

"No kidding. That's great. Hell, you ought to be at the club tying one on, not out on one of these six hour ball busters."

"The way I figure it, the more missions I fly, the sooner we win and I get to go home."

They stopped at the wingtip of Hank's Mustang.

"You think we can beat the odds til it's over?" Chris asked, knowing they had lasted longer than most.

Hank stared up at Mt Suribachi, its ugly black slope stark against the blue morning sky.

"If it was the Luftwaffe and we were at Leiston with another year to go, I don't know. But here and now I have to believe we can make it." The two friends looked at each other for a moment, the bond as strong as ever. "Besides, I'm nasty and you're good. There's nothing the Japs have that can top that."

Both of them laughed and Chris turned and walked over to his aircraft. "I'll buy you a cold one when we get back."


As many times as he had rendezvoused with B-29's since his arrival on Iwo, Hank never ceased to be impressed with the sheer size of the big bomber. Bad Betty had taken off before the fighters and was holding at 15,000 feet north of the field. Nine P-51's quickly joined on the Superfort and took their briefed positions as the photo aircraft began her climb to their enroute altitude of 29,000 feet. One weather front lay between them and Japan, but they wouldn't encounter the leading edge for an hour.

Once level at 29,000 feet, the fighters loosened up the formation, allowing each pilot to monitor his own instruments. During the flight, Hank knew Chris would move the fighters around to help break the monotony. Those periodic reshuffles would also allow everyone to move around in their own cockpits, preventing stiff necks and sore butts. Hank was glad he'd passed on a last cup of coffee. He'd never had much luck using the relief tube in the Mustang, particularly while flying formation.

An hour later they could see the dark forward edge of the weather front that the meteorologist on Iwo had briefed. Still early in the day, Hank couldn't see any obvious buildups that might indicate imbedded thunderstorms. He'd learned early in his pilot flying days that no one in their right mind flies into a thunderstorm and he had no desire to violate that rule today.

Hank estimated another thirty minutes until they would penetrate the clouds, which would require all the fighters to pull in tight to the B-29. While flying tight formation to transit the front was the best course of action, it did eat up the fuel from constant throttle corrections. Normally a little extra fuel use wouldn't be a big problem, but today's route was almost 400 miles longer than their normal missions. Just have to be careful, he told himself.

The front turned out to be laced with multiple bands of clouds which took almost forty minutes to fly through. While flying close formation for that long was not fun, the lack of turbulence made it tolerable.

Breaking out into clear sunshine and scattered low level clouds, the aircraft were now forty minutes from Nagasaki. The clear weather would make navigation easier, but it would also give the Jap gunners and fighters a clear shot at the Americans. Hank knew that lone B-29's normally didn't draw much attention from the Japanese air defense system. He hoped today would be no different.

So far the radio had been silent, the flight having gone as briefed. Out of habit Hank checked to make sure he was still dialed into the correct radio channel, then glanced over his instruments, noting all reading were normal. Running like a top, he thought, reflecting how this group of maintenance personnel had taken new aircraft and made them better.

He remembered those first days at Leiston. Flying the old B model Mustang, many of the problems that were now solved had made each day a challenge. Seldom did Hank return from a mission over Europe without five or six maintenance issues, many of which took days to resolve. Now it was unusual to bring one of these new Mustangs back to Iwo, even after six hours airborne and have any problems. The B-Model, with a thinner wing, had the .50 caliber machine guns mounted at an odd angle to fit inside the wing. The problem came when pulling strong g-force while the gun was cycling, often jamming them up. Now the D model's guns were mounted as designed and jammed guns were almost unheard of. A change like that might have taken years in peacetime but happened very quickly in response to feedback from combat operations. Good pilots, good aircraft and an unending support chain from the States convinced Hank that victory over the Japs was only a matter of time. But how long he wondered?

In the distance, the small costal islands off the coast of Japan began to show against the blue green sea. Checking his chart, Hank knew they would start down at any time for 25,000 feet for photographing the target areas. Almost on cue, Bad Betty began a slow descent. The fighters pushed out to each side, taking up their pre-briefed defensive positions. Hank checked his switches, making sure he was ready to quickly jettison tanks, and charge his guns. Perhaps today they would return to the rock with their tanks still attached, the indication to all ground personnel that the fighters had not engaged the enemy.

There was little intelligence on Nagasaki's defenses. The few missions the 20th Air Force had flown against the coastal city had not been significant, nor had much opposition been encountered. Checking his chart, Hank could break out the distinctive coast line that led to the city. Much different from the flat plain surrounding Tokyo and Yokohama, this was much rougher territory complete with hills and valleys. Bad Betty now began a turn to the right, lining up for the photo run. A quick check of his compass told Hank that the B-29's navigator was right on the money from his pre-flighted plan.

Scanning the sky, Hank saw no other air traffic. But he knew that could change in a heartbeat and he kept his scan rapid. Suddenly an ugly black anti-aircraft burst erupted in front of and below the bomber. A second and third were close behind and seemed to be following the formation. There were two methods of using anti-aircraft batteries, barrage fire where all guns fire at the maximum rate to put a wall of fragments in the air for the targets to fly through. The second method was aimed fire. Each gun was individually aimed at the target and corrections added after each shot. It appeared the Nagasaki batteries were using aimed fire. Maybe they didn't have sufficient guns or ammunition to put up sustained barrage fire. Both methods were dangerous and the Japanese had learned a great deal about air defense in the last year.

More bursts appeared, now co-altitude with the bomber, although Hank hadn't seen any too close to do damage so far. While the intensity of the fire was much lower than they were used to up north, these gunners seemed to be more accurate. He'd be happy when they moved out of range. Perhaps that would bring out the Jap fighters, but between flak or fighters, Hank would take the fighters, at least he could fight back against them. Another ugly black burst erupted just aft of the B-29, close enough to do damage, but the big bomber maintained altitude and airspeed. A quick look down told Hank they should be almost done with the Nagasaki photo run and he checked his chart for the heading to Hiroshima.

Three more flak shells burst directly in front of Hank, the concussion shaking his Mustang, rolling the aircraft to the right. That's too damn close, he thought, quickly checking his engine instruments. With relief he saw oil and hydraulic pressure steady and engine temperature unchanged.

Over Germany, now would be the time the Luftwaffe would pounce, having held back while ground gunners engaged the bombers. Since arriving in the Pacific, Hank had not seen any kind of coordination between the anti-aircraft crews and the fighters. But they could always start and better to be vigilant than dead.

But the sky remained clear of enemy aircraft as the small formation continued northeast toward the Inland Sea and Hiroshima. Maybe the bombing was finally affecting the ability of the enemy to launch fighters, Hank thought. The entire Japanese petroleum storage and refining industry had been one of the main B-29 targets. In addition, the U.S. Navy's submarines and minefields had severely cut down the ability to move crude oil from the south to the home islands. Perhaps we're seeing the beginning of the end, Hank hoped, his thoughts briefly turning to Kate.

What would life be like when this was all behind him? It seemed sometimes that he'd been flying combat for his entire life. The time he spent as a young banker working for his father was a distant memory of another world. Could he go back to that? Flying a large wooden desk instead of a high performance fighter? Perhaps, but the Hank Mitchell that would return to the bank would not be the same man who left.

"Ghost Zero Five from lead, I've got a problem."

Chris's radio transmission broke Hank out of his reflections. "What's wrong?" Hank asked.

"Must have taken some flak damage. I'm losing fuel."

The matter of fact tone could not disguise the real danger that now threatened Chris. The nearest friendly field was hundreds of miles away and depending on how much fuel Chris had lost, or would lose, it might mean he couldn't get there.

Hank had thought about this problem before and there were never any good answers. The best solution always included using the most efficient fuel profile and heading for the nearest field right away.

Pushing the throttle forward slightly he moved up underneath Chris's underside to look for damage. His heart sickened when he saw the bright line of avgas streaming back along Chris's fuselage and from his drop tank.

"Chris, pass the lead to Terry. We need to head for the barn right now. You're losing fuel from your fuselage and drop tank."

"Rog." Chris knew what Hank's report meant.

Quickly Hank checked his chart and changed his radio selector from the group common they'd been using and the main strike frequency.

"Lima Baker One Two, this is Ghost Zero Five. We've got flak damage and need to divert two aircraft at this time. Request a divert heading."

"Roger, stand by."

The two Mustangs dropped below the B-29 and began a turn to the east. Hank was now on Chris's right wing.

"Estimate one five zero," Hank called on the group common.

"Roger, that's about what I thought," Chris replied.

"Ghost Zero Five, one four five magnetic, I say again one four five magnetic."

"Roger, thanks."

"Good luck," came the final transmission from Bad Betty as the formation continued northeast toward Hiroshima.


Lieutenant Dick Nyhof rubbed his eyes then put the sunglasses back on, adjusting his New York Yankees baseball hat. Dumbo Two Three had been airborne for over two hours and Nyhof estimated they were 180 miles northwest of Iwo Jima. The big PBY-5A was on the standard air sea rescue patrol the Navy conducted every day from Iwo. Nyhof had originally wanted to be a fighter pilot. Now the young aviator felt he had the best job in the Navy. He and his crew had rescued a total of thirty eight aircrew over the last two months, saving them from almost certain death. The Catalina's ability to conduct open ocean landings had allowed the Navy to provide a chance for survival to aircrews that couldn't make it back to Iwo Jima after suffering damage over Japan. Combining surface ships, submarines and the PBY's, the Navy had created a safety net over the vast Pacific Ocean.

"Here's the last of the coffee," Chief Petty Officer Stan Morales said. Kneeling between Nyhof and his co-pilot Bill Hannan, the PBY's crew chief held two white china coffee mugs.

"We need to find another big thermos. Maybe we can cumshaw one from the Air Corp guys next time one of them diverts into Iwo."

The two pilots carefully took the mugs from Morales and set them on the side consoles.

"Anything going on?" The crew chief asked.

Nyhof shook his head.

"A little early anyway. There's a large strike coming back from north of Tokyo. But the lead aircraft won't be in our area for at least another hour."

"Rog," Morales said and headed back aft.

For twenty minutes the big seaplane continued north, then turned almost directly east. This leg of their flight would complete one side of a box which was centered on an imaginary point in the water. Given the code name "Chicago," it allowed aircrews to have a reference they could use to send their approximate position to other aircraft. In the world of search and rescue this ability to coordinate locations without giving your real world location was very critical, especially if there were enemy forces in the area. If an aircraft declared an emergency, Dick Nyhof could tell anyone monitoring the frequency that a Navy PBY was currently 35 miles north east of Chicago, ready to provide assistance.

"Hey, Dick. We might have a customer," navigator Larry Beiman called over the intercom.

"What you got, Beemer?"

"Sounds like a couple of Mustangs headed for Iwo with one low on gas. One of our picket destroyers is relaying their position. Hang on a minute."

The twin radial engines of the PBY continued to drone as the aircraft made its way east. In the cockpit, Nyhof and Hannan could only wait for further info.

"They're a long way from Iwo. I make their current posit about two hundred and eighty miles bearing 305 magnetic," Beiman passed from below where he was hunched over his nav plot.

"They're still making their way toward Iwo?" Nyhof asked.

"That's what it sounds like," Beiman said. "The frequency is a little garbled. If I heard them right, one of the Mustangs is about out of gas."

"Shit," Hannan said. At max speed, the PBY could meet the fighters in about an hour and a half if the single seater didn't go in the drink.

"Well, that's what they pay us for," Nyhof said, banking the PBY to the right, allowing the compass to track right to 305 degrees. "Let's hope he can stay airborne for a while."


Both Mustangs were dialed into the same frequency, but neither Chris nor Hank had said anything in the last fifteen minutes. What was there to say? After running fuel consumption numbers and checking the chart, it looked like Chris would run out of fuel about 400 miles from Iwo Jima. They'd been able to contact one of the long range radar picket destroyers that covered this part of the ocean and found out a Navy PBY was the closest search and rescue unit to their position. Unfortunately the seaplane was over two hundred miles away.

Expecting to run out of fuel within the next twenty minutes, Chris had descended to 10,000 feet, not wanting to bail out any higher. He and Hank discussed jettisoning the canopy and slowing to 150 knots to make a controlled bail out. Once everything had been discussed, there wasn't anything else to say. Chris could only hope the PBY had a good heading and if they were lucky, the radar picket destroyer might be able to provide vectors if he could see all aircraft on radar. Finding one man in a raft in the ocean was extremely difficult without some reference.

"How's your fuel, Hank?" Chris said, breaking the silence. He knew that his friend was now off the optimum fuel profile for return to Iwo, burning precious fuel by sticking with Chris.

"I'm doing fine," Hank said, knowing that he was right on the edge. If he went to his max range profile right now, he might make Iwo. But today's winds were out of the east at all altitudes, which would probably mean he was going swimming too. His thoughts flashed back to that day in the English Channel. He never wanted to be in that situation again, he also knew that if he left now, the chance that PBY would find Chris was slim at best.

Hank pulled out his large scale chart of the area. Doing a quick computation in his head, he saw a chance. With one of the very strong high altitude winds which sometimes hit 150 knots, he could make Okinawa. There were several air bases where he could land, fuel up and return to Iwo tomorrow. He knew it was a chance, but his only other choice was to bail out and join Chris. Hank wasn't willing to write off a brand new P-51 that easily.

The distance between the Mustangs and PBY was now closing at almost 300 miles per hour. On the radar screen aboard the U.S.S. Wadsworth (DD-516), the air controller had a constant paint of Dumbo Two Three. While he didn't have the Air Corps Mustangs yet, he could now hear them talking to each other.

"Dumbo, Dumbo, this is Ghost Zero Five, Ghost Zero One is bailing out, I say again Ghost Zero One is bailing out."

Hank had seen the canopy jettison clear of Chris's aircraft and knew it was time. He watched Chris twist in the cockpit and suddenly pull himself out into the airstream, falling behind the right wing. Immediately Hank pulled the Mustang to the right, looking for Chris's open chute. Before he'd turned thirty degrees, he could see the white canopy against the blue green ocean. A chill went through Hank, history repeated.

"Estimating your position in twenty minutes, Ghost. Request you remain to mark the position if able, over."

Hank knew the answer before he keyed the radio. "Wilco."

Descending to 4000 feet Hank thought the descent was taking a long time, but knew Chris was busy getting ready to go in the water. The small one man raft was in the survival pack in his seat and Chris was trying to get it out and inflated. Almost on cue the bright yellow raft opened underneath Chris and now swung on a lanyard in the wind. Okay buddy, now just get in the raft and we can wrap this up.

Ten minutes later Chris floated in his raft as Hank flew a circle around his position.

"Ghost, this is Dumbo, give me a long count."

Hank keyed his radio and began to count slowly hoping that in the PBY's cockpit, their radio direction finder needle was locking up on his signal.

""We've got you, Ghost.  Dumbo is at 6,000, letting down."

Hank kept watching the sky, hoping they could connect quickly.  He looked down at his fuel and knew it was going to be very close.  Then he saw the big blue PBY, perhaps five miles from him.

"Dumbo, tallyho.  Raft is just left of your nose, estimating four miles."

"We've got him, Ghost, you're cleared to detach," came the transmission from the PBY which had just crossed over Chris's raft and turned to set up a landing.

"Thanks, Dumbo, the first bottle's on me."  Hank turned toward Okinawa and pushed the throttle forward, starting his climb.  Now he had his own battle to fight.

# Chapter Twenty Three

New York City
June 11, 1945

While very different from London, Kate knew she could learn to love this city. She had watched spring unfold in Central Park and as her strength increased, her walks extended to almost every corner of the park. Susan Mitchell kept the days filled with exploring the city and their friendship had grown stronger each day. She continued to see Doctor Glenn, and the reports had remained positive. But the highlights of her days were Hank's letters. His inability to talk about what he was doing made the content that much more endearing. He talked about their past, the things he wanted to show her in New York and where they would go on their honeymoon. The war's uncertainty put any specific plans on hold. Hank couldn't offer any idea of when he might return from overseas.

"Can I get you some tea?" Susan asked.

Kate had been reading the latest novel by F. van Wyck Mason which she'd found at the closest branch of the New York Public Library. The front sitting room had become her favorite reading place.

"Yes, thanks, although I can do it."

"Nonsense, I'm up and I'm getting myself one. I'll just be a minute."

Kate heard the door open and Tyler Mitchell entered carrying a large black briefcase.

"Hello, young lady. How are you today?" He smiled and set his briefcase down next to the couch and sat down opposite Kate.

"Quite well, actually. Susan and I were going to have some tea. Can I get you some?"

He laughed and got up. "I think in the battle between a cup of tea or a martini, the long stemmed glass with the olive will win out." Tyler walked over behind the bar and began to get out the ingredients for his afternoon cocktail.

The doorbell rang. From down the hallway, Dexter appeared to answer it.

The large man reappeared at the doorway. "Sir, it is Western Union for you. Your signature is required."

Tyler walked past Kate, who had returned to her reading.

A moment later, she looked up and knew something was terribly wrong. Tyler stood with a Western Union telegram in his right hand, just as Susan came down the hall carrying a small tray holding two cups.

"Tyler, what's wrong?" she asked, seeing the look on her husband's face.

For a moment her husband said nothing, appearing almost confused. He took two steps to his wife and reached out for her arm. "Hank is missing."

Kate shivered as if a cold wind had blown over her bringing with it a terrible reality. Missing, what did that mean?

Tyler and Susan sat down side by side on the couch as he read the message slowly, "The Department of the Army regrets to inform you that your son, Lieutenant Colonel Henry Tyler Mitchell, III is missing in action and presumed dead. Details of his loss are still classified, but rest assured the Secretary of the Army will contact you if there is any change in status. At the time of his loss, he was engaged in active combat operations in the Western Pacific as a member of the 20th Air Force."

"I've got to find out what happened," Tyler said, breaking the silence.

"My, God," Susan said quietly and buried her head in her hands.

Kate looked to Tyler, who walked over and put his hand on her shoulder. "I'll find out, don't worry.

Private Kaito Ugaki slid the metal plate aside and peered into the small jail cell. Curled up on the thin cotton mat, the American flier appeared to be asleep. Ugaki was one of eighteen Japanese Army soldiers who stood guard in the two cell blocks which adjoined the Urakami Prison in the center of Nagasaki. The cells were in an annex of the main building which housed the regional headquarters of the Kempetai, the Japanese Military Police.

When the prisoner had arrived, the young soldier was curious about the big American, having only seen Korean or Chinese prisoners and the occasional Japanese civilian during his two years as a guard. Seeing his own countrymen under arrest bothered Ugaki, however any Japanese civilian who demonstrated a "defeatist" attitude was liable for detention and questioning by the secret police. In his time as a guard, he had seen few prisoners of this division of the Kempetai leave the cell block alive.

Ugaki thought it strange the American had not been sent to the prisoner of war camp outside the city. However, according to Ugaki's sergeant, this prisoner was to have "special handling." Not only a senior officer, this pilot had been captured very recently and must have information that would help defend the home islands during this time of great threat. For that reason they had placed Mitchell in the lower tier that was seldom used. His cell was the only one occupied in the dark, dank section of the cell block.

Sliding the plate back in place, Ugaki returned to the small desk reserved for the duty guard. He noted the prisoner was secure and all conditions appeared normal. Leafing back in the book he noted the date the tall American with the terrible scars on his face had first arrived in the cellblock, 12 June, almost nine weeks ago. He had often wondered why this man had not been sent to Tokyo to the central headquarters. Surely they had the best interrogators in Tokyo. He did know that the most senior Kempetai officer in the district, Colonel Kitano had taken a special interest in this particular prisoner. Perhaps the Colonel was trying to gain favor by extracting crucial information from the American. Whatever the reason, the senior interrogator, Sergeant Major Nagata visited the man's cell every day, often late at night, always accompanied by the interpreter, Sergeant Ozuwa and Corporal Yamada. The men would spend at least an hour per session. Ugaki could hear what was happening as the Sergeant Major and Yamada tried to extract information from the American.

He'd seen Nagata in action on several occasions and he knew the man enjoyed inflicting pain. Using manila rope and short wooden sticks, the Sergeant Major could produce intense pain on a prisoner's joints, cut off circulation and even break bones. Corporal Yamada, a huge man from the northern island, provided the muscle to inflict the pain under close supervision of the Sergeant Major. While Ugaki knew his duty and would gladly die for the Emperor, the constant torture of the American had begun to disturb him. Kaito Ugaki wondered if perhaps he lacked the true warrior spirit. But he could never share those thoughts with anyone, he could only do his duty.

Hank Mitchell laid on his left side, curled up with his hands drawn close to his body. Remaining completely still helped to diminish the pain he felt from the constant torture. It frightened him when he lost track of the days, afraid he was losing his mind. Fighting back through an ongoing nightmare of violence and lack of food, he tried with all his will to focus on getting through each day.

In the last week, Hank had realized that he would probably never leave this building alive. But somehow that helped him gain strength in his determination not to give in to the bastards. And they were bastards. His main antagonist stood over six feet tall, and seemed to enjoy the pain he caused Hank. His helper was a thug who did whatever the older man ordered. The interpreter always stood to the side, never taking part in the actual abuse.

He thought back to the first Japs he'd seen, fishermen who spotted his raft two days after he bailed out of the Mustang. The small group of scruffy men who manned the 40 foot wooden fishing boat hadn't been friendly, but neither had they been abusive. Severely dehydrated from his time in the open raft, they allowed him food and water that probably saved his life. No one in the fishing boat's crew spoke English and the only word he recognized when they tried to communicate was 'Nagasaki.'

Five days after his rescue, Hank saw land to the northeast. Within two hours a Japanese Navy patrol boat had pulled alongside. The sailors, expecting only to conduct a routine inspection, became very excited when they found an American pilot aboard the boat. Hank's treatment immediately took a turn for the worse. Dragged aboard the patrol boat, he was bound hand and foot with manila rope and shoved into a small compartment where the extra lines and fenders were stored.

Several hours later, the diesel engine had shut down and Hank had been pulled roughly on deck. Around him he recognized the busy port of Nagasaki, ringed by high hills. While he had only seen target mosaics, the distinct pattern of the bay and peninsula confirmed it was Nagasaki. Despite the presence of several industrial sites, Hank knew the city had been spared any significant air raids.

The patrol boat crew had turned Hank over to a detachment of army guards waiting on the pier. Pulled roughly onto the pier, he was immediately blindfolded and pushed into the rear seat of an old sedan. That quick view of the city had been the last thing Hank had seen of the outside world. All interrogations and the accompanying beatings had taken place within the confines of the cell block. He couldn't remember hearing another prisoner and he'd certainly not seen anyone except his Japanese captors. While Hank had considered what it might be like to be a prisoner, he had never imagined anything like this.

A bucket in the corner served as his privy, but when they allowed him to empty it, he only walked to the end of the corridor where he dumped it into a larger bucket on a rope from the level above. His meals came sporadically and always consisted of rice and some mixture of vegetables with the occasional piece of gristly meat. He made himself eat every bit of food, as disgusting as the taste or smell might be. Over time he learned to live with the hunger pains as his body adjusted to the lack of food.

Hank heard noise outside in the corridor. Despite his manacled hands, he pushed up from the thin pad and sat back against the concrete wall. The metal bar that served to lock the cell slid from the closed position, the grating sound making Hank's stomach turn queasy knowing what was about to happen. He now knew they could force him to talk. Why did he ever think a person could resist torture? Name, rank and serial number – what a joke. When the enemy has all the time and power, they will break you. It's just a matter of time. The first time Hank gave up a piece of information he felt like a failure. The information meant nothing from an intelligence standpoint but he had let them break him. In his cell after that session he vowed that he would fight back. They might break him, but he'd rebound and fight back each time. It gave him a reason to keep fighting.

The cell door swung open and Sergeant Major Nagata stepped in, a short wooden bat in his right hand. The expression on the big man's face was totally impassive. His eyes quickly examined the cell as he moved out of the way for Yamada. The Corporal walked over to Hank, grabbing him by his ripped shirt and pulling him to his feet.

Not trying to help his assailant, Hank stood on his own only after the man pushed him against the wall. The feeling of helplessness was overwhelming. Without any way to defend himself, he stood waiting for Nagata's instructions.

"Put his arms behind his back and make it tight," Nagata said quietly to the Corporal.

The small interpreter, Sergeant Ozuwa, stepped into the cell and partially closed the door as Yamada spun Hank around and looped a rope around his elbow. Running the other end of the rope around Hank's back and elbow, he now had Hank's hands in the manacles pulled hard against his stomach. Now Yamada cinched the rope tight and inserted a small stick into the loop. As he twisted the stick, taking up slack in the rope, Hank's elbows were slowly and painfully pulled back until they almost touched behind his back.

Nagata began to speak as Yamada turned Hank around to face the Sergeant Major.

"Now that you are comfortable, we will continue our talk," Ozuwa translated.

The pain shot through Hank's shoulders, sending searing sharp jabs down his arms. It felt as though they were pulling his arms from their sockets and his breath came in short labored gasps.

The door to the cell opened, and Corporal Ugaki carried a small chair to Nagata, setting it down on the concrete. He glanced quickly at the American, seeing the pain on his face.

Sweat ran down the prisoner's cheeks, the summer heat penetrating into the dark cellblock.

"Get out," Nagata said.

Bowing quickly, Ugaki backed out of the cell. But not before his eyes met those of the flier.

Sitting back at the desk, Ugaki heard the sharp sounds as the interrogation continued. He was an educated man and felt he knew what was right and what was wrong. How could Nagata keep up this punishment day after day, making sure that the prisoner was injured, but would survive long enough to answer his questions? The honorable thing would be to execute the man and allow him some self respect, not keep him like an animal in a cage. But at the same time Ugaki dreaded the possibility that they would decide the prisoner had no more use to them. Unknown to any of his friends in the barracks Private Ugaki had gotten to know Mitchell. The young man had known that unnecessary contact between guards and the prisoners was forbidden. But over the weeks, Ugaki's curiosity about the American had prompted him to visit the man during his guard shifts.

Unlike most Japanese Army conscripts, Kaito Ugaki was not only a Christian, but he had spent his elementary and secondary school years at a Christian missionary school in Akita Prefecture. Two years at the university had broadened his view of the world and he had never accepted the military's view of the world outside Japan. His knowledge of English was something he kept to himself, not wanting to be sent to the front as an interpreter. Now he found himself able to talk to the prisoner. The more he talked with the man, the more his faith in the triumph of Japan wavered.

He remembered the first time he spoke English to Mitchell. It was late one night two weeks after he had arrived at the prison. Rather than looking through the viewing slot during the prisoner count, he opened the door and stepped into the cell. Nagata's interrogation sessions had commenced the first night of Mitchell's arrival and the pilot showed the effects of daily torture. Ugaki could see ugly bruises on Mitchell's arms and face.

"Your name is Mitchell," he said.

He watched the prisoner nod, his eyes watching Ugaki warily.

"I have been watching you."

238

While the daily food and energy shortages were a reality to all Japanese, they had been told that the sacrifices were needed to provide the armed forces with the material to finish the war against the Americans. A constant stream of news reports had described the destruction of the American fleet off the Philippines and a complete failure of the landings by MacArthur. But at the same time American bombers continued to wreak devastation to Japan's cities. If Japan was truly winning, how could that be happening? What was the truth?

"Why does your country continue in this futile war? With your fleet destroyed and your army defeated in the Philippines, you have lost the war."

"Unless something has happened in the last two weeks, it was your fleet that was destroyed at Leyte Gulf. MacArthur took Manila in March."

"But that can't be true."

"We've also taken Okinawa. But I guess no one has told you that either?"

Ugaki found it difficult to not believe Mitchell and his visits became more regular. That had been almost two months ago. Now he felt that he knew the tall American. The visits by Nagata disturbed him more and more each day.

An hour later the three Japanese emerged from the cell. Nagata walked past Ugaki without a glance.

"Clean him up. And clean up my tools," Yamada said as he followed the Sergeant Major.

"Yes, Corporal," Ugaki replied.

The small interpreter said nothing as he followed the other two.


He found Mitchell lying on his side, the ropes still twisted tight. His nose told him immediately why they had left. Mitchell had voided his bowels and lay in his own filth. Ugaki thought Mitchell must be unconscious. A deep breath followed by a low groan came from the American as Ugaki unwound the cords.

Hank's shoulders painfully returned to their normal position. He felt the last cord slip from around his arms, which felt dead and lifeless.

Ugaki rolled Hank onto his back, looking down to see if his eyes were open.

"Mitchell, they will let you clean yourself. Do you think you can stand up?"

"Yeah," Hank said slowly, disgusted with his own condition.

"I will take you to the washroom. It is late, so we have time."

The Corporal reached down and unlocked the hand manacles.

"Here," Ugaki said, helping Hank to stand.

"Thanks," he said softly. Still in pain and confused after Nagata's beating, he staggered slightly. Ugaki grabbed Hank's shoulders and helped him out the door. Concentrating on each step, he slowly made his way to the end of the corridor and into the small washroom.

Hank slowly stripped down and threw his shirt and pants in a bucket provided by Ugaki. Standing in front of a porcelain basin, he took the bar of soap and began to wash his chest gingerly. As he scrubbed away the dirt and filth, he began to feel more in control. After drying with a rough cloth, he went to work washing his soiled clothes. Squatting on the floor, he worked the soap and tepid water through his shirt and pants for fifteen minutes. As he worked, he wondered how long he could take this punishment. While he never had given the Japs anything of importance, they must know any information he might give them was no longer relevant. Why did they keep at him? The pains from the sessions now stayed with him constantly and his strength was ebbing away.

Hank had always thought he would die quickly in the air. Now the reality was he had begun to die slowly from beatings and lack of nutrition. All he could do was fight on as long as he could. He knew he would never regret sticking with Chris, it was what he had to do. But never seeing Kate again was going to be a high price to pay. Shit, what a war, he thought, just let me make it through tomorrow.

"It is time to go back," Ugaki said quietly.

Hank turned and looked into the man's eyes, but said nothing.

Ambassador John Winant stood as Kate was shown into his office by Alice Tinsley. A call from Tyler Mitchell alerted him that she was returning to England and wanted to thank him for his part in getting her to New York.

He came around the desk and offered his hand. "Miss Murray, it is indeed a pleasure to finally meet you. Please have a seat."

Kate started hesitantly, although she had practiced what she wanted to say. "Thank you for seeing me. I know you're very busy."

He examined her face as she talked. Her honest features seemed to carry a sadness, a quiet pain. It was her eyes that told the story.

"I'm glad Tyler called. I wanted to meet you before you left for New York but Hank had you on quite the schedule."

At the sound of his name, Winant saw a flash of pain.

He continued, "Tyler tells me that the treatment has gone very well."

Kate nodded. "I'm a very lucky person, Mr. Ambassador." She paused. "Hank....Hank gave me a new chance at life. Without everything he did, things likely would have turned out much differently."

She looked down at her lap, trying to maintain her composure.

"And if you hadn't helped us, I know I could never have received the treatment. For that I wanted to thank you."

The older man said nothing for a long moment. She looked up and their eyes met.

"Nothing can ever take away the hurt of losing Hank. Time will dull it, but it will always be there." He paused, mulling over his words. "This has been a terrible war and you know it better than most. I don't know how we'll ever make any sense of it. But I do know that you two helped each other through very difficult times and fell in love. Remember those good things."

Tears appeared in Kate's eyes and she reached in her purse for a handkerchief. "I told myself I wouldn't cry," she said, smiling slightly.

"I've always found that tears work wonders helping us get past the unbearable times."

"I'll be fine. At least that's what I've been telling myself ever since I left New York. Once I'm back home maybe this will all seem like a dream."

"Are you going to work in the hospital again?" he asked.

"That was my intention. I'm sure they will have plenty of work helping the wounded coming home from overseas."

The ambassador thought of the upcoming invasion of Japan and he shuddered. As bad as the butcher's bill had been so far, he knew the loss of life, both military and civilian, would be staggering. While the British Empire had been bled dry over the last six years, he knew there would be British troops in the invasion force. The pain and agony of Singapore had not been forgotten and now it was time for retribution.

"Yes, I'm afraid you're right." He got up and walked over to the window, the blue summer sky reminding him of that summer of 1940 when the European war was very much in doubt. Thank goodness we've whipped the Nazi's, he thought. "If you don't mind, I'll send a cable to Tyler and Susan to let them know you arrived safe and sound."

Kate smiled. "Thank you. Please say that I miss them both terribly." She remembered the tearful good bye when she boarded one of the fast liners returning to England to load aboard another group of soldiers coming home to be demobilized. While they both asked her to stay with them, Kate's final decision to go home to help her father had been respected. The time she had spent with the Mitchell's had been some of the best memories of her life as she and Susan became close friends and confidents. Not having a mother as she grew up made their relationship even more special. She had to promise a return visit to see them. She wanted to remain in touch with them. It might help all of them deal with the loss of Hank. Something had to. Something had to help her lose this feeling of emptiness.

"Can I provide a car to take you to East Grinstead?"

She really was going home.

# Chapter Twenty Four

Kempetai Headquarters
Urakami, Prison
Nagasaki, Japan
August 9, 1945

Lieutenant Colonel Hank Mitchell lay on his small mat, his clothes still damp from their hasty wash job the previous evening. He thought it was funny how your priorities change and how he actually considered himself fortunate. Not only was he cleaner than he'd been in weeks, but the friendly guard, Private Ugaki had given him a double serving of rice porridge this morning. The inevitable visit by Nagata was something he had forced to the back of his mind.

In the next building, his tormentor Sergeant Major Nagata stood at rigid attention in front of Colonel Isoruko Kitano. Slowly reading from a notebook, the senior officer frowned.

"So you believe there is nothing more of substance we can learn from our prisoner?" he asked, his eyes hard on his subordinate.

Nagata bowed as he replied, "No, sir."

Kitano stood and walked to his window that looked out across the district of Urakami. "This prisoner is of no further use to the Kempetai. I would prefer that our failure to extract any significant information not become known. Do I make myself clear?"

"Yes, sir."  Nagata had taken care of dispatching prisoners on many occasions, but never an American.

The Colonel turned to face Nagata. "Do not delay."

Bowing quickly, the big man backed out of Kitano's office.  Standing in the corridor he looked at his watch noting it was a little before 11:00.  He had already decided that he would use a single shot to the head after bringing the prisoner to the washroom.  He preferred executions in the shower area where the cleanup was much quicker.  Better to be done with it now so he could enjoy his lunch, he thought.  Turning to the window, he tried to remember where Corporal Yamada was working this morning, knowing that he would need the big soldier to help with the execution.

Nagata's thoughts were interrupted by a blinding white light, brighter than a thousand suns.  Closing his eyes, the Sergeant Major's hand came up in a reflex action to shield his vision.  An instant later the imploding glass window shredded the upper part of Nagata's face and torso, throwing him against the wall with enough force to break his back.  Lying on his side, consciousness slipping away, Nagata's last thoughts were of Yamada as a searing wave of heat and blast washed over him.

Dust filled the air of Hank's cell, only moments after a terrible roar had engulfed him.  Thrown against the wall, he rolled onto his stomach and rose up on one knee.  His ears rang and he was very unsteady.  His only thought was some kind of explosion or aerial bomb had hit the cell block.  Knowing his cell was below ground, he wondered if he could be under debris and trapped if the building had collapsed.  Moving to the door he put his ear against the steel door, but he could hear nothing.  The cell block's generator was silent.  Something was wrong.

Kaito Ugaki lay sprawled on the floor, his senses overwhelmed.  His ears roared like the ocean and he couldn't focus his eyes when he slowly opened them.  He remembered the brilliant white light that penetrated the cellblock corridor and the tremendous blast that tore much of the tile roof off the cellblock, exposing the support beams.  A wave of searing heat had accompanied the blast, setting fire to anything wood or paper.  He coughed, his lungs rejecting the dust and smoke that now lay over the skeleton of the cellblock.  Struggling to his feet he staggered to the large steel door at the entrance.  It was off its hinges and he pulled hard to move it several inches.

The young soldier stared with disbelief at the scene outside the door. The main Kempetai admin building had been reduced to a jumble of wreckage, most of which now burned brightly. As he looked up his heart pounded to see the awful dark swirling clouds that were tinged in colors of red and orange. Truly this is the end of the world, he thought. What do I do? He slumped to his knees and lay against the masonry wall. Staring into the smoke and dust, Ugaki realized the two prisoners on the upper level were calling from behind the cell doors. Both were local citizens who had been denounced for making anti war comments. He rose shakily, noting that there was a fine white dust everywhere which added to the unreality. He reached the first cell and slid the lock open.

"What happened? What is wrong?" Mr. Sentaki asked.

Ugaki shook his head. "I don't ...." Then it came to him, this must be the same attack that was made on Hiroshima two days ago. One of the men in his detachment had been on leave, and brought word back yesterday of the attack. Although the press had been very vague about what happened, his friend had heard from some of the people who fled the outskirts of the city. According to them, the entire city was destroyed. Not from incendiary bombs but in one massive explosion. He ignored Sentaki and moved to the next cell.

"Come out," he ordered when he pulled the door open.

An older man, a Mr. Fukome bowed as he stood in the door, awaiting instructions.

"Fukome, Fukome," Sentaki said grabbing the man by his arm.

The older man looked bewildered and the two stood watching Ugaki.

"Go home," he said. They were all going to die anyway, just like Hiroshima. What difference did it make?

The two men's eyes opened in surprise.

"Go, get out of here."

Confused and scared, the two men looked at each other and then moved for the door.

Ugaki picked up the overturned chair near the guard desk and sat down heavily. Lying in a pile of debris on the floor he saw the guard's logbook. He laughed at the absurdity. Perhaps he should note the end of the world for the official record. Somehow it all seemed so futile. Years of sacrifice by our people, the entire energy of Japan directed at what we were told was a weak coalition of enemies and now they are able to destroy our cities one by one. It is the end of our civilization. Two thousand years of unbroken history and now he was watching the end.

The fire in the roof's support beams was burning fiercely. It was only a matter of time before the remaining roof collapsed. He was tired and despite the smoke, which now made him cough, Kaito debated whether to just sit on his chair and wait for the end. It was the honorable thing to do.

He remembered the American. They have done this to my country and my people. Anger flared briefly, his hand reaching down to the pistol on his leather belt. But this man didn't do this, he thought. He remembered their conversations. This man Mitchell was a brave and proud man who was doing his duty for his country. And Ugaki knew he couldn't kill another person. A burning beam broke free from the overhead structure jolting him out of his thoughts.

The smell of smoke was strong in Hank's cell. The first threads of panic were beginning to grip him. Trapped in his cell as the structure burned around him brought back those terrible moments over the channel when he first felt the flames. After the burns, he knew he would rather die in one swift hail of bullets or striking the ground with a parachute failure than burn again. After everything else, not this.

A dull scrape came from the other side of the door and quickly it slid open to reveal Private Ugaki standing in the door like a ghost. His entire body was covered by a fine dusting of white powder. The look on his face told Hank that this was a man who had been shaken to his core.

"What happened?" Hank asked, expecting the guard to enter the cell.

"We must leave," Kaito said, his voice as urgent as his eyes were scared.

Without looking back, Hank followed Ugaki who had turned toward the steep steps, which led up to the ground floor. At the top of the stairs, Hank looked around with shock to see that most everything wooden had begun to burn.

"This way," Kaito said, not bothering to look back. He squeezed through the large door to the cell block which remained off its hinges, but open enough for a man to squeeze through.

Hank surveyed the landscape, his mind desperately trying to comprehend the scene in front of him. He stumbled over broken bricks and wooden beams which littered the courtyard. Above them the clouds boiled like a witch's cauldron. The sky had an ugly orange tinge to it, adding to the spectacle of fires burning as far as a person could see.

The two men scrambled over a low brick wall to find a man and woman on the ground. Remnants of burned clothing barely covered their singed bodies. Hank and Kaito continued on, passing a small river where bodies of men, women and children floated in the dark water. Around them survivors wandered aimlessly through the remains of the city, their faces showing a state of disbelief or shock. Hank saw more evidence of the terrible fire, people with large burned areas on their bodies, in many cases most of their clothing had been burned off. No one seemed to be doing anything to help. Nowhere did he see fireman or police responding to the disaster. What could have possibly happened here?

Kaito finally stopped in the courtyard of a large building. Most of the structure had been leveled, but the courtyard remained clear of debris. He and Hank sat down on a low masonry wall that ran next to the road, both of them breathing hard from their forced walk. He looked at his companion, the white dust in Ugaki's hair giving him a ghostly appearance. The young soldier said nothing but stared out at the destruction which stretched as far as they could see.

"What happened?" Hank asked.

Kaito began speaking without looking at Hank. "I think this is the same attack that happened two days ago in Hiroshima."

"What?"

"We heard that a single bomb destroyed Hiroshima in one blinding flash. It seemed impossible to believe. But now it seems we are the second."

A single bomb? Hank had heard nothing about this. Some kind of secret weapon? And why only on Japan, why not on Germany? Nothing made sense. But it really didn't matter now, he had to survive. What would become of him, a single American alone in a devastated city, at the mercy of people who had just been viciously attacked? This quiet Japanese Private might be his only chance to live through this.

"What do you think we should do?" Hank asked.

"My friend Mr. Kobayashi lives in this direction, we will go there. He will know what to do."

Two hours later the men left the main road and made their way up a winding road that climbed away from the low valley. The houses became fewer and finding their way in the darkness became a challenge. Kaito told Hank he spent much of his off duty time with the elderly man who was a friend of his father's family. In single file they negotiated the last winding steps to a small wooden house which sat by itself behind a wooden fence.

Kaito pulled the chime next to the door and they stood quietly. Behind the opaque paper sliding wall they saw a light approach and the panel slid open.

A candle appeared first, illuminating a small gray haired man who looked with curiosity at Hank before recognizing Kaito.

"Kaito, what has happened? I saw the light and the cloud this morning and knew it must be another attack as on Hiroshima. Thank the Lord you are alright."

"Sir, I couldn't think of anywhere else to go. Everything in the city is destroyed. I brought an American with me. The prison has been destroyed and we couldn't stay there."

The man looked at Hank, his eyes showing only curiosity.

"Please, sir, tell me what you think we should do?" Kaito made a short bow with his head.

"You shall come in while we decide the most prudent course of action," he said quietly. "I am thankful it is dark, I wouldn't want my neighbors to know there is an American behind my walls."

After a quick meal of noodles and vegetables, the men decided that sleep was their greatest need. Both men felt completely exhausted by the events of the day. Hank and Kaito lay down in a small room that was almost devoid of furniture. Two tatami mats covered most of the floor space, the only piece of furniture a low table in the corner.

Hank, tired as he was, couldn't sleep. Instead he continued to try and understand what he had seen today. He also thought of the young Japanese man who lay only inches away. Why had he taken it upon himself to look out for an American, one of the people who had destroyed Nagasaki? There had always been a difference between this man and the rest of the Kempetai guards. Hank knew it was natural to consider every Japanese or German as evil and an enemy of his country. He'd never met any Germans while he was in Europe. They were a faceless enemy and that had been fine with Hank. But now to see two extremes of behavior from that bastard Nagata to Kaito and Mr. Kobayashi made Hank reconsider what he had accepted for years as truth.

Rolling on to his left side, Hank sighed, the emotion of the day keeping sleep from him.

"I cannot sleep tonight," Kaito said in the darkness.

"I can't either," Hank replied, turning on his back.

"Do you think the war will end now?"

He hadn't thought that through yet, and honestly told Kaito, "I don't know. But after today, I don't see how the war can continue." The invasion might not even be needed. Perhaps they had seen the beginning of the end.

"Not if there is to be a Japan in the future."

Although Hank would always hate what Japan had done to his country, he did not hate this man. Maybe that's how peace does begin, Hank thought, one person at a time.


"It's over, Kate. Have you heard?"

Duncan Frazier stood at the door to the medical records section, his white lab coat open at the front, a clipboard in his hand.

Kate Murray turned from the small pile of records she had been filing in the storage area.

"Sorry, no, I've been here all morning. What's over?"

He smiled. "The war, the whole lousy bloody war. The Japs announced they will surrender."

Finally, she thought, but not in time for Hank. The pain of his loss never really left her. She hoped working hard and taking care of her Dad might dull the hurt. But she was wrong. Maybe as time passed she could move away from him. But now the pain would stay with her.

"That's marvelous, of course. Maybe now we can get back on with life."

Duncan knew of her loss and said, "That's all any of us can do, Kate."

Now working full time in the hospital administration office, Kate turned back to the records. Duncan Frazier had been instrumental in getting her this position and had been very supportive since she returned from New York. Her thoughts returned to the letters she had received from Chris and Roger. She knew they were trying to offer consolation and sympathy as they both described Hank's time on Iwo Jima and the last mission. His leadership and bravery had made a real difference to the men around him. Chris told her that many pilots were still alive because of Hank. For one instant she had been angry at Hank for sacrificing himself to save Chris and then regretted it. It was what he would have done, just like Chris staying with Hank over the Channel. Roger's letter had echoed Chris's and she could sense how deeply Hank's loss had affected him. Good men, trapped in a world of honor and friendship, they had all done what they had to do. That didn't make it any easier for her to deal with the loss of Hank. She picked up a file and tried to read through her tears.


Tomatsu Kobayashi was a member of the local Catholic community, which was one of the largest in Japan. Only luck placed him at his home which was over six miles from the point of detonation. Normally he would have been at the Urakami Cathedral where he worked as a volunteer in the rectory.

Devastated by the deaths of so many of his friends, the old man looked at Hank the next morning and forgave the allies for the attack. "Perhaps this terrible fire was God's way of cleansing the dishonor our military leaders have brought upon this country." He kept the two men inside his house to protect Hank from any reprisals from the local Japanese. News and official government communication was sporadic. Each day Mr. Kobayashi would walk down to the local police precinct station to try and get information, although most directives dealt only with trying to restore order in the local area.

Unable to go outside, Hank and Kaito spent many hours talking about their lives before the war, their countries and their hopes for the future. They tried to make some sense of the effect the war's ending would have on the world. The more Hank talked with the young man, the more he liked him. Studying economics and finance at Harvard had not left Hank much time to learn about the world around him. Now he felt he had some grasp of Japan and the Orient.


Three days after the atomic attack, Kaito began to show symptoms of some type of illness. Mr. Kobayashi thought it might be related to contaminated water and they began to boil any water they would consume. But the young man remained nauseated and soon could not keep food or water down. Hank suspected some type of intestinal infection but Mr. Kobayashi had no medicine that was appropriate. They tried to keep Kaito nourished with a watered down rice gruel but he would throw up soon after being fed. His strength began to ebb away.

"Do you think it is from the attack?" Kaito asked Hank after taking a bite of the rice.

"My friend, I wish I knew," he said, taking another spoon of rice and gently feeding it to Kaito.

"I think now that I only want to go home." Kaito lay back, staring at the ceiling.

Hank thought of New York and Kate, setting the small bowl on the table.

"Kaito, I wish we were both home."

Hank heard Mr. Kobayashi returning from his daily trip down to the valley. The elderly man slid a panel aside and stepped slowly into the room.

"The emperor spoke to the people this morning," he said. His words are being passed throughout the city. I have a copy, let me read it to you."


*"Despite the best that has been done by everyone — the gallant fighting of the military and naval forces, the diligence and assiduity of Our servants of the State, and the devoted service of Our one hundred million people — the war situation has developed not necessarily to Japan's advantage, while the general trends of the world have all turned against her interest.*

*Moreover, the enemy has begun to employ a new and most cruel bomb, the power of which to do damage is, indeed, incalculable, taking the toll of many innocent lives. Should we continue to fight, not only would it result*

251

*in an ultimate collapse and obliteration of the Japanese nation, but also it would lead to the total extinction of human civilization.*

*Such being the case, how are We to save the millions of Our subjects, or to atone Ourselves before the hallowed spirits of Our Imperial Ancestors? This is the reason why We have ordered the acceptance of the provisions of the Joint Declaration of the Powers.*

*The hardships and sufferings to which Our nation is to be subjected hereafter will be certainly great. We are keenly aware of the inmost feelings of all of you, Our subjects. However, it is according to the dictates of time and fate that We have resolved to pave the way for a grand peace for all the generations to come by enduring the unendurable and suffering what is unsufferable."*

When he finished Mr. Kobayashi turned and left the room, his head down, the paper held lightly in his hand.

Kaito stared at the ceiling, while Hank tried to grasp that the war was coming to an end.

Later that night, Mr. Kobayashi told them the mood in the streets was one of acceptance. While the city had been destroyed, at least they would now be able to rebuild their lives without the war hanging over them.

"We must look on it as the will of our God," he added, then paused to look at Hank. "Do you not feel well?"

Sweat glistened on his forehead and Hank knew that something wasn't right. An hour earlier he had thrown up the small bowl of rice he'd eaten for dinner. Now he started to wonder if he was coming down with Kaito's illness.

"I seem to be following the path of Kaito."

Mr. Kobayashi walked over and placed his hand on Hank's forehead.

"I fear you may be right. Have you been sick yet?"

Hank nodded.

"At the prefecture, there have been reports of this type of sickness throughout the city. There must be some connection with the attack."

The irony hit Hank. To have survived in an area of almost total destruction was almost too good to believe. He felt a weariness he had never felt before, either in prison or the hospital. Maybe this attack included some type of chemical that sickened the survivors. Hank lay down on his mat and tried not to think about what might be. For now he had to regain his strength.


For only the second time in over two weeks, Mr. Kobayashi left his small house. Today he would visit the prefecture to get news and hopefully find food to buy. He'd been afraid to leave his two wards as they both had been very ill. Taking care of the two had been hard work for the older man, but he didn't complain. He appreciated having something to occupy his time. It had been a slow recovery process for the young men. Now both of them were improving.

Yesterday, deciding that nutrition might be important to their recovery, he'd been able to buy some fish from a local man who had ventured into the city. Some of the fisherman from the outer islands had just begun to sell their fish in Nagasaki.

Throughout the city people fought to survive and the needs of everyday life now became critical. The civil authorities did as much as their resources allowed, but each man, woman and child had to look out for themselves.

Today, Mr. Kobayashi would see if any late summer produce might be available from the farms in the Kerama Valley. He was pleased to see that several wooden produce carts were grouped in the large courtyard near the highway. Several of the farmers he knew by name and they exchanged greetings.

"Kato san, I am pleased to see you."

An older man in a one piece coverall made a short bow to Kobayashi.

"We were told to wait until it was safe to venture into the city," he said, his grin marred by two missing teeth.

"Of course it is safe," Kobayashi replied

One of his companions laughed. "You are too old to fear anything, even the Americans."

Kobayashi stopped and stared at the man.

"Have you seen Americans? Here?"

"Yes, Kobayashi-san. One mile down the highway they have taken over a large building as their local headquarters. We saw it this morning on our way here."

Sergeant Alan Lindquist lit a cigarette and took a quick sip from the steaming canteen cup of coffee Corporal Hemmings handed him.

"God all mighty, that's the shitiest coffee you've ever made Hemmings."

"Sarge, get off my back. This crap we got from supply is three years old. Whaddya expect?" The Corporal turned to leave the office then stopped and turned back to Lindquist. "Wouldya look at this."

The Sergeant looked out the open door to the flight of steps leading up to the open veranda. An older Japanese man was climbing purposely up the steps in violation of the warning posted in Japanese that forbid entry to locals. Lindquist walked outside and saw the man must be confused. Damn Nips, he thought.

"Hey you, No. Can't come here. Understand?" The Sergeant pointed to the painted sign hanging from the railing.

The small man stopped on the porch and bowed carefully, his eyes not showing the fear the Americans had seen so far from the locals.

"I have an American pilot at my house who needs help. Will you come?" he said in very good English.

"I'll be damned."


Hank sat on the floor opposite Kaito, sharing tea while awaiting Mr. Kobayashi's return. Still weak, they both had been doing more each day and had resumed their long discussions.

Hearing the panel slide open, they turned as Mr. Kobayashi entered. Seeing uniforms behind the old man, Hank thought they had finally been turned in by the neighbors. Scrambling to his feet, Hank realized the man was an American Army Captain in fatigues followed by a soldier carrying an M-1.

For a moment the two men looked at each other as Mr. Kobayashi stood aside.

"Colonel Mitchell, my name is Gates, I'm with the 476th Military Police detachment. We're here to take you home."

# Chapter Twenty Five

Iwo Jima
Bonin Islands
September 17, 1945

A single jeep sped up the dirt road, pulling into the parking area in front of the 321st Fighter Group headquarters and slid to a stop in a cloud of dust. Corporal Jamie Thomas jumped from the jeep and ran to the large tent, which stood on a raised wooden floor. Leaping over the small two steps built up to the platform, Thomas ran into the partitioned tent, heading straight for the rear office.

"Colonel, you're not gonna believe this," he yelled, breaking in on Colonel Max Gogan, who sat reading a Stars and Stripes newspaper.

"Relax, Corporal, I'm not going to believe what?"

"Here, sir. I just picked this up at the Comm Center."

Gogan took the message form and began to read aloud, *"Priority Message from Combined Allied Forces Japan to Commander 20th Air Force, info 321st Fighter Group. For all addees, Lieutenant Colonel Henry Tyler Mitchell, previously listed as missing in action, presumed killed has been returned to Allied Control as of 1400 15 Sept 1945. Subject named member had been held by Japanese Secret Police in Urakami Prison, Nagasaki following capture. Due to his proximity to the atomic detonation 9*

*August, he will be sent immediately to the 32nd Evacuation Hospital, Kadena, Okinawa for medical treatment/evaluation. For Deputy Chief of Staff for Personnel, please expedite casualty notification procedures for next of kin."* I'll be a son of a bitch." He grinned at Corporal Thomas. "Go get Major Christiansen, Major Hanson and that bottle of brandy out of my locker."

"Roger?" Chris Christiansen called at the flap entrance to Hanson's medical admin tent.

"Back here."

Chris passed through the boxes of records that were being packed for shipment home with the Group. He found Hanson sitting on a wooden box, tinkering with a small telescope. The doctor spent his off duty hours satisfying his astronomy interest, the clear skies of the Pacific markedly different from England.

"Hi, Chris," Hanson said, looking up from his telescope.

"Hank's alive."

Roger paused before speaking.

"Say that again, please."

"Damn it, Roger, he made it. They found him in Nagasaki over a month after the blast. Gogan's got the message. I think we've got a reason for a helluva celebration."

Roger reached across and grabbed Chris's arm.

"You're sure?"

"That's what Thomas told me and Gogan wants both of us over there right now."

Putting the telescope down, Roger raised both hands to his face, the emotion evident in his voice.

"Thank God."

Colonel Max Gogan was setting out three glasses on his desk when Roger and Chris announced their arrival. He picked up a bottle, withdrew the cork and began pouring measures of brandy.

"Come in, you two."

He handed each man a glass and raised his. "To Hank Mitchell," he toasted.

Chris echoed the Colonel's words while Roger chimed in with, "Hear, hear."

Putting down his glass, Gogan handed Roger the message.

"See for yourself, Doc."

Roger read through the message twice. "I'll be damned," he added, but the mention of medical treatment due to his proximity to the blast disturbed him. He'd heard some of the rumors from Hiroshima describing a sickness due to absorption of radiation. So little was known about over exposure to radiation that lessons from this new weapon would be critical for the future.

"I wish there was more information on his condition," Roger said.

"Can we try sending them a message?" Chris asked.

Gogan nodded. "We can try, nothing lost in that. The only question is who to ask that might have the latest info."

"We could ask the evac hospital in Kadena. They must know something. I could use the medical connection as his flight surgeon. They might be willing to release that info."

"Hell, why don't we fly there and see him ourselves?"

"Chris, that's the best idea I've heard all day," Gogan said. "Besides, most of the movement plans for the Group are done, so there isn't much for us to do now anyway."

"I can wrap up the medical records in no time," Roger added, his voice upbeat.

"Okay, let me work on getting us over there. I don't want to take any of our aircraft, don't have time to fix them if they break." Gogan furrowed his brow for a moment. "Hell, I know. We can get Homer Moore to take us over in the B-25." Outside of all official channels, the 20th Air Force detachment on Iwo Jima had procured an early model B-25 which they used for logistics and parts runs. Lieutenant Colonel Homer Moore was the Officer in Charge and flew the B-25 regularly.

"I've got a bottle of Old Grand Dad that I'd donate to pay for our passage," Roger said.

Gogan laughed, "Is that the going price now days?"

"That's what I heard," Roger answered.

"Then let's get busy, gentlemen. We've got a date in Kadena."

Tyler and Susan Mitchell had greeted the news of the Japanese surrender with subdued joy. Since receiving the War Department telegram on the 11th of June, they had both dealt with their grief differently. Taking care of getting Kate Murray safely home occupied Susan for a short time and Tyler threw himself into work with an even greater vengeance than normal. But nothing could ease the pain of their loss. Having to say good bye to Kate, realizing that all their plans and future were now gone, was the most difficult thing Susan had ever done. They both knew that time would help them deal with their pain but it would never be the same again.

Susan found that long walks in Central Park, particularly where she and Kate used to go did help her find some peace each day. More young men were appearing on the streets as the European demobilization took place and she found herself searching faces anytime she saw someone that resembled Hank. She knew it made no sense, but she couldn't make herself stop.

Today's walk had been refreshing after the recent heat and humidity. Climbing up the steps from the pathway to the sidewalk on Columbia, she felt ready to face Tyler. As her pain ate away at her, it hurt her even more to see the fire gone from her husband's eyes. Tyler and Hank had not only become friends, they respected each other. Losing his son dealt Tyler Mitchell a blow that she knew was worse than anything he had ever suffered. Walking slowly toward their house she felt the urge to hold her husband and forget about the world.

Turning the corner she saw an olive drab sedan parked in front of their house. Not sure what it could mean, she suddenly realized there might be news of Hank. To find out what really happened would be the greatest gift the two of them could receive, to finally know.

As she began to climb the stairs, the front door opened and a man in uniform stepped out, a smile on his face. Standing behind the man she saw Tyler and in an instant knew that something wonderful must have happened. She froze as their eyes met, her expression asking Tyler what was happening. He brushed past the man, running down the stairs and grabbing her by the shoulders.

"Hank's alive," he choked out, and threw his arms around her.

She looked up at the man as she held Tyler and he nodded "yes" to her.

Susan Tyler's world changed in an instant from despair to joy. Her son was alive.


"We're really not supposed to let you walk," Captain Elliot Russell, Medical Corps, U.S. Army, said as he stood at the back of the ambulance parked next to the Army transport. Captain Russell had been taking care of Hank since his arrival at the 390th Mobile Field Hospital, which had been set up in Fukuoka to process the allied POW's held on the island of Kyushu. The two had become friends as Hank regained his strength from the radiation sickness. There hadn't been much that Russell could do other than provide good nutrition and treat his infection and mild dysentery. The knowledge of radiation sickness was almost non existent throughout the medical world.

"Russ, I'm still a fighter pilot. And fighter pilots don't get carried onto transports in a stretcher if there is any way they can walk. And you know I can walk." Hank sat in the back of the ambulance wearing a khaki uniform the hospital had been able to scrounge from supply. With his fresh haircut and shave, he looked relatively healthy.

"What the hell, I'm only in for the duration. What are they gonna do, send me to Japan? Let's go," he said and helped Hank out onto the tarmac.

The two walked slowly over to the boarding ladder.

"They told us you'll be in Kadena no more than a week. There's a small group of POW's from Hiroshima who will be there with you. The plan is to make sure everyone is ready to travel then straight back to a treatment team they're putting together in San Francisco."

"San Francisco," Hank repeated without thinking. The idea of putting his feet back on American soil made Hank feel good. The two stopped at the bottom of the ladder.

"Good luck, sir."

"Thanks for taking good care of me,"

They shook hands and Hank climbed the ladder.

A First Lieutenant stood at the door of the aircraft. He saluted as Hank climbed up to the platform.

"Colonel, I'm Tim Sparks, the co-pilot. You're our last passenger. As soon as you're strapped in, we're ready to go."

"Lieutenant, you can't imagine how ready I am to do just that. Where do you want me?"

"Colonel Mitchell is out for his morning walk," the Army nurse told the three men who stood in front of her desk.

"Where can we find him?" Roger asked.

"Right out that door is a path that turns into a long circular road. That's where I've seen him the last few days, just making circuits on the road.

"Thanks."

Gogan, Christiansen and Hanson saw a lone figure walking up the road toward them. They watched him as he approached, his hands in his pockets, head down.

"Know where we can get a beer?" Roger called.

Hank looked up and stopped.

"What?"

The three walked toward him and they saw his face as he recognized his friends.

"I'll be damned," he said quietly to himself as he walked toward them.

Gogan extended his hand. "Welcome home, Hank."

Roger grabbed him in a bear hug. "Don't ever scare us like that again!"

Chris stood next to Roger and Hank and as they let go he did the same thing. "Thanks for saving my ass, pal."

"You'd have done the same thing for me, right?"

They all laughed.

Twenty minutes later they all sat with cups of coffee in the hospital's cafeteria.

Hank had been recounting his journey from departing over Chris to Urakami. They were full of questions both as friend and from professional curiosity.

"What about the A-bomb attack?"

"I figure the only reason I'm here is that my cell was underground. The destruction I saw when I left the prison was hard to believe. Everything was leveled for miles, fires everywhere and the people terribly burned. We've taken killing to a new level."

"Well it ended the war. We didn't have to invade and that saved as many Japs as Americans."

"I'd hate think of someone dropping something like that on the states." Hank said.

They nodded.

"Hey, I was told they notified my folks as soon as they found out I was alive."

Gogan said, "That's what the message directed."

"So Kate will know?" Hank asked.

"You didn't know that she went back to England?"

Hank didn't know, but it did make sense to him. She felt very responsible for her father. He had to figure out how to get the word to Kate.


Sitting in her office, Kate Murray rechecked the patient roster. She'd never realized how many things have to work correctly for a hospital to function efficiently. To her surprise she found that she enjoyed managing all of the details involved in everyday support of the doctors and nurses. Her time on the wards had given her a wonderful feel for the problems the staff faced every day. Duncan Frazier's recommendation of Kate was now recognized as superb and the hospital administration saw a big future for her.

The door opened and Duncan came in, leaving the door ajar.

"Hello, Duncan."

The tall man took a seat in front of her desk.

Kate had come to know Frazier's moods, but she couldn't read him now.

"Life is an amazing journey, Kate. I continue to be surprised everyday at the depths of tragedy I see and at the same time joy unbounded."

What is he talking about, Kate asked herself. This is very unlike the Duncan Frazier I know.

He continued, "There is someone outside you know, and he has the most joyful news for you. I just wanted to prepare you."

With that he rose and swung open the door behind which Ambassador John Winant stood, impeccably attired in a three piece pin-striped suit.

"Mr. Ambassador," Frazier said, ushering him into the room.

Kate remained sitting, the surprise at seeing Winant overcoming her natural manners.

"My dear, in all of my years in public service, never have I had the opportunity to convey a message with such complete happiness."

Kate rose slowly, her heart telling her not to hope for the impossible, but...."

"Kate, he's alive and on his way home."

She heard what the Ambassador had said, but couldn't reply, her mind overcome by emotion.

The two met at the side of the desk and she buried her head in his chest.

"Tyler called me as soon as they were informed," he said.

Kate wiped her eyes, and Winant handed her the handkerchief from his breast pocket.

To one side, Duncan Frazier beamed.

"What can you tell me? Is he all right? When will he be home?"

The Ambassador smiled. "According to Tyler, he's undergoing some medical tests and then will be on his way home. They'll fly him to San Francisco for follow on treatment and.."

"He's hurt?"

"Actually he appears to be fine. He was in Nagasaki when the second bomb went off, so they have to do some tests. But right now you have to decide if you would like to return to New York to await his return?"

"Can I do that?" she asked.

"My dear, with Tyler Mitchell at work, nothing is impossible."

With scheduled trans-Atlantic service beginning next month, Pan American World Airways had scheduled several flights to work out the logistics and support for the new route. By virtue of his friendship with the Chairman of Pan American, Juan Trippe, Tyler was able to get Kate a seat on a Douglas DC-3 for the fourteen hour flight from London via Shannon Ireland, Gander Newfoundland and into La Guardia.

Ambassador Winant took care of getting her to the airport on time and with the appropriate paperwork for U.S. Immigration. As she left for the airport she remembered the ambassador's words, "...nothing is impossible."

Kate hadn't told John Winant she had never flown in an aircraft. But she'd never sailed across the Atlantic until six months ago and now she had done it twice.

The morning sun warmed her face as she was escorted to the aircraft. A movable set of steps led up to the cabin entry hatch at the rear of the DC-3.

"The cabin attendant will show you to your seat," the man said as he stopped at the foot of the steps.

"Thank you," Kate said, the words catching in her throat.

"Have a good trip. And watch your head."

Kate ducked slightly and stepped into the plane.

"Welcome aboard, I'm Dale Jones. I'll be taking care of the cabin during the trip. The man looked to be in his 30's and wore a military style uniform. "You'll be sitting in the second row on the right in the window seat."

Kate followed him up the slanting floor. Two other men wearing suits were already seated in the row in front of hers.

"I can take your coat for you and you can get settled."

As she sat back in her seat, Kate looked out her window at the men working on the ramp getting the aircraft ready. Is this what it's like for Hank, she wondered? Everyone seemed very busy although she didn't know exactly what they were doing. A fourth passenger came up the aisle and took the opposite window seat in her row.

In a moment, Dale Jones came up the aisle and turned to face the four passengers.

"Welcome aboard Pan American World Airways. We're almost ready for engine start and I'll ask everyone to fasten their lap belts for takeoff. Our first leg to Shannon will take about two hours depending on the winds. There's a lavatory in the rear of the aircraft. Also we have sandwiches and coffee in the galley. Just let me know if you want anything."

Kate heard a sharp report as the left engine started, the aircraft picking up the strong rhythm as the propeller came up to speed. Almost immediately the second engine roared to life behind her and she jumped involuntarily.

In another minute she heard the power increase on the engines and they were moving. She looked at the man by the opposite window and he seemed totally relaxed, probably a veteran air traveler. As they rolled down the taxiway, a loud squeal would come from below the aircraft which she hoped was normal. The plane now turned sharply and came to a stop, the engines roaring to full power. She decided this must be the moment of truth, the takeoff. Looking down at the ring she wore on her left hand, she realized her knuckles were white from gripping the armrest.

"All set?" Dale Jones' voice came from the row behind her above the sound of the engines.

Kate nodded, afraid to turn her head or talk.

Then the big airliner was rolling down the runway. When the tail lifted off, she knew they were about to fly and suddenly she wasn't scared. The sensation of power, speed and movement culminated with the DC-3 lifting off and transitioning to flight. While the noise level was high, it was smooth flying as they climbed out and Kate wondered why she had ever feared doing this. Now she knew what Hank must feel as he climbed out in his fighter. The thought made her smile.


After the flight from London to Shannon, the DC-3 departed for the long over water flight to Gander Newfoundland. Dale had told them they expected to take between 9 and 10 hours adding that the weather was clear. Kate looked forward to the second takeoff and she enjoyed every sensation. Watching out her window, the dark green hills of Ireland gave way to the blue green Atlantic as they all settled in for the long flight.

Kate found the rhythm of the engines comforting and she was alone with her thoughts. While the other passengers seemed to be leaning back to go to sleep, she found herself still too excited for her mind to slow down. In less than twelve hours she would be back in New York City. Her memories of Susan and Tyler came back as she looked at the ring, her ring. They had insisted she keep it when she returned to England, but she found that she couldn't keep wearing it. Now she would never take it off.


Hank awoke with a start, having dozed off for almost twenty minutes. He was tired and the long flight from San Francisco via Olathe, Kansas seemed to drag on forever. Stretching his back, he looked around the cabin of the R5D transport. Most of the passengers were sleeping or reading, almost all were in uniform and only a very few were speaking with their fellow travelers. Hank suspected many were on their way home and their thoughts were of where they were going, not where they had been.

The thoroughness of the medical exams surprised Hank during his short stay at Letterman Army Hospital in San Francisco, as did the intensity of the intelligence debrief by the team sent out from Washington. Anything connected with the attacks on Hiroshima or Nagasaki had become top priority for the services. Talking with the debrief officers he realized how fortunate he'd been to be in the lower cell tier at Urakami Prison. His physical condition was better than the men from Hiroshima and allowed his release to come home early. He would have to take part in an ongoing monitoring program beginning as soon as he finished one week of convalescent leave.

Glancing out the window Hank saw wooded hills through the thin clouds. He looked at his watch and figured they must be over Pennsylvania. His thoughts turned to Kate and he laughed when he remembered their very awkward conversation on a terrible connection from New York. She'd just arrived and Susan Mitchell was getting her settled. His parents had only taken the time to say hello, then left the two of them to talk.

Hank and Kate should have had so much to talk about, but they were both at a loss for words after their initial greeting. For them, simply knowing the other person was on the line seemed to be enough. Now he couldn't wait to see her. As if in consonance with his desires, Hank heard the power come back on the four engines and the aircraft began its descent.

A Navy crew chief walked back through the aisle and told them they needed to stay in their seats with their lap belts fastened until landing. The pilot estimated thirty minutes until they would be on deck.

Standing on the grass outside the Operations Building at Floyd Bennett Field, Kate and Tyler scanned the clear sky for any sign of Hank's plane. Several groups of people stood around them, obviously waiting for the same aircraft they were.

Kate remembered stepping out of the DC-3 yesterday, suddenly unsure of herself. Susan's hug and the warmth of Tyler's greeting told her everything she needed to know.

"Tyler, shouldn't they be here by now?"

"I'm sure it will be any minute, dear," he replied smiling inwardly at his wife's impatience. Tyler turned to look at Kate who had been very quiet this morning. He could only imagine what was going through her mind. He stepped over to her, gently placing his hand on her shoulder.

"Not too much longer, I'm sure."

Kate turned and smiled, but the look on her face made him ask, "Are you all right?"

"Just nervous." Her voice was soft so that only Tyler could hear her response.

He'd come to respect and care very much for this young woman who had helped his son and fought her own battle with cancer. He squeezed her shoulder and quietly said, "You'll be fine."

"There's a plane now," Susan said and pointed to the east.

Kate saw the transport approaching the field, its landing gear already down for landing.

Tyler reached for his wife's hand and they stood together saying nothing as the plane landed, small white puffs of smoke coming off the tires. The quiet of the airport was broken as the aircraft approached the parking ramp, despite the outboard engine on each wing being shut down. With one last addition of power, the transport moved into its parking spot and two men threw chocks under each wheel. Almost simultaneously the two inboard engines shut down, their propellers slowing until the individual blades became visible, then stopped.

From the side a portable stairway was pushed into place beneath the cabin door. A man ran up the steps to the hatch. A recessed handle moved on the door and it swung open and inward, the ground crewman now attaching two lanyards from the stairs to securing points on the plane.

The small group watched as men in uniform began to emerge. Most of the passengers appeared tired. A few looked across the people gathered on the grass, perhaps expecting to be met. Two small tractors pulled up to the aircraft and men began to unload baggage.

Kate subconsciously had moved closer to the concrete, now standing on the edge of the grass, her eyes fixed on the top of the stairs.

Then she saw him, standing in the sunshine, searching the crowd. He started down the steps, still looking across the throng in the waiting area. Then their eyes met. Kate raised her hand almost by reflex and began to run toward the stairs. Hank, carrying only a raincoat, hurried down the stairs, never taking his eyes off her as she ran up to him and into his arms.

# Epilogue

Queen Victoria Hospital
East Grinstead
West Sussex, England
June 4, 1956

An early summer breeze blew through the trees which lined Hollye Road as a large limousine drove up to the main entrance of the hospital. A small group of people stood on the steps awaiting the arrival of the car. As the car pulled to a stop at the base of the stairs, one man moved down the steps and leaned down to look in the rear window.

Roger Hanson smiled broadly and reached for the door handle. As the door swung open he reached forward and helped Kate Mitchell out of the car, giving her a warm hug. They held each other for a long moment then stood facing each other, their hands joined.

"It's so good to see you," Roger said.

"We've been away far too long," Kate replied and moved slightly for Hank Mitchell to get out of the car.

The two men bear hugged each other.

"Long time," Roger said.

"Too long," Hank replied.

The three turned to walk up the stairs as a third man came around from the far side of the car.

Hank stopped to make the introduction.

"Roger, I'd like you to meet the head of our investment banking operations in Tokyo, Kaito Ugaki."

The slim and handsome young man extended his hand. "Doctor Hanson, it is an honor to finally meet you. Hank has talked of you for many years with the greatest respect."

Roger took Kaito's hand. "I can say the same about you, Mr. Ugaki. I think we have you to thank for having Hank with us today."

"Doctor, I think it is more appropriate to say that we saved each other."

Everyone laughed and they continued up the stairs.

Later, after the dedication of the new Cancer Research Facility funded by the Tyler Mitchell Charitable Trust, Hank broke away from the crowd and walked down the hallway toward his old room. How things have changed, he decided, no one in uniform or sporting the latest in skin grafts. Queen Victoria had returned to being a municipal hospital. He was happy that Roger, who had realized he loved England almost as much as he loved medicine, was now the Medical Director. Duncan Frazier had been the heir apparent, but a motorcar accident last year had taken his life.

He thought back to the old group. All of them had walked the halls of East Grinstead. Chris remained in the Air Corps, now officially the Air Force, and was commanding a jet interceptor squadron in Florida. Max Gogan was now retired and through Tyler Mitchell's connection with Juan Trippe, ran Pan American's operations at Logan Airport in Boston. Dan Wilskie hadn't died over Germany, but did spend eight months as a captive of the Germans. He was now the head of Hank's west coast financial operations from his office in Seattle. The threads of life, woven together in this far land during a terrible war, were now bound together permanently.

It had been ten years ago that Hank had returned to Japan. Drawn back by a desire to learn more about the orient, he had an additional purpose for his first journey back to the orient.

269

Hank would always remember Mr. Kobayashi's look of surprise when he opened his cottage door.

"As before, you are welcome in my humble house and always will be." A gracious host, Hank thought he looked tired. But his faith was as strong as ever and his outlook positive. Over cups of steaming tea, he told Hank that the rebuilding of Nagasaki was not progressing as many had hoped. Bureaucratic procedures coupled with material shortages had left much of the damage as it was following the attack. "But we will continue our efforts. This city has existed for 1700 years and will surely be reborn from the ruins."

Hank found the old man's sense of purpose and serenity uplifting and renewed his belief that there are good men to be found everywhere. When it was time to leave, Hank asked him what he could do to help. Mr. Kobayashi asked that Hank help the local Catholic community rebuild the Urakami Cathedral which had been almost totally destroyed in the bombing.

"I would be happy to do what I can to honor you."

Kobayashi smiled, "I think Kaito was a good judge of men."

Hank leaned forward and touched his friend's sleeve.

"Can you help me find him?"

Kobayashi looked out across his neat yard. "I don't know if Kaito would want to see you."

The response surprised Hank.

"As the war was ending, your bombers made one last attack on Japan, almost a week after the bomb dropped here."

Hank remembered hearing about the confusion during the last days of combat, the question of an immediate surrender or fighting on longer.

"That attack was on Kaito's home city of Akita. No American bombers had gone that far north and the population was not as prepared as they should have been. Kaito's mother and father were killed in that attack. I don't know how he would greet you."

The journey to Akita Prefecture had been challenging. Many of the roads were in disrepair, while others were simply cart paths. A friend of one of Tyler's closest friends who worked in the growing American administration had been able to find a 1935 Ford sedan and reliable driver who spoke passable English.

Mr. Nomo was large for a Japanese, but his size was accompanied by an outgoing personality just as big. He'd been a civil administrator in Yokohama and now hoped to return to a government position as the occupation progressed. Until then he picked up work wherever he could.

Hank's interest in the orient and Japan had not lessened and he felt that there were tremendous business opportunities as the Far East recovered from the war. Nomo's commentary allowed him an inside view of the country that would have been difficult to gain in any other way. But Hank's primary purpose on this part of his journey was to find Kaito and learn what had become of his friend.

Mr. Kobayashi's last contact with Kaito's sister told of the young man's return to Akita after being released from the army. Apparently Kaito had been able to get a job as municipal worker for the City of Akita.

"Kaito Ugaki did work for the city but left over two months ago." Mr. Nomo had spent twenty minutes in the City Administration Building trying to find Kaito.

"Did they know where he went?"

Nomo shook his head. "They gave me his last address. It's on the northern side of the city."

Three hours later the car moved slowly down a narrow road past several single story wooden houses. Ahead a man walked toward them, a pole over one shoulder with a bucket balanced on each end of the heavy bamboo.

Nomo rolled the window down and asked for directions. The man pointed up the road, saying something that Hank couldn't make out.

"He says the house is around the next turn on the right."

Hank wondered if they were on a wild goose chase. But he'd come this far to find Kaito and he had to try everything.

Mr. Nomo pulled the small string attached to a metal bell. The door was opened by a young woman in her early twenties. She wore the traditional kimono, her black hair tied straight back. Her surprise at seeing an American was apparent and she quickly looked to Mr. Nomo who held up one hand.

"Our apologies for disturbing you. We are looking for this man's friend, Kaito Ugaki. Do you know where he lives?"

Her surprise increased and she asked Nomo, "This man is Kaito's friend?"

Nomo nodded. "His name is Mitchell. They met in Nagasaki at the end of the war."

Suddenly the look in her eyes changed from surprise to wonder.

"He is Mitchell?" Her brother had talked of the American named Mitchell and their time after the bomb.

"He has traveled from America to find his friend. Do you know where Kaito Ugaki is now?"

"Kaito is my brother. He is here," she said, her excitement obvious. "Please come in."

The two men removed their shoes and stepped into the entryway, Hank ducking under the low beam over the door. As they turned to follow the woman, Kaito entered the hall from a side room.

"Kaito," she said and turned to Hank. "This man is here to see you."

For a moment Kaito looked at Hank, who had gained weight from his days as a prisoner and wore a sports coat and slacks. In an instant there was a look of recognition followed by a smile.

"Mitchell, it really is you."

"Hello, Kaito," Hank replied trying to gauge his friend's reaction.

Kaito stepped forward, nodding his head in a small bow. Looking in Hank's eyes he said, "You honor our house."

Hank saw the friendship was still there, the man he remembered. He extended his hand which Kaito took, the two men shaking hands slowly.

"It is good to see you, my friend."


Later, after his sister Megumi had served tea, he and Kaito sat alone on a bench in the small garden behind the house.

"Mr. Kobayashi told me about your parents. I am sorry for your loss."

Kaito sat quietly for a moment.

"It is still hard to realize they are gone."

"So it is you and your sister? Do you have any other family?"

"Only distant relatives."

"Have you decided what you will do?" Hank asked, looking at his friend.

"Mitchell-san, in today's Japan we work everyday just to survive. Before the war I wanted to become a university professor. I think now I must take care of my sister."

"Kaito, have you ever thought about going into banking?"

"I thought I might find you here," Kate said from behind him. She took his arm, laying her head against his shoulder.

"So long ago. But the memories are as vivid as ever. That first day when Trevor told me all about you."

They both smiled, each remembering the young RAF pilot who would return to combat only to die over France the following August.

"He was a dear," Kate said.

"He didn't want to go back to flying. But he wouldn't dodge his duty." He remembered the look in Trevor's eyes the last time he had seen him. "What is it that makes men sacrifice themselves for an idea?"

"I think you know the answer. You were willing to die rather than leave Chris alone in the Pacific."

Hank thought back to that day. He hadn't cared about the war or his duty, he only cared about his friend. "And he did the same for me."

"As you've said before, there's nothing noble about war. But the way men act in response to war can be noble."

"My love, you're a philosopher," he laughed and put his arms around her.

"No, just a very lucky woman."

They stood in the deserted hallway holding each other for a long moment then turned and walked down the corridor, their heels clicking on the polished tiles.